H O

C000152613

HOMEWORK

Suneeta Peres da Costa

BLOOMSBURY

First published 1999
This paperback edition published 2000

Copyright © 1999 by Suneeta Peres da Costa

The moral right of the author has been asserted

Bloomsbury Publishing Plc,
38 Soho Square, London W1V 5DF

A CIP catalogue record for this book
is available from the British Library

ISBN 0 7475 4728 9

10 9 8 7 6 5 4 3 2 1

Typeset by Hewer Text Ltd, Edinburgh
Printed by Clays Ltd, St Ives plc

For my father, with love

CONTENTS

CALIFORNIA SUNSHINE

I had not set out to steal sunshine that winter. Even at six years old, I could no more believe I was a burglar than that sunlight might be bought. When the time came it is true I had neither alibis nor appeals to my advantage, but if my crime was premeditated there was a reason for this: I could feel my mother growing cold.

It was July; the suburban trees had lost their leaves; the street lamps were on by five o'clock in the evening and each day I had to wear to school a tie and ribbed stockings beneath a heavy box-pleat tunic. That is to say, it was winter in the Antipodes and as our days dawned and drew to a close it was not infrequently that Mum, intent on humiliating us with her occult rite of insulation – body oiling – pursued us, nude after our baths, through all the rooms of the house, brandishing a bottle of Johnson's Baby Oil.

My efforts at eluding her oleaginous touch were, however futile, quite genuine. So I surprised myself one morning around this time when, having sensed the strain in her voice when she summoned me, I peaceably complied. Mimicking small, slick Shanti's example (if we nicknamed Shanti Samosa, it was no doubt owing to this era when she had stood, pliable as pastry, based in grease), I came at once and endured the cool oil as placidly as possible. I let go my usual refusals and let Mum lubricate my limbs and, smiling, submitted as she smeared and saturated the tiniest of my anatomical cavities. In the end it was not I but Deepa – at eight, reading Solzhenitsyn (Tolstoy and Turgenev having been polished off the summer before) – who had risen with resistance.

'Can't you see this is *torture*, Mama!' she had cried.

But Mum was strangely unmoved and her imperturbability at that moment brought to my mind other recent curiosities. It was the height of winter, yet even in the middle of the day, I had been discovering Mum bundling herself in blankets. Of an evening, I would spy her carrying hot water bottles to her bed and lying down for hours. Her teeth chattered and did not stop when only for a moment – to the laundry or the backyard – she left the house and returned. It was cold, yes, but not that chill. For failure in simple tasks, I would see her endlessly reproaching herself: forgetting to buy milk; mislaying the clothes she'd picked up from the laundromat.

Shiny and uncomplaining as she slathered me with baby oil, I could not help but notice that she was shivering even while kneading us and, at times, sighing a little aching sigh as she drew her hand across our gleaming forms. *Was she sad?* I had silently speculated of this beleaguered sculptor whom I so dearly loved. Were my mother's small grouses about the Sydney sun, small though uttered sometimes with tears, concealing a deeper longing? I had quietly considered. And had *I* brought it on? Had I, with my nodes, been the nemesis in her life, as she so often charged?

Oh, my nodes, those feelers I was born with! Those protuberances, no bigger than fingertips, that at my birth had been discovered atop my skull! How often I speculated as to the bereavement they must have brought Mum and Dad at the moment I had emerged, bawling, eyelids resolutely closed, into the world. What lamentations, rather than sweetnesses, I frequently conjectured, had been elicited by the proportions of my bald, slightly misshapen head and murmured to me during those first few sips at my mother's breast? How tightly had they, my parents, squeezed each other's hands, marvelling, wondering, or in plain terror trembling, at those strange distortions of my sconce?

'Look!' I could even recall people having whispered aghast, indicating my innocent form as it lay, suckling a pacifier, in the King George nativity crib. 'Can you see that kid? What are those small things on her head? Why, they look like antennae. Oh, how awful!'

Sophisticated diagnostic tests had been performed on me during my first days on earth, yet despite countless reassurances that the swellings were benign, Mum and Dad had continued to harbour the suspicion that I might, on account of those excrescences, turn out to be a dud child. *And how might I have even held their prejudices against them?* In the subcontinent, from where they came, physical disability is understood to be the work of karmic intervention. I had thus been ordered from birth to carry, alone, the onus of universal malevolence, global errors and atrocities practised before my very conception. Only four months old – when many children still failed to turn over by themselves – Mum and Dad had been waiting in earnest for evidence of complete speech from me, had had me potty-trained. And of course, it didn't help me that Deepa, the brilliant event of whose perfect coming-into-existence they were still recovering from – and who was three at this time – was filling in tax-return forms on my parents' behalf, reading *Candide* after preschool.

The pressure on my infant mind to retain, recall, and express myself had been heavy from the moment I blinked. At one, they had moved to placing huge volumes of World Book Encyclopedia directly on my lap, burdening and straining my as yet unformed limbs. No rabbits, no Aesop, Grimm, or Andersen. I did not have in my possession a single pop-up book, and the instrumentalism of my education in reading was so laboured that when covering the most astonishing revelations, I did not even realise that a wolf had changed places with a grandmother, that there was anything very much wrong with kidnapping children and putting them into ovens. By two they'd forced a bow into my hand, had felt no qualms in shoving before me the sheet-music of Mozart's Concerto No. 3 in G Major, K. 216, demanding that I memorise that strange arrangement of half notes, quarter notes, and modulated keys.

All the while the feelers protruded but were obscured by my mop of hair, which, try as Mum did, refused to be pasted down. For some time, all around failed to realise that the nodes were wired to my heart, programmed with small but rapidly expanding ranges of psychic and social sensation. But then in my fourth year, the public reality of my abnormality suddenly took on a life of its own. This was not so difficult to abide at first for people only stared Soon, though, the feelers became a force of their own reckoning and I a specimen of public intrigue. The phone continuously rang with pleas for my parents' guest appearance on puerile television shows about human tenacity in the face of adversity and some with more dubious orientations. Colleagues of Mum asked if – in the interest of human progress, naturally – they might present me as a finding to various medical journals: *Current Therapeutics, The Journal of Paediatric Pathology, The Medical Examiner*.

It is also true that while the antennae had remained relatively governable, with no real discernible effect during my infancy, they began – as I did – to grow and, as it was discovered, in times of great anxiety or distress, pricked up straight as aerial antennae. Where previously they had lain low, like a surplus mass of skin on my head, they became, in my fourth year, organs of a kind of self-determination. When this first became evident, specialist consultants were sought, multiple operations performed, but as it turned out, the antennae failed to be excised. I could hardly forget the expression of complete defeat on Dad's face, when, after the final operation, Dr. Levy called us into his office and broke it to my parents that it was going to be impossible to remove the nodes surgically since they were rooted in the brain matter of my skull.

'You can't do anything!' Dad, normally the calmer of the two, wailed, pacing about the room.

Dr. Levy explained that while the nodes were a curiosity about which nothing could apparently be done, they were benign and it was that for which my parents should remember to be grateful.

'But what will this mean?' Mum, herself a daughter of science, shrieked.

'Oh, she might be a little sensitive, that's all. There are

enough nerve endings in those things for lightning to strike them! Let's just monitor her progress for some time.'

And, just as Dr. Levy had said this, I, lost in the huge leather chair to which I'd been assigned for the ordeal, had felt the feelers slump in despair.

The bottom line was this: I had to live with them, a fact which to me as an infant had not really seemed any more horrendous than living with a sixth finger on each hand, a third eye. I did not cry as Mum not just scraped the comb against my scalp, but with all her quotidian strength tried to braid each node into my plaits. I protested but did not lock my jaw around anybody's hand as I was, on a regular basis, taken to hairstylists to have my hair arranged in coifs that would skilfully conceal my deformity.

'Oh, they're nothing. It just means she's a little more sensitive . . .' I began to notice that Mum and Dad would, as though to warn people before their having even made my acquaintance, appeal on my behalf.

'She's just a bit sensitive,' my parents would try, in Woolworth's checkouts and car parks, on public transport and in church, to appease those who gawked as I – up to the very *ordinary* antics of a child my age (smashing tubs of yoghurt against the metal spokes of the trolley, threatening defection from the family, wearing myself out up and down the aisles, and striking up conversation with proximate parishioners) – drew *extraordinary*, sell-out crowds.

Sometimes the feelers served as my most formidable childhood weapon. Boys my age and older – bullies – I could, by getting the blood to run fast enough to the proper place, turn screaming for the mother's legs they would otherwise have publicly eschewed. Girls whom I despised for whatever infant whim was mine were even easier to scare. To make *them* run, I might simply have to point in the direction of my crown, mention the Bogey Man or Wee Willy Winkie or ask if they had heard about extraterrestrials.

'Extra what?' they would inquire, wide-eyed.

'Extraterrestrials,' I'd repeat and then proceed, like a zealot, to explain the phenomenon of outer-planetary life forms.

But then, such opportunities for triumph, for indiscriminate acts of tyranny, proved in my case rather rare. When Shanti was born (another perfect sibling against whose unblemished body my own would be routinely compared), she did not cling to my finger as she would every other member of the family, every other relation whose doting hand came in sight of her crib; no, where I was concerned, Shanti each time reached for – and time and again caught in her tiny, obstinate, saliva-steeped fist – one or the other of my nodes.

It had been especially instructive to observe the response my antennae elicited from those we knew, relations, people to whom we were supposed to have been 'close.' Incidents involving Aunty Sylvia and Uncle Vincent, telling my parents what 'an *awful* shame' it was that I'd turned out the way I had, and Mum in chronic rescue mode saying, 'You know, she's very artistic; have you shown Aunty Sylvia your knitting?' would hit me with sudden gravity. In those days I had over and over retreated to dutifully retrieve my sad black and blue and green scarf whose width was all wonky because I'd keep losing stitches somewhere. While I was gone, Deepa, not a flaw on her body, would emerge and they'd all remark on what a 'tremendous personality' she had (Uncle Vincent's expression).

In Bombay when my grandfather had taught me how to burn holes with the sun, he had held the magnifying glass over my feelers, studied them for some time and told me they resembled the horns of Lucifer. He had notified me that Jesus sat on the Right Hand of the Father and that while it was normally a pretty uncomplicated trip to heaven, with those demonlike projections on my head, Jesus, Mary, and St. Peter might have trouble determining whether I was truly a Child of God. The best thing to do, he had reported, was to work up a good rapport with my guardian angel.

'Who is my guardian angel?' I had inquired, sipping from a warm flat bottle of Limca, harbouring a measure of private doubt about all of this.

He had asked that I stop bothering him, was pressing his hand to his chest as though he had some pain in there.

'Papa, who is my guardian angel?' I'd repeated, mangling the straw in my mouth, the feelers by now on end.

'Go and ask your mama, Papa isn't feeling so good today,' he had said before retiring to his bedroom, putting on some long socks, and getting in the bed to die.

Save this fatal encounter with my grandfather, I had been able to abide the insensitivity of strangers and the brazen gazes of blood relations. But I did not feel I possessed the tenacity to endure yet another public humiliation of the kind to which I had in recent days been subjected by Daniel Hoolahan in physical education.

I had known that the feelers were sources of intrigue to my peers. I had even secretly suspected that I might have been regarded with a certain awe on account of them.

Parents aware of my 'condition' had been advised to have their children refrain from teasing me. Like a disabled child, I had relished the special attention I had been given.

But suddenly this winter of my sixth year these once-sympathetic classmates had complex questions of their own.

'Do they hurt?' I was encircled at lunchtime and summarily questioned.

And it became more malicious.

'Look! Look at Mina Pereira!'

And the more abased I was, the more the feelers moved, drew attention to themselves, indeed, exposed my whole internal psychological anatomy, their sole pitiable function.

We were do-si-doing and Miss Lancaster had just said, 'All right, everybody join hands.'

Daniel was scowling as he reluctantly placed his clammy hand in mine. His grip was itself loose and limp. His boyish brow was furrowed in frustration and I became quite bewildered myself then, had the impulse to say, 'Come on, Daniel, it's okay Look, they're just like little fingers!' But his hand remained so dead inside mine, his face contorted into an expression of disgust or lurid curiosity, I really could not tell. The more sensitive I became then, the more movement I had felt from those noxious projectiles; the more hurt, the more embarrassed, the more they swayed in like sadness. The steps of do-si-do were doomed, for Daniel's palm soon began sweating like candle wax and, just as we were to change partners, he let go and shouted, 'You're a mutant, Mina, that's what you are!'

With this single act of alienation, I sank to an unprecedented low. My grandfather's prophecy fulfilled, my life seemed beyond hope. I waited around for my guardian angel all day at school, but whomever this sweet sprite was she never did arrive. It was I who now wanted to run and in desperation hide my face behind my mother's legs. But Mum's legs (bony at the best of times) were no longer available. Not even her lap.

I discovered this when, trying to climb into it the evening of Daniel's cruelty, I was doubly rejected. Gently lifting me away, Mum told me that I was getting too big for her. When I resisted, she touched her stomach, sucked her teeth in as though, in simply resting my head against her abdomen, I had caused her great pain.

Too big? I mulled over these words while finding my way to, and comfortably ensconcing myself in, Dad's sturdy lap. Why, I thought, I had not to my knowledge grown even an inch all year (I had studiously been surveying my height, competing each week for millimetres with Deepa), so what was she talking about my being too large for her lap?

Oh, how I longed for nothing but her warm, if scrawny, lap again! *Oh, how I longed to uncover the mystery of Mum's sudden frigidity!* More than a demon, I felt like a kind of human barometer, my feelers registering the depths of her woe; though now I see that lying there, wondering if her knee was forever lost to me, I was still staring with Icarian delight at the earth; my life was not yet tinged with sadness, for I could not believe that people really died.

All this culminated when Lucy Malone returned from America, where, on account of her father's job, she had been going to school for the last two years.

Lucy had been my best friend before she'd left.

'I like them,' she had said, petting one of the antennae on our first day in kindergarten. 'They're cute and soft, like a snail or something.'

Given that I already entertained notions of alienation, statement made of my likeness to a mollusc had at the time seemed to me a great compliment. But I was now convinced that Lucy was irredeemably changed.

Shrewd witness when Miss Martin requested that she tell the class about her time in the United States of America that chilly Monday morning, I watched Lucy shy toward the front, with pity observed the blood rush to and flood her face. *Poor* Lucy! I thought, for I often knew how it felt when my own skin got hot – had felt it that day do-si-doing with Daniel – but was always intrigued to see how this sensation occasionally produced physically in my freckled-faced colleagues the same extremes of involuntary exposure I constantly experienced with my nodes.

Lucy, I mused at this moment of her crimson suffering, wasn't very popular before she'd left; she had been shy and quiet and small; but, having returned from the United States of America, she was now talking like a real American, saying 'like' and 'right' with those hyperbolic *R*'s rolling round her mouth and 'sure' and, oh, there were so many strange things she was saying, her mouth was like a motor racing and, looking about at my possessed peers, I with perturbation understood that everyone, but everyone, wanted her!

She spoke to us for some time about her 'terrific time' in the United States of America; then Miss Martin asked Lucy whether she had anything to show us, something she may have brought back as a souvenir.

'Souvenir. Do you know what that means, class?'

No one really knew, but it sounded very exciting to see a thing brought all the way from the United States of America!

Lucy a now reached into her bag and retrieved a small aluminium can embossed with a gaudy, smiling sun and the words CALIFORNIA SUNSHINE, and the class grew very quiet. She informed us that in California the sun is always shining just right, not too hot, and that people sat on their porches shelling and eating peanuts all day and, oh, that Californian peanuts had to be the best ones in the whole world!

Miss Martin asked the class whether we'd like to ask Lucy any questions, but all around remained subdued, their eyes fixed on that can of sunshine.

Suddenly, Adrian Simpson shouted, 'Hey, Lucy, what's in the can?'

Lucy said it would be all right if he held the can, but that he had to be very careful. She passed it over to him.

'Why, it's empty!' Adrian Simpson said to Amen Anthony, chuckling and shaking it, 'It's just an empty can!'

And then Roger Nolan started tittering, too, and Miss Martin was shouting, 'That's enough!' and the girls started giggling, and poor Lucy with her freckle-fury was shouting, 'Give it back! You don't know anything!'

And then, out of the blue and with those funny *R*'s bonking inside her mouth like marbles, she added, 'Adrian Simpson you're just – you're just a – a stupid idiot!'

A hush descended on us again.

She grabbed the can from him and I could see from my colleagues' expressions that they were very impressed with these words she had uttered. 'Stoo-pid', she had said, as if with a hollow inside the word. *Stoo-pid*. Yes, all the girls agreed and stared at Lucy very inspired, and the boys seemed especially surprised with the wisdom of it all: Adrian Simpson was a Stoo-pid Idiot!

'Lucy,' Miss Martin said, 'we don't use that language at a Catholic school. Please apologise to Adrian right away!'

But Adrian Simpson was already crying.

At lunchtime I went to sit next to Lucy but found that on our usual undercroft bench my place had been usurped; she was now surrounded by others like Melanie O'Brien and Cathy Small, all the eminent members of the class, all of whom were being exceptionally friendly, fawning and falling all over her. From a distance, I could see the boys were watching them also, longingly and full of fear. The girls were eating Orchy ice blocks together. *Orchy ice blocks!* Sucking away the juice until the ice was without colour, without sweetness, just as I had done with Lucy before she went to the United States of America, before she became *so* interesting.

I thought Lucy was trying to ignore me because when they started doing Double Dutch and I asked whether I might play with them and they said only if I didn't mind holding the rope, she didn't even look at me. So I then resolved I wouldn't speak to her either.

Mum always said, 'If you give someone your tail, they'll probably pull it'; this previously elusive dictum now took on a poignant and particular significance.

Only when the bell rang did she finally come to confront me.

'Mina, Mum said to ask whether you'd like to come over on Sunday? We're having a barbecue. I'd really like for you to come.'

I thought, *This is my chance!* and now maintained *my* silence.

'What's wrong?' she said, with the marble *R*'s still knocking about, 'Why are you *ignorrrring* me?'

I didn't answer. And then, just before we got to the top of the stairs, Lucy turned to me, and would you believe what she called me, quiet Lucy Malone whose own heart had once been like mine, so full of fear and timidity?

'You know what you are, Mina Pereira?'

I stood there defenceless, the aforementioned tail firmly between my legs, my feelers inclining.

'Why,' she went on, 'you're nothing but a fair weather friend!'

And with this she stormed away.

I must admit that like *souvenir* it took me some time to fully grasp the meaning of these awful words, but I knew from her tone that there could be no doubt that they had been intended as insults, just as 'stoo-pid idiot' had been. *A Fair Weather Friend!* Where had she learnt this language that was mean and at the same time so wondrously sure of itself? I entered the classroom, dejected and alone, contemplating what a Fair Weather Friend might be and why Lucy Malone, who, with her newfound and wonderful rolling *R*'s, was being lavished with such affection.

Mulling over Lucy Malone's Fair Weather charge, I noticed that the can of Californian Sunshine was sitting on Miss Martin's desk.

How do you enclose sunshine in a can? I philosophised. And I thought of Mum, poor Mum, always complaining that the Sydney sun never lasted long enough for her, or saying that it was always a harsh, hungry sun that made her feel as though it were burning a hole right through her heart. Dad said Mum even sleep-talked about the sun; he said that sometimes he would wake to discover her dreaming aloud of the Bombay light jumping along the dark grey roofs of Byculla and, at dusk, turning the Hanging Gardens into a live zoo creeping with long and mammoth shadows.

And I myself could remember gazing upon Mum's face as she and I had walked the streets of her Bombay youth bathed in such an illumination. We would stop at the fish market where the fisherwomen would always tease me, requesting that Mum leave me forever in their company. I'd shriek, for I could not bear to think of being orphaned to these women with their toothless smiles, their bloody hands all day lodged inside the intestines of fish, of their deep, parched, and wrinkled cleavages. I would bury my head in Mum's skirt until she'd reassure me that of course she would never, ever leave me; that it was only that the women liked to vex me in this way. She'd then buy me a Kwality ice cream and we'd walk home, me taking charge of the bag of fresh bream and occasionally tripping on the cobblestones of Clare Road.

But this reverie was cut short as I now heard footsteps on the stairs and Peter Donaldson being chased by Tracy James, who had loved him ever since kindergarten. And before I was even aware of it, before I had even thought the word *thief*, I was adroitly smuggling the can of Californian Sunshine into my lunchbox and running downstairs to put it in my bag.

Are the giftgivers really thieves? Was it really so heinous to steal some sunshine for Mum?

Catching my breath as I returned to my place at my desk, I reasoned with myself: The United States of America sounded like a very big country; surely, I self-counselled, it could be arranged that some more Californian Sunshine be sent to compensate Lucy. *And wasn't it Mum who needed the sunshine more than anyone?* Frigid Mum with her toes curled like thorns in the winter, Mum who painstakingly oiled our bodies to protect us from the wind when we played bulrush late into the darkening afternoons, late into the diminishing Sydney evenings?

Thief: this was the appellation that was suddenly conferred on me at home and they threatened to tell the school, only Dad said he could never show his face again at parent-teacher interviews.

Mum, washing out my lunchbox, had discovered the can.

'You shouldn't be drinking that soft drink rubbish. Do you want to get diabetes and go blind like Aunty Beatrice and have to have big fat insulin injections in your arm every day?' she asked me.

Then she said something to Dad in Konkani, that secret, parental idiom. *Mother Tongue*, I'd once heard Dad declare it, and I had often wondered whether, having ripped out my mother's own oratory muscle, I'd be any better equipped for the many traumas of my youth.

Dad repeated what she said, only with less enthusiasm.

'Mina, do you want to get diabetes?' he indifferently added.

That fear they'd driven inside me. *Soft* drink. I was definitely on the periphery of linguistic sophistry. *Soft*: How was it soft when in fact it assaulted the throat and ran to the belly, bringing tears to the eyes?

I now rambled, conciliation my intent, into the kitchen, where Mum was cooking potato bajhi.

'Mmm,' I said searchingly. (*Oh, but I did love the*

aroma of the mustard seeds and onion frying) 'Mama,' I said, picking up the can from where she'd put it aside for the rubbish. 'Look it's still sealed, Mama, I brought it – I bought it (I was six: Diction was not yet my forte) – for you.'

Mum picked up the can and took a long look at it. She began speaking to Dad and I knew they were talking about something wrong or rude, because I was again denied access. The words exploded from their mouths and sounded at once vulgar and beautiful and in all their urgency seemed to tear their way through to my own, tiny heart.

Dad grinned and passed the can over to Deepa.

Deepa rolled her eyes and began reading what it said aloud; all intelligent, I thought, and full of that Tremendous Personality.

' "ONE HUNDRED PERCENT PURE LIGHT FROM THE BLUEST PASADENA SKY. LET SOME CALIFORNIA SUNSHINE INTO YOUR LIFE TODAY!" '

'It's sun!' I now explained, feeling their mockery suddenly enshrouding me. 'It's sun!, Mama, I brou – bought – it for you.'

Mum, shook her head reprovingly, sighed, and said, 'Oh my God!'

'All the way from California!' I continued.

'Where did you buy it?' Deepa, whose selective curiosity was beginning to annoy me, asked.

I made my snake eyes at her and went to seek refuge in the room I shared with Shanti.

She was playing with blue plasticine and had some on her tongue. She looked unwordly, an unlikely saviour, still glistening with the now rancid oil of that morning. I thought, *Now I've done it. Now I'm going to be skinned alive*! No volume of Johnson's Baby Oil could provide me with protection or immunity now.

Mum entered the room after me.

'Mina, where did you get the sun?'

Oh my God! I, too, wanted to say. A great emptiness suddenly entered me and I could feel my perforated heart sinking. No guardian angel came to rescue me, even though I knew it was the end of my life and even though I lifted up my right hand.

'Jesus is listening.'

She had to say that, she *always* had to say that; just when I supposed that I might be able to tell the truth about something, Mum would say, 'Jesus is listening,' and that was enough to turn my resolve. I would rather dissemble just to keep a good record, if indeed he was listening.

By now Deepa, meddlesome Deepa, had come to the door, only further demanding a performance. I thought about how my six-year-old credibility would be shot should I be found out.

Then, with innocent eyes, I said, 'Lucy gave it to me as a – a *sou-venir* – of America.'

So, I thought, *I had been saved by Lucy Malone!* Little able was I to foresee the humiliation, the public scandal that would follow from my misdemeanour. Later that evening Mrs. Malone telephoned Mum. They talked about the United States of America and Mum affected the taut unlovely voice she used when trying to imitate local inflections. *The lemon voice*, Dad would call it, alluding to the lemons brought by our next-door neighbours, who'd sigh and say that they wished we were all the same and who never ceased asking Mum what she was cooking because, they'd say, it *smelt very strong*.

I observed her pitiful struggle to sound just like Mrs. Malone. *Is this my mother?* I wondered. *Is this my mother's tongue?*

My feelers suddenly rose, tense and wary.

'Lucy has been a bit upset that Mina would not speak to her'; this is what I imagined Mrs Malone to be saying. 'Lucy invited Mina over for a barbecue, but Mina snubbed her.'

Mum covered the receiver with her hand.

'Mrs. Malone has asked whether you'd like to go over to a barbecue at Lucy's on Sunday.'

My ears burned. My feelers now drooped and weighed me down.

'Okay,' I agreed, thinking maybe this was my way out. Jesus' way of letting my lie slide was simply having to endure the barbecue.

But Mum returned to Mrs. Malone, chatting away in her phoney telephone voice.

Then, as I blew cool air on my bajhi, I noticed her growing silent, very, very silent.

Instead of responding in words she again vaguely murmured, 'Mmm,' to Mrs. Malone, 'Mmm' and 'Mmm.'

Then, very abruptly, she said, 'I'll have to call you back, I'm afraid, My youngest is screaming.'

At this moment Shanti *was* screaming but that was nothing unusual, and we let her scream, hoping that with her screams and the very strong smell of biryani our neighbours who brought lemons in their hands, lemons and smiles at the door, that they'd die or go away.

I was now at the table. I looked over at smug Deepa, the

sister who had never, ever come to my aid in battle and, as far as I was concerned, had set a childhood precedent for enmity even in peacetime. She was certainly not going to start up an alliance now. She had finished her khana, like a good girl, and was sitting with that face of hers so incapable of mischief. She shook her head, mimicking Mum's look of reproach.

I was just a little girl! What could they possibly do to me? I ruminated. I was innocent and much-abused. Did they not know how abused I was, how any of act of impropriety was a consequence of what six years of life in the world had done to me? And it was *their* fault I used to fall asleep in kindergarten; I mean, I was only three-and-a-half when everyone else was five! Again, it was *they* who had enrolled me thinking I 'could cope' given that Deepa's development was so rapid her third grade teacher had had her writing book reports on *Nausea*. Oh, what chagrin and long faces when, at awards night, I would shame them year after academic year with the mediocrity of 'The Most Improved,' while shining Deepa startled everyone with her arms bursting with Excellence!

And all my other personality 'problems' seemed to my six-year-old consciousness quite rational. I mean, what were they expecting, that I'd come home after having slept all day in class and that they could then force me to sleep – *again* – on their bed? On one such occasion I had been so bored that, like the poor, famished caterpillar of Hungry Caterpillar fame, I had senselessly bitten the green tassels off the bedspread. They had transferred me to my own room. No sooner had the shift been made with my unheeded protests resounding in the corridor than they'd found I'd eaten the wallpaper off the wall in frustration. I hadn't been fatigued – I had, in fact, felt well-rested – but had they listened? *Had they?*

I now weighed up my felony. First the theft and then the Jesus-lie. I stuffed a spoonful of steaming potato bajhi into my mouth, but I couldn't taste it tonight; I could barely perform the most primitive sensory motor task, making my mouth chew or swallow. They might have once observed such behaviour and sought advice from *Baby and Child Care*.

Had I not heard them read aloud for my two-year-old pleasure that,

' "*The trouble is that a child is also born with an instinct to get baulky if he is pushed too hard, and an instinct to get stroppy. So it's human and normal and inevitable that we should feel quite differently about each of our children, that we should be impatient with certain characteristics in certain ones of them*" ' *(here they'd turn to me)* ' "*and proud of others*" ' *(their eyes, at this, on Deepa)*.

Mum hung up the phone and again began talking to Dad in the interdictory idiom.

She went to the bookshelf to consult with Dr. Spock.

' "*Often there's no sense to the stealing . . . He seems to have a blind craving for something . . . What does he really want? In most cases the child is unhappy and lonesome to some degree.*" '

The even-tempered tone of Dr. Spock did not seem to allay her conscience, though, and she began pulling me toward the hallway picture of Jesus and His bleeding heart.

She demanded I kneel down – 'until I say you can get up!' – to ask his forgiveness.

Oh, it was the separation that hurt most! He did not hurt, not He of the Sacred Heart and yellow face and hands that made Him look more like a sickly, dying man than one who would rise again; He just seemed old and tired; no Son of God but a world-weary illusionist.

Thief: That's what I was called. Dad covered his face and cowered in shame when Mum told him of my crime.

Then, very systematically, he took the can, popped the top, released the silent, invisible sun in front of my eyes and said, 'If you ever, ever steal again – ' but he didn't finish and I saw his eyes well with tears as he put the can in the garbage bin.

The Californian Sunshine vanished, just like that. I hadn't seen it, it had neither made us any warmer nor the weather fairer. In fact, it rained, rained, and rained. Maybe it had never even been there to begin with, I reflected. *Maybe the United States of America was full of such foolish, empty souvenirs!* More than the shame of my crime, I felt duped. Why were the secrets of the sun so invisible to the human eye? How could I make Mum warm, if I couldn't steal that for which she longed?

Mum came into my bedroom to kiss me that night after having released me from the stare of Christ.

She must have sensed that my cheeks were wet and so put her graceful arms around me. I could feel her own tears splash onto my skin. The moon's crepuscular shadow faintly outlined her face, a face I loved so dearly that it sometimes hurt, and I hoped that soon, one day very soon, I would stop my own reckless mastication and, having stuffed myself with all small pieces of the world, metamorphose into such a beautiful creature as she.

She and Dad had decided that no one in the family was to say anything at school. If Miss Martin mentioned the can of Californian Sunshine, we would have, for the sake of the family name, to pretend ignorance.

'I know you only wanted to give Mama a present,' Mum whispered.

Shanti sat up and flopped down again at this moment with a kind of kidlike censoriousness which suggested we were disturbing her dreams.

'Mama loves you, Mina,' she told me. 'But she doesn't like a thief.'

I couldn't shake it, the word was so horrendous. My feelers rose and fell in shame.

'Ma,' I whispered.

'Ya?' (*The poetry of her natural inflection!*)

'What about the barbecue? I don't want to go.'

'We'll see about the barbecue.'

We never saw about it because the day before it was to take place someone called to say that Mr. Malone, Lucy's father, had been seriously injured in car crash; there was a possibility he might die.

The word fell on me, levelled me when I heard it. I had known no one other than my grandfather who had Died.

I was intrigued by the notion of the Christian Soul.

In Church we would sing,

And I will raise him up,
I will raise him up,
I will raise him up
On the last day.

And I had more than once wondered, was it true, that like Shanti stumbling about reality in her dreams, we would one day be awoken to eternal life or something sweeter than this hurricane-life full of moods and moons and losses? What of the Gates of Heaven, of that place where my soul was to be measured by St. Peter; what if he, too, didn't want to hold my hand (after all, he had a record for disavowals) and, on a whim, sent my soul to purgatory. And worse, imagine if I felt right at home there; purgatory – paragon of equivocality – where I would have to contend neither with the terrors of hell nor the pretensions and pressures of being a heaven dweller either. Perhaps St. Peter would take one look at my crime and the feelers on my head and consult with God and say, 'She's one for Lucifer, I'm afraid.'

I felt very bad for Lucy and asked whether I may go and see Mr. Malone, but Mum said she wasn't sure whether this would be 'very appropriate.'

'You know Mr. Malone has got to be Lazarus to get well. The best thing you can do is say prayers,' she told me.

The whole of the first grade said prayers; prayers to God for Mr. Malone to get well, for Lucy and her family, for the poor children of the Third World, for the world seemed to grow quite enormous around a dying person. And I said my own prayers; I said prayers for Shanti and Deepa and made massive apologies to God for all my wickedness.

I went into St. Sophia's Parish confessional and told Father Murphy that I had stolen sunshine from a dying man's daughter. Father Murphy told me to say three Hail Marys and to pray for the dying man's soul. I did.

Then, a week later, we got news that Mr. Malone had 'slipped away.'

Mum said she would like to make a dish and send it over to the Malone family. She spent the whole morning thinking about what would be 'appropriate.'

'Make them a *mild* chicken curry,' Dad suggested.

But Mum gave Dad a look that suggested that this would not be very appropriate.

She started clambering about the kitchen. She took out flour and some butter and measuring cups and set a recipe down which was, in bold letters, headed, PLAIN SCONES. She stared at it for some time and seemed to become very daunted by the word *Method*. With great concentration, she traced and mouthed the words of the recipe with her fingers.

Dad came in and, seeing her battle with scone dough, asked if she might like some help.

'Please leave the kitchen – that's what you can do to help!'

I was reading aloud from my *Endeavour Reader*. Though I would have much preferred at that moment to be reading about that starved caterpillar boring holes in the world, I was reading,

Judy and John like to take Digger to the park and play ball with him. 'Look,' says Judy. 'Look at Digger run.' John says, 'Yes, Digger can run very far and fast. Digger likes to run.'

Dad grabbed Mum by the wrists and they wrestled with each other for a moment until Mum finally fell onto his chest and wept and let him lead her to the dining table.

'Mama, what's wrong?' we three now crowded round to ask.

She took Shanti on her lap and, wiping her face on her sleeve and her hands, coated in flour, on her skirt, said, 'Mama's got to go to the hospital for an operation.'

No way, I thought, as she said these words, *hospital* and *operation*; operation, with its huge swallowing *O*, and hospital, a place in which people 'slipped away.' I would not let her go. *I would not!*

'What do you have to have an operation for?' Deepa asked.

'Well,' she said, staring blankly at Dad, 'Mama has a small sore inside her and they think it might grow big and make her sick if they don't remove it.'

'Where's the sore?' Deepa asked.

'On my o-varies,' she said. Again the swallowing, well-like *O*'s.

'Okay?' Daddy said.

Deepa shrugged and Dad said that Mum would only be in the hospital for a few days.

Shanti now began to cry and Dad took her onto his own lap.

'Don't cry, Shanti,' he said.

Now I said to her, 'Mama, are you going to die?'

'No,' said Dad, 'of course Mummy's not going to die.'

And then I began to wonder whether he was lying.

'Mama!' I screamed, 'are you going to die?'

No, I was told but I didn't believe it. I was not certain any one of us was going to live or that anyone would ever really rise; I was not certain that they would not put her in a coma, a kind of never-ending cocoon, and then call us up and say that she, too, had 'slipped away.' My feelers gyrated, afflicted. I wondered whether she had got sick because she was hungry for the sun. The world was so cruel, I thought, making people sick with sunless gloom and all this Jesus stuff that made you hope for things that He, He who was just a poor, ailing man with yellow skin and a bleeding heart, could not provide. In my *Endeavour Reader* I could see the barren, shadowy words,

> *Digger is a good dog. Digger can bark. Hear him bark, Judy! Woof Woof!*

And even these words did not seem certain, they seemed as though they may have been lain on the page just moments before I had read them; that they may just as easily 'slip away'. It seemed to me as though anyone else seeing these same words may have read,

> *Digger is a dumb dog. Digger yelps. Hear Digger yelp! Digger is a sad dog. Watch Digger run! Digger can run away.*

IMMORTALITY

In the week Mum went into hospital, Dad, hoping to cajole us, brought home a treat: Sea Monkeys. Deepa had been ceaselessly campaigning for them after having seen a television commercial in which they were profiled. She was enthusiastic about anything fluvial; it was the one shared bond between us. We both wanted, after having read Kingsley's magical tale of an aquatic republic, to be Tom from the *Water Babies*, and fought when we were only three and six for the part in the paltry tub in which we were bathed. Dad often had trouble getting us out of this bath, such was our love affair with water. When we'd swim in the small infants' Council pool at Rain Hill, our fingers had shrivelled into small walnut shells before we'd be willing to come out. Eventually – a luxury to be sure – Dad had built a small swimming pool at the back of the house.

Deepa was always quick to remind everyone that it was she who was born the true water-daughter, that my first encounter had not necessarily suggested such formidable marine ease. What she was refusing to let me forget was how, when Dad was teaching me to swim, I had climbed on his head and almost drowned him. ('Problem trusting grown-ups,' Dr. Blaby would perceptively diagnose some years later.) Sometimes, when I wasn't feeling so good about myself, such as the evening of the Daniel Hoolahan hand-holding hostility, I would stand on the bathmat as Dad gently dried me, watching the soapy water gurgle down the drain, wishing to God I would be small and viscose enough to slip through, to experience the pleasure of the Sydney Water Board's drainage kingdom first hand.

The Sea Monkeys were supposed to 'cheer us up' and 'keep us good' until Mum returned from her operation. According to Dad, we would have to share them. There was a problem with this, though, because Shanti couldn't see them and therefore did not believe they actually existed. As she was small, Deepa and I tried to explain that this imperceptibility was the source of their mystique, the very reason why they were *Magic* Monkeys. Shanti would not concede, suspend for our enjoyment the boundaries of her three-year-old disbelief. She also maintained that if they were *really* monkeys they certainly wouldn't live in water, for – *What did we take her for, a fool?* – she had been to Taronga Zoo several times and not once had she seen a primate residing in water there.

Deepa and I looked at each other and shook our heads bemoaning, exasperated: '*Kids.*'

Of course, the real problem began not with Shanti's scepticism but when Deepa – Deepa, who could always see things that others could not – made an outrageous claim.

She had monopolised the contents of the box, which included a special handbook for cultivating Sea Monkey society, a small transparent plastic bowl in which to accommodate them, and three essential sachets: Water Purifier, Instant Live Eggs, Growth Food.

I, left with the torn remnants of the box, devoured the instructions. Like those on the packs of noodles Dad had been feeding us, the directions for hatching sea monkeys seemed rather simple: *'Just add water and they come to life!'* In the corner of the mangled box, another series of bold letters entreated, FEED THEM, GROW THEM, BREED THEM! After you had spent some time feeding them, the monkeys were supposed to grow and, perhaps then, if you were really gifted with magic faculties – the powers of aquatic soothsaying, no less – you would see the monkeys performing aquatic acrobatic feats, pairing off and crafting for themselves a distinctive Sea Monkey social economy.

I tried to piece the torn box together and found a fabulist depiction of what the monkeys might look like: a king and queen reclined with their prince and princess Sea Monkey progeny. *Why, this was no republic!* In the fever of planning the rearing of these creatures, I had also noticed and not entirely dismissed the disclaimer in tiny print in one corner of the box:

Illustration is fanciful.
Does not depict contents of pack.

And then a note that would come to have import only sometime later, evidence for my subsequent scepticism, and a reminder of a not-so-distant misdemeanour involving an empty can of sunshine. As if to account for everything that would later happen, it read,

Made in the U.S.A.

Deepa, no patience for the steady needs of nature, expecting all around to simply partake of her own staggering developmental momentum, suggested that we feed the Sea Monkeys really quickly – maybe double their food requirements for the day.

'Okay,' I naively agreed. Although I had read the warning on the pack – *Do not overfeed!* – there didn't seem much harm in it.

The first two days bore no Sea Monkeys, and Shanti sighed with contrition at our disappointment with the barren bowl. She shook her head with great disapprobation as Deepa and I spent the weekend, like a couple undergoing in vitro fertilisation together, surveying our synthetic, disembowelled womb for changes. I myself had begun to wonder whether we had induced a reproductive crisis by adding so much food at once.

But on the third day of our nurturing the monkeys, Deepa woke early before school.

'Come and see them!' she commanded from the bottom of the stairs.

Somnolent, I arrived rubbing my eyes and made my way toward the little shrine we had erected for the monkeys in the middle of the dining table.

I found Deepa, already dressed in her school uniform, with her bloated features suctioned to the bowl.

I raced over and put my face where hers had been, where it was cloudy.

'I can't see anything.'

'I can,' she pronounced confidently.

'What can you see?'

She put her face to the other side of the bowl and I watched her wide, dark eyes come alive.

'Oh!' she said in turn-of-the-century English, 'it's gorgeous! It's marvellous!'

'Gorgeous'; 'marvellous': I started to suspect her, for I myself could perceive nothing but abandoned shreds of Sea Monkey feed floating on the surface.

'Tell me, then, what can you see?'

'Oh, they're all babies,' she replied convincingly without even having to so much as search for the words. 'Like Water Babies only they've got faces like monkeys, you know.'

I did not know. All I could think at that moment was how she had keenly flung herself into the deep end of the adult council pool many years ago while Dad had patiently coaxed me into the infants' pool.

Baths I had been able to handle, as the boundaries of the public and private were there clearly defined, but as a swimming initiate I had had to scream as I was reminded of that horrific event not long after my birth during which a burly man wearing a dress had, not only with parental consent but in a mood of celebration even, tried to drown me in a public forum. Had they come to my aid then? *Had they even called my name, let alone made an effort to rescue me?*

'Mina is a scaredy-cat! Mina is a scaredy-cat!' Deepa had shouted her competitive accusations of pusillanimity, drawing all nearby swimmers' attention to my novice blundering, until Dad, gasping after my having clung to his back and held him under for so long, screaming and flailing my arms, desperately censured her.

'What are they doing?' I said stonily.

'Why, swimming and playing and eating,' she improvised.

Her capacity for invention, I'll admit, was breathtaking.

She then took her face from the bowl, and with a look of utter astonishment and pity, too, said, 'You mean you really can't see them?'

'Maybe if I get Papa's magnifying glass.'

I ran into Mum and Dad's bedroom and reached around in the depths of Dad's top drawer of miscellaneous items and retrieved the brilliant instrument. I ran back and looked through at the enlarged image of a bowl of water: still nothing.

'What are they doing now?' I asked, my feelers falling.

'Oh, Mina, they're talking!' she said, delighted.

'English?' I asked.

'No . . . it's a kind of *patois*.'

'Can you understand anything?'

'Shh!' she declared, silencing me, putting her finger to her lip, '*I'm trying.*'

Early the next morning, before she'd woken, I got up and sought the bowl whose surface was now polluted with monkey feed. *Where*, I wondered, *were those creatures that capitalism had promised?* I pressed my nose to the plastic. I closed my eyes and imagined probing below the surface like an underwater diver. I imagined an army and family, a city and a cave and a dinner table and a country of Sea Monkeys, singing, dancing, invading, and conquering, crying and embracing and travelling from one colony to another and speaking in wild and glorious tongues.

I opened my eyes and stared at the dull, still water.

And it was now that I hatched my own plan.

I climbed the stairs and stealthily made my way to Deepa's room. Then, without making a sound, I turned the handle of her door and peered within to find my sister – angelic by night if duplicitous by day – still sleeping. Following this, I made my way back down the stairs and to the back door.

From here I could see Dad by the incinerator, preparing things to be burned; this annual ritual now recalled to me the imminence of another event: *Next weekend*, I thought, *the Queen's Birthday Celebrations: Fireworks Night!* This was when the Rain Hill neighbourhood wandered down to Clearwater Park with sparklers and bags of multifarious firecrackers in their hands. Revelling in the beauty of the naked sky, Dad would say that it was with such clarity that the Aborigines had once penetrated nature; that this was the spectacle of night that had existed before the British ruined the country.

I now longed to go outside and blow smoke into the chill air, but the late-July cold was caustic enough to give me chilblains.

There was some frost on the glass of the sliding door. As I watched Dad hauling huge branches toward the burner, I wrote my mortal name in the icy surface of the glass, but it disappeared with the whim of frost and I remembered that I had a task to complete.

Shanti was sitting in front of the television with only her pyjama bottoms on; she must have lost the top in the bed during the night, a common occurrence for her, she whose dreams were almost as animated as the cartoons with which she was infatuated. I would sometimes wake in the middle of the night to find her wrestling with an imagined enemy, conducting whole conversations with an array of like-minded individuals. At this moment, she was watching Sylvester catching Tweety and laughing contentedly, completely untroubled by the cold or by the prospect of slaughter.

While her back was turned, I quietly lifted the bowl from the centre of the dining table and, on tiptoe, carried it to the bathroom.

Safely there, I sat on the edge of the bathtub and opened the taps. Next, I coolly emptied the monkeys. *Good-bye, good-bye!* I facetiously saw them off in my mind's eye. *Have a nice time in Sewerage Kingdom!*

I then refilled the bowl with water and, careful to gauge I'd filled the accurate volume, deposited it back in the middle of the dining table.

Pleased with my work, I scattered a whole handful of food on the surface.

Shanti roused herself during a commercial and, just as I had nearly stilled the water, entered the kitchen.

She placed a large number of Weet-bix in a bowl.

'I hope you're going to eat all those,' I cautioned, trying to distract her from the still-trembling water.

She looked up at me, sighed, silently poured some milk into her bowl, and resettled herself in her beanbag.

Sylvester was now exiled from the house and I thought, *I want to have the bird murdered sooner or later!* for Tweety surely could not have been as innocent as she consistently seemed.

Moments later, Deepa strutted in, donned in her pyjamas.

I now feigned indifference and contented myself with some of the illustrations in a medical journal of Mum's that was lying on the table. A feature article on itchy rashes in children came to my attention. A pair of blistery red legs stood centrepiece and the caption read,

Atopic dermatitis. Flexural involvement with linche-nification.

I heard Tweety saying something about Sylvester being a naughty Putty Tat.

'Oh my God, there are more, so many more!' Deepa suddenly exclaimed. 'You really can't see anything, can you?'

I shook my head without looking up from the illustration. *No.*

'Oh, there are babies and mothers and little monkeys playing, and they're all talking. You mean to say you really can't see anything, Mina?' she had the gall to go on.

I went directly to the back where Dad had by now collected a huge amount of leaves and branches and paper to be burned.

From the look on his face I wondered whether he wanted to throw his heart in the incinerator.

'Deepa is a liar,' I unequivocally stated.

I detailed her crime thinking this would shift the balance of power, that he might, as he had at the public swimming pool all those years ago, tell her to hush.

Dad, the obliging arbiter of such disputes, now accompanied me into the house.

Deepa was asked to give her version of events. I again gave mine.

Before I knew it I was being accused by Deepa of murder and worse – the words again – of being a Stupid Idiot.

Thereafter, I was chased around the dining table.

Competing with Deepa's howls and the old grand-mother who had just admonished Sylvester and put him out of the house, Dad told me that my own behaviour left something to be desired. (*What*, I wanted to ask, *was that missing something that could enhance my life?*)

He found what I had done, he said, 'very disappointing.'

Deepa was crying out that I be sentenced according to the extremity of my misdeed. 'Butchery,' she said, and no one seemed to tell her that she might be exaggerating. 'Massacre,' she kept on saying.

'But, Daddy,' I opined, 'she said she could see them, She said they were playing and talking and she really couldn't see anything at all.'

Then, with Dad's next statement, I had to dispose of any plan of juridical order in which I had ever invested a shred of hope; completely reassess my perception of my father as servant of justice and exponent of human rights; indeed, I had to do away with the very doctrine of social democracy.

'Deepa has a good imagination,' he said.

And Deepa smiled.

Imagination. So that is how it happened that Imagination became the preserve of the liars and Carnage the preserve of the truth seekers. She got Imagination and I got Murder. Then, in the midst of it all, as I deliberated the paradox with which I was suddenly confronted, wondering whether there was any fairness in the universe at all, Dad declared that my punishment would be that I was not to attend Fireworks Night.

My already unsteady world thus collapsed. The world which, to my young eyes, only seemed truly beautiful when the moon and the stars and the iridescent bombs of light exploded and exposed the sky in all its nude glory. It was only on Fireworks Night that the worlds of my childhood – of that faraway place which I loved but rarely saw and this one in which I lived but rarely loved – became whole; it was only on Fireworks Night that my own doubt was suspended and the frontiers of the planet withdrew; it was only then, in the July sky, if I threw my head back far enough into the night, that I could see the lights shimmering about the Bombay docks at Colaba; only then that I might make out the blanket of smog sitting over that vast city and the edges of the shore of that cleaner entry to the Indian Ocean at my father's ancestral home at Benaulim, where at dusk the fishermen would collect their nets, nets always brimming with fish of pure silver it seemed, and visible only for the moon and the small lights thrown on the beach from Carlos's sand shack, which, it was said, kept burning all night to exorcise demons that came to interfere with the souls of two Siamese twin babies – the progeny of Carlos and his sister – who, because of their deformity, had been buried alive at birth. It was then, on Fireworks Night, that I would remember lying in my father's splendid lap, listening to the Christmas carols coming from the nearby church, the zealous, if a little off-key, voices of the parishioners, and my grandmother, her head resting on my father's shoulder, snoring and fitfully cursing the name of my dead grandfather; it was then that I, too, dozing off, would see as if in my dreams the servant boy, Tomas, fixing neon lights to the Christmas tree, making the face of the infant Jesus in the nearby crib flicker over and over, like a tenuous star.

Dad now entered the kitchen and emptied out some packs of two-minute noodles. He grumbled that it would be the last time he'd be bringing something home for us to share until such time as we could deal civilly with each other; after all, he said, we were *sisters*.

That Deepa was my sister seldom crossed my mind; she infuriated me so frequently.

'Oh, I don't care,' Deepa suddenly said, 'They're immortal, they couldn't die even if the stupid idiot drowned them!'

Immortal. They're immortal! It came suddenly, itself like an explosion. Immortality: This word bedazzled me, had me hypnotised in an instant. So, I did not possess the capacity to find life in a bowl of water, I had not even the imagination to invent them, to pretend to having seen those monkeys. *Oh, but immortality!* The same thing Tweetie Bird had, that was what I wanted – for Mum and for Dad and Shanti, and, yes, even for Deepa. Immortality! I had a vague notion of what this might involve; I knew it was a property unique to only select artefacts in the world and I tried at that moment to bring them to mind: the Holy Spirit, magnets, trees. Momentarily forgetting my transgression and the punishment that had ensued from it, I sat at the table wrapping endless noodles round my fork.

I went to the massive *Webster's Dictionary* by Dad's typewriter and looked up Deepa's big word.

Immortality: undying, famous for all time.

Preoccupied with endurance, I was hardly relieved when – the occasion for which I had been waiting for days – Mum returned from her operation.

'Mama, has the sore gone away?'

'Yes, they removed it all, everything,' she snapped and fluttered into the bathroom without so much as even looking at me.

Next she went about reordering the kitchen. She opened the refrigerator and for a good hour-and-a-half dreamily contemplated its cool interior. Following this, she hastily stuffed inside it a range of things that had been left out on the kitchen bench, perishables and – I observed with some alarm – even some nonperishable items: kitchen scissors, a dishcloth, a packet of paper napkins, and – was it just an oversight on her part? – Shanti's one-eyed plush giraffe.

There was yet another peculiar feature of her home-coming. Though I had been punished for theft and much else in recent months, we were all disconcerted to observe Mum unpack her bags in which were carefully stashed a host of stolen hospital goods: pillowcases with NSW PUB-LIC HOSPITAL stamped on their seams, spoils of bed linen, shower caps, and gowns; she'd even managed a host of implements and instruments, among them a bed pan, a spittoon, and a set of steel cups. Fruit, biscuits, and cheeses she had saved from her mealtime trays, scavenged and carried home with her. *The profound hypocrisy of it all!* And with what despotic urgency she now went about filling the kitchen cupboards and the pantry with these goods, refusing Shanti – who'd gone to retrieve the frigid giraffe and there discovered them – the small bars of chocolate she'd also collected for her hoard.

Of all the items in this strange booty, I myself was most fascinated by the small plastic identity bracelet inscribed with her name and blood type, which I could see fastened to her wrist.

Deepa, as it turned out, wanted it too.

This time I was perhaps prepared to share.

When we pleaded with her for it, though, it was Mum,

who, with a moony trill and the faraway eyes of a glorified pigeon, stingily said, 'You can't have it. I'm keeping it.'

At this moment, Dad was standing on the dining table replacing a lightbulb that had just blown.

'Why not?' Deepa begged her.

'I may need it one day to get back.'

'Get back where?' I asked.

'Home,' my mother chirmed.

Dad, startled, had then looked up, letting the globe in his hand fall and crash to the ground.

Given these events, I waited a very long time before Mum remembered to take me in her arms and kiss me. When finally she came to me, I was so sleepy I did not think twice about the peculiarity of what she did. Instead of stooping to kiss me spontaneously, as these things usually went, she asked if she might 'have' a kiss.

'Of course,' I said and grabbed the beautiful nape of her neck and plunked on her cheek the wettest kiss I had all week been waiting to give her for not dying on me.

'Make sure you keep your caps on!' she was exhorting Deepa and Shanti as Dad took their hands. In the course of the week, Dad had taken pity on me and decided to let me go to watch the fireworks; it was Mum who had insisted that I should have to see my punishment through.

She had opened *Baby and Child Care* at the chapter entitled 'Discipline.' She felt she was on a first-name basis with Dr. Spock, calling him Ben as though he were an intimate companion.

' "*A child knows when he has displeased a parent or broken a rule. If his parent tries to hide his irritation . . . it only makes the child uneasy. He imagines that all this*

42

suppressed anger is building up somewhere ... and worries what will happen if it ever breaks out,"' she had read aloud to Dad.

From the window in Deepa's room I could now see the park at the end of the road and the minor crackers already being fired.

I opened the window and blew a cloud of smoke in front of me and thought over and over to myself of the same mesmerising thesis: *Immortality*.

'Close the window or put a cap on, otherwise you'll get a head cold!' Mum crowed.

All the neighbourhood children were thronging the park, inflated in their anoraks, their faces blithe moons illumined by the fireworks. At a distance, I could even make out the tiny figure of Shanti playing with some other children and Deepa lighting a spinning top from the branch of a eucalyptus tree: *Immortality*. The top ricocheted around and around, and spectators moved away watching, in dynamic action, Deepa's vibrancy, her Imagination, her Tremendous Personality; indeed, the whole tree lit up beautifully when the top began to spiral between the deep cola sky and the tips of the branches. And then, as fast as it had brought that joy, the dynamite died and the thrill receded into darkness.

I could now smell basmati rice and frying eggplant and wandered downstairs in the hope that Mum would call me and ask me, as she often did while preparing dinner, to read from my *Endeavour Reader*.

She did not ask and so I went of my own accord to my school bag to retrieve that inane text.

I settled myself onto the kitchen stool and began reading aloud about Digger and Jane and Jim who had been taken, in this particular series number, to the seaside for a summer holiday. As she turned the delicious aubergine over and over in the pan, randomly adding spices and flavorings that she felt appropriate – cumin, turmeric, cardamom to season, fresh lemon – I continued reading with my best diction.

When she did not look up and request, as she usually did, that I come to her – whereupon she'd take a teaspoon for me to test the pungency of the masala, consult me about what it needed *More salt? More ginger?* – I simply kept reading. I read until I could no longer bear the easy cadence of my voice.

Then I snapped my book shut, sidled over near to where she was standing, opened the rice cooker, and let the steam rise into my face.

Immortality, I again thought to myself.

'You know you can die doing such things,' Mum told me.

Die? How was it that she knew so much more than I about death, I who had been thinking exclusively on that subject for several months now? At this moment I wanted to say to her, 'Whatever sore they removed from you, I am your daughter and I want them to put it back and for everything to be the way it was before I began knowing that you might leave me forever.'

I could not say it. Instead, I returned to the solitary kitchen stool and continued reading aloud of Digger and Jane and Jim and the meagre paradise in which they spent their days building sandcastles, pretend edifices that would no doubt crumble as soon as the tide came in, and, if not then, before the summer ended. I knew the end of summer. The end of summer came like the death of light and in its spectre I could see my father desperately embracing his weeping mother; and I knew this weeping was because he could not know whether she might die – *his own mother!* – before Dad might return again to the village in Goa. Seeing Dad in such despair – was it *that* which he had been contemplating as he had stood before the incinerator? – I would cry bitterly, too, until the servant, Karena, smelling of cloves and sweat and chapattis, would draw me to her, smother me in her generous bosom and wipe my tears away with the hem of her singed dress.

Mum now set me some pieces of eggplant on a plate and, eating with my bare hands, licking the piquant masala from them, I devoured them as though were they were gifts of the greatest maternal munificence.

Once or twice I sensed something move in the house next door, the Soyers' house, into which, from my position at the table, I could see directly.

It was true: Quentin, the boy next door, was waving at me.

I waved back.

I knew why he wasn't partaking of Fireworks Night. He had told me once with no bravado at all: He was scared.

He drew away from the window and I kept on eating. As I ate, I thought, *He knew what it was not to depend on the immutability of any planetary configuration; he knew about the fading and dissolution of the stars.*

And it was now that we heard keys at the door. It was far too early for them to be returning. As they entered, I saw Dad was carrying Shanti in his arms. My feelers pricked up. I dropped my *Reader* and screamed. Mum darted toward them. I could not focus. Their figures were blurred by the steam still rising in my eyes. Deepa's nose was running and she had long tears dripping down her cheeks. Dad said that someone had thrown a throw-down at Shanti and it had exploded close to her eye. Mum went to examine it. She took Shanti from Dad's arms while Dad rushed to get the car out to take her to casualty. I could see that her eye was ruined and bleeding. Shanti had the habit of holding her breath when she was injured – why, we never knew – but now she was alert, wrestling with them all as I would sometimes wake to find her wrestling those that peopled her dreams. This was no oneiric fantasy, though. Mum, too, had started screaming.

I watched them with their mouths agape as if they were astonished by the sight of firecrackers shattering. *Were they forgetting to swallow?* I wondered as I watched my rapt mother and father. We were waiting in the Casualty. I had thoroughly apprehended that word by then. I knew my mother worked in Casualty, that we sometimes lived with casualty about us, but rarely, I believed, did we ever meet with casualty.

I began tap-dancing down the Casualty corridor with the shoes I had been bought as a birthday present from China Town, where we'd gone to buy the firecrackers.

Dad watched me out of the corner of his eye.

I wondered whether he thought I was being wicked. When I was wicked – as at this moment when I showed no awareness of my dear sister's plight, shuffling around on the linoleum – Dad's cheeks bloated like those of a popper fish.

I kept dancing, hypnotised by the clicking of plastic on plastic.

Deepa was reading *Crime and Punishment* and kept looking up at me and then lowering her eyes, as if to say, 'No, I am not going to give you the satisfaction of seeing my eyes meet yours. Look here, don't be seeking a bond of any kind between us.'

Soon enough there was an audience of Casualty strangers, perturbed, as I, a mutant child, my nodes turgid – easily offending the memory of Shirley Temple – performed for them.

Mum and Dad remained silent; noise was the load I carried; their mute load was this: They could not hold the world in one hand and their daughter in the other and they were tormented by that inexorable interface.

Shanti, the doll of the family, almost went blind on account of a Queen's Birthday Casualty. That was how we were to forever after name the day and circumstances of the accident in which her left cornea was almost damaged with fire.

When she awoke from the surgery that saved her, she sat up the same way we had known her to; the way children, unconscious of their own blessed bodies, such that if one were to remove a limb here or a sense there in their sleep, would wake only believing that they had never had faculty in that area.

I kept dancing even when the surgeon came out and informed us that the vision had been salvaged; the prognosis was normal. I had heard such a reassurance once before and what folly it had been to depend on it!

My antennae extended, all I could do to save myself was dance.

'She's fine,' the surgeon said of my little sister, 'just fine.'

Dad was now cursing the name of Queen Elizabeth,

muttering something under his breath. 'Birthright of butchery,' he kept on saying 'Carnival of carnage.'

'Look,' I wanted to cry out as everybody watched me shuffling like a lunatic a series of made-up steps on that floor, 'I, too, am scared that you cannot hold the world in one hand; I, too, am scared of crashing headlong with the night.'

Dad's hand, which I had never felt falling on me, suddenly struck the back of my leg. My feet stopped like those of a wild animal that has just been shot. My leg throbbed for hours after but just at that moment it pained me so much so that I lay down and wept in front of all the tired nurses, the grim relations, and mortified lovers.

Having struck me, Dad's eyes clouded over with the sadness of that morning by the incinerator. He turned to Mum, whose mouth now seemed as tight as a ravenous but eternally malnourished caterpillar; she could not fly, at least not yet, and I myself would have to quit waiting for her transmogrification. Her words would no longer give way to her heart and her kisses would now come to me only involuntarily.

At this moment I imagined a huge void opening between them. She felt responsible for not going, for staying behind; he felt responsible for going, for not remaining. It was now that I imagined that sterile amniotic fluid in which the Sea Monkeys had refused to breed; now that I knew only the dead were timeless; that what they had removed from my mother would not be reissued; and that we ourselves sitting in this waiting room, that we were as perishable as bread.

'Mama, can I have a look under Samosa's patch?'

They'd let her out since the retina had stopped bleeding.

Dad turned to face me at the red light. His cheeks were puffed again. Shanti was oblivious to the fuss everyone was making of her. Deepa possessively hooked her arm inside hers. No one answered me. During that most precarious journey on the way to the hospital, Mum had stubbornly pulled her tiny limbs into a fresh pair of panties and a singlet. Shanti had complied. Now she yawned and Mum, occasionally turning her head to see her sitting weary in the bleached underwear, began to coo and cry again, to shift in her seat, to chirr something to Jesus that made us three very scared in the back.

Then Shanti asked it, as though she were again talking in her sleep.

'Mama,' she asked, touching the patch that covered her wounded left eye, 'am I going to be like Quentin?'

DOUBLE VISION

I thought that Quentin, who was born blind in one eye, suffered a great deficit. But then his father left him.

Perhaps it was portentous that as the Soyers had moved in next door Quentin prostrated himself and cried on the lawn. His mother came out and pleaded with him to go inside, but he remained inconsolable, his seven-year-old heart broken. Diminutive and misplaced as Alice in Wonderland, he simply closed his eyes and feigned death while the removalists deposited hulky pieces of furniture onto the lawn around him.

Deepa was at the bay window commenting on the action.

'Oh, it's a boy!' she exclaimed despondently, as though he had just emerged fresh from the womb or from an egg.

I came over and craned my neck to see and Shanti, too, demanded a peep.

'Don't spy,' Mum said.

It was a Saturday morning in early autumn. She was dressing to go to the job she had taken on weekends in Casualty ('Cas' as she came affectionately and odiously, to call it), a second job at a hospital on the faraway Western periphery of Sydney.

I could see steam rising from the polyester blouse she was pressing. Work as a palliative physician, among the living dead, was taking its toll on her. She needed 'time away' she had told Dad, to administer to people she felt she could '*really* save.' Death from Monday to Friday she could endure if only she felt she was giving life elsewhere.

'Of course,' Dad had said, 'you ought to go.'

'We could use the money,' she had said, indicating us, her easy justification, the feet that required ballet lessons, the talent that required violin tuition, the young minds that would profit from camps, retreats, courses of educational enrichment.

'You ought to go,' he had repeated.

Terminal pain and chronic illness were by now old hat to me. I knew and, when convenient, boasted, about Mum's occupation. That palliative medicine might be the most debauched discipline of an otherwise noble scientific episteme did not cross my mind. I believed Mum was a regular, if diffident, Florence Nightingale.

'I help people to die with dignity,' she would say to those who inquired, and I was too vain and young to have denuded the euphemisms, seen the perversity of what others must have, equally, regarded as magnanimity: My mother helped people to die.

To my mind, her work was as lofty as Dad's; he counselled on the legal status of refugees and immigrants for the Department of Immigration and Ethnic Affairs. This, I supposed, was something like what the President of the United Nations presided over, just on a smaller scale.

I waited in earnest for his promotion.

But while I may have internalised mortality from a young age, Casualty was indeed a novel concept. *Casualty*: I toyed with the word in my mind as she came to escape each weekend. I strove to comprehend her departures by way of vague associations; victims of natural disaster, the leukaemic children of Chernobyl, the famine-stricken Ethiopians who were made to look like freaks on TV, the citizens of Nagasaki: These people were all 'casualties' of a kind.

When these references failed to satisfy, I asked her straight out.

'Salvageable emergencies,' she told me; people, I imagined, with their limbs fractured, their ligaments torn, their flesh slivered. 'Remedial accidents.'

Casualty. I soon became inured to its meaning, habituated it just as quickly as I had the contents of her journals that arrived in the mail week by week and that were frequently strewn across the dining table – *The Medical Examiner, Contemporary Australian Physician* – all with their fascinating pictures of fatality, of human waste. I knew that if I wanted to sneak a look at the heart of a myocardial infarction survivor, the ravages of hepatocellular carcinoma, all I had to do was turn to the appropriate edition of one of those texts. It had also occurred to me that those harrowing anatomies might one day earn me fame at school; again, I was simply waiting for the most auspicious moment.

As Quentin was lying on the front lawn of his new house, I went to the door and pressed my nose to the fly-screen mesh.

I watched Dad reverse the car out of the driveway to take her, Florence Nightingale, to the railway station. He looked sad, damaged; he stuck his head out of the window and a shower of rain from the side hedge struck him. He glowered. It had become a habit of mine to spend this time enviously imagining, in symptomatic detail, the various maladies of the patients she might encounter. *How*, I would think, with silent wonder and with scorn, *could my mother suture a stranger's flesh, when she couldn't even mend my own wide and gaping wounds?* Not just sorrow but real needs were at stake. I needed more than palliation, more than any salve.

The hem, for instance, of my school uniform, had been coming down for months. When I had showed it to Dad, he, knowing no better, had conscientiously taken the stapler to it.

I stayed guard at the door, but, once they were out of sight, wandered into the garden where the once splendid roses had fallen to the frosted ground. In their place were blunt, ruined centres and I was bereft to find that the bees that had just weeks before come for the rich pollen were now nowhere in sight. The concrete of the driveway was cold and enlivening and I felt delightfully naked barefoot.

I glanced back at the bay window and noticed that Deepa had retreated. The house was faintly illumined by the light of the television, which Shanti was watching, passively mesmerised. A devotional yogi, she rarely swallowed during such trances and would feel aggrieved to find her muesli or Weet-bix sloppy as porridge when Porky Pig dutifully disclosed that it was all over. Now I could hear at a distance the thunderous, foppish timbre of Quick Draw McGraw as he guffawed; he seemed to shake the foundations of the whole house.

'I don't think you should lie down there, you'll die of cold,' I said.

The whole figure of the small boy moved as he raised his shoulders into an impudent shrug.

'What's your name?' I asked.

'What's yours?' He closed his eyes, affecting tedium.

'Mina,' I said. 'Don't you like your new house?'

He shook his head from side to side.

I sighed at his melodrama and made to return inside.

'Want to see something?' he suddenly asked.

I turned back. 'Okay.'

'You have to come here.'

I carefully climbed over the small rose bed that was cobbled at the edges with stones.

Now I felt I was down the Rabbit Hole, dwarfed by a huge grandfather clock, giant-sized oak dining chairs, a huge scroll of a rug.

'What?' I said as I drew near to him.

His eyes were still closed. He had a pale complexion, was wearing a tracksuit that was sodden and oversized. I was often told *I* was puny, elfin, but compared to that supine child I felt gigantic. I was not going to be made a fool of by an imp, I thought; he had not yet even given me a name. I drew back from him, impatient, as he, with his eyes still shut, giggled demoniacally.

'What is it?' I pressed.

He now opened his eyes, stared at me with ominous good humour and, before I knew it, had extracted his left eye ball and was sitting upright, holding and displaying it in his open hand.

I felt I may have been hallucinating, had, like Alice, perchance drunk some strange elixir and this was its potent side effect.

'It's glass,' he said and laughed nonchalantly.

I scowled, expressing my distaste.

'Oh, don't worry,' he soothed, 'it's just like a big marble. Want to have a feel?'

I thought on this proposition a moment and then, curiosity replacing terror, squatted down to him.

I could feel my antennae quizzically rising.

'Hey,' he laughed touching the tip of the left one, 'what's that?'

'Don't!' I drew away from him again.

He stood up then, glaring at me with his one real, cyclopean eye, ennui suddenly turned into competitive wonder.

'Quentin.'

'What?'

'My name's Quentin,' he said, fitting the artificial eye back into its socket.

I can't remember exactly what we said to each other then, although it was clear that we were locked into a primal confidence, that we had, in those few pointed moments, revealed to each other more than some lovers lay bare in a whole lifetime, enjoined ourselves more metaphysically than siamese twins.

Mrs. Soyer, so lively and vivacious, came out then.

'You must be our new neighbour!' she said, smiling brightly.

I nodded.

'Say, Quentin, aren't you going to be neighbourly and invite your new neighbour in?'

The grandfather clock chimed nine o'clock.

Quentin again lay down on the grass and closed his eyes.

'Playing dead, I suppose. Charming,' she admonished him and then gave me a complicit wink.

'Would you like a glass of Ribena?'

'Oh, I've got to go to my violin lesson,' I lied and excused myself and quickly made my way back over the stones and rose bushes dividing our houses.

The flannel of my pyjamas got caught on a thorn. I unhooked myself, my antennae almost sweeping me off balance, and made my way inside.

'Come over and say a proper hello later!' I heard her calling after me.

Quick Draw McGraw was desperately trying to assert some authority, exclaiming something in his Southern drawl.

'I say,' he blundered, removing a shotgun from his buckle, 'seems to me we've got a crime occurring in our midst.'

He faltered with the gun and shot the tyres of the car he was supposed to drive off in. I'd always suspected Baba Looey was the real brain behind the pair.

Shanti, though, humoured by his buffoonery, giggled, rustling the foam in the beanbag where she lay, her mouth encrusted with milk. Beside her a bowl of cornflakes stood, swampy and inedible.

My own stomach grumbled and I realised I had not eaten the night before. Having been a Lenten Friday, Mum had forced us to eat fish, and not just boneless bream, but a cheap, lean fish, with thin bones all through it. I had given up halfway through a bite, decided I'd rather starve than struggle with that alimentary conundrum. I had always felt a certain pity for the Five Thousand; I myself would have accepted the bread, but politely declined when the fish appeared as part of Christ's miraculous overture.

I opened the fridge and, from amongst the weird stock

of perishables that had begun to amass itself there – most intriguing was a pair of black suede heels Mum had, in a fit of spendthrift deviation, recently bought but not yet worn – retrieved some leftover chicken curry and rice.

'Want some?' I called to Shanti, indicating the Tupperware container with cold, congealed drumsticks.

She didn't answer but turned to her bowl and, shattered at seeing her cereal soggy, lay back in her beanbag, slapping her head.

'Playing dead,' I commented, 'Charming.'

'My Mum was in a camp,' Quentin was telling me.

In recent weeks he had braved his way over to our territory and was now sitting on our porch, letting me handle the eye. It was Good Friday and, as Mum had prophesied, the sky was in mourning for Jesus. Earlier in the afternoon we had gone to Mass, where Christ's trial had been reenacted. Jesus was brought before Pontius Pilate, had testified against the Jews, and been crucified all within the hour. I was enraged when the soldiers threw die for his clothes. I cried when Father Murphy quoted from the Gospel according to St John:

'Jesus saw his mother and the disciple he loved standing there; so he said to his mother, "He is your son."

Then he said to the disciple, "She is your mother." From that time the disciple took her to live in his home.'

I had looked up at Mum; could she not see the depth of my own suffering? Oh, how I longed not to be cast away from her! Did she not know her station in life? She was my mother, *my mother!* And I thought of poor, bereaved Mother Mary having to forsake her home, to abandon all her belongings and take up with a complete stranger, John, cooking and cleaning in somebody else's house. And where, I wondered, was the carpenter Joseph through all this? Did his mortality somehow save him from despair? As I sniffled, Father Murphy blew out the candle signifying Jesus' presence; he left the tabernacle ajar. He did not, I noted, genuflect on his way out. *How did he maintain this annual woe*, I wondered, *the prognosis always negative, even as it was repetitive?*

Ever since the homily when he'd said that Jesus had died to save the soul of Christians, that it was an honourable and courageous act, and would we humans sacrifice so much for even our closest kin? Father Murphy had seemed unusually agitated. 'Yes,' I had wanted to say, looking sideways at my family, I had wanted to raise my hand and say yes, that I, personally, would. I had firmly gripped Mum's arm as the congregation burst into the words of the final hymn:

Oh, Jesus Crucified
For us you suffered, for us you died
On the cross!

Now sitting on the porch steps with Quentin, I realised I hadn't changed out of my plum cord pinafore, in these days my standard apparel for what were called 'special occasions', Jesus' death among them. Mum was going to call me in to change, I knew, interrupt us when the dress was ready for a wash anyway. I'd already dropped the afternoon meal – fish fingers and sauce – down the front, so to my own eye the dress couldn't get much grubbier.

'What kind of camp?' I now asked Quentin.

'A concentrating camp.'

'Oh,' I said.

Dad was always trying to get us places at such things during school holidays; Deepa, particularly, he knew would thrive if given the opportunity for such academic advancement, and so enrolled her, willing and sometimes unwilling, into every conceivable mode of extracurricular scholarship about which he'd hear.

'Oh, but she's just a child!' her teachers would try at Parent-Teacher Night to assuage Mum and Dad, who were anxious to realise Deepa's genius. 'You must remember she must partake of normal child activities, too,' they'd say.

'Convicts!' Dad had charged them in a fit of rage when he'd arrived home once, immediately entering Deepa's name into a brochure that advertised a camp for the mathematically gifted. 'Descendants of convicts, why of course they'd be happy with the mediocrity of every child. They know no better!'

Of me they'd said, 'Mina needs to pay greater heed to spelling. Her sentence construction and grammar are fair, but she tends to make careless errors. With greater care and concentration . . .'

A Concentrating Camp! A camp specifically for those who required instruction in Diligence and Patience. If he knew about this, Dad would try to send me! The thought was painful, the idea of exile – of, to put it plainly, enduring fellow children – brought tears again to my eyes.

Tenderly, I handed the eye back to Quentin who slotted it into the socket.

'She's got a stamp on her hand to prove she's been there and everything.'

This might not be so bad, though, myself, I didn't care for the stamps my sedulous peers received on their hands – Smiley stamps, Busy Bee stamps – but I could not abide the idea of a Concentrating Camp, even if such gratuities were on offer.

'How come you don't go to Church?' I asked Quentin.

He shrugged.

'Are you a Child of God?'

The shrugging, I could see, was a habit with him.

'Well if you're not Christian, you're not saved.' I informed him directly of Father Murphy's words.

'Oh, yes I am!' he suddenly cried. 'I was one of five.'

'Hah?'

'The other four died. God blessed me especially. That's why I'm alive.'

'What?'

'Mum had five babies, but they all died inside her tummy. I was saved. Only me.'

I now pictured stout Mrs. Soyer with her face as gentle and kind as Mary; I imagined four babies simultaneously sighing and suiciding inside her womb and Quentin the only one to have emerged breathing, the others shrivelled into tones of pain like the roses in our garden.

'They all died, did they?' I asked him, dismayed at the thought.

But again he shrugged.

'Quentin?'

'Mmm?'

'What happened to your eye?'

Mum had told us not to ask about it; as with spying on

our new neighbours, inquiring about their child's disability came under the burgeoning category of impertinences. 'Did I like to have my nodes examined?' 'How did I feel when others commented on the aberrations at the top of my head?'

'Oh, that,' he said, pointing to the single, bright organ from which sight was available, 'that was saved, too!'

We went inside to ask Deepa whether she wanted to play bulrush. She had been fiddling with a school project she'd been assigned for the Easter break. The task was to empty an egg of its yolk and white, break open a small section of the top of the shell, and attach a few balls of cotton with glue to the centre. With a little imagination, a cardboard beak, and two small Magic Marker eyes, a simulated chick was supposed to provide the third-grader with a delightful, self-rendered monad of the Easter thesis: New Life.

Mum had made a great fuss about allowing Deepa that one egg.

'Here,' she had said, carrying it in a dishcloth and bestowing it before Deepa as if it were a jewel. 'Only because it's for school.'

'How about an omelette for lunch?' Dad had said to Mum when he'd seen the extracted viscera sitting on the table in a tumbler.

Eggs? It had been so long since I'd eaten one – hard-boiled, scrambled, or sunny-side up.

Dad reminded me of this when he'd muttered, scratching his head, 'Don't know when it was that I last had an egg.'

At this, Mum had done a strange thing. She'd grabbed

the carton of remaining eggs from the kitchen bench and pressed them to her chest.

'I'll make an omelette out of you if you're not careful!' she told him.

No sooner had she said this than she had hurried out the back, carrying, as if she were the dignified member of an offertory procession, the tumbler of mucousy liquid. Dad and I both stood watching, baffled, as my mother, a gardening spade in one hand, then emptied and interred the contents into a fertile patch of soil near the mint and coriander.

Her knees bare, she then knelt on the wet soil and made the sign of the cross.

'What's Mama doing that for?' I asked Dad.

'She feels bad.'

'Bad for what?'

'Bad for the chick,' Dad had told me.

Deepa was now sitting cross-legged at the table, having completed the first part of her assignment; two plain white balls of cotton emerged from the eggshell, faceless and bald. She was bored, I could tell. The malformed chick was set aside and she was reading from *On the Genealogy of Morals*.

Thoroughly engaged, she did not answer our request to play bulrush, but looked up and deadpanned, 'God is dead.'

'What are you reading?' Quentin asked, moving toward the colossal pile of library books on the table.

'Oh, Quentin,' she sighed, 'you wouldn't understand.'

I didn't like her speaking down to Quentin, although I realised that with his slight build it was difficult to talk any other way. Deepa had been in an abominable mood ever since having returned from School on Holy Thursday, where in class they had been reading 'Batter My Heart, Three-Person'd God.' Some unknowing child had asked the teacher whether the Battered Heart was akin to a battered savloy and Deepa had taken great offence at this.

'You know,' she had said at the dining table that evening, grim as Christ's own disciple, 'Donne was a true genius. You know, Daddy, many of his best sonnets were composed when he was blind.' At this she had slightly tilted her head in the direction of the Soyer house.

Mum was making fish amothik. I could smell the sour aroma of tamarind simmering with turmeric and garlic. The scent seduced me, filled me with a terrible longing, but I thought again of the maze of bones through which I'd have to find my way to the paltry flesh. *Why, I wondered, was the internal reality of the world so unnecessarily complicated?* I wanted to be moved, feel something sudden and urgent; I wanted to suffer a fast and real kind of casualty, to have my senses thoroughly assaulted. I flipped at random through a journal lying on the table and I arrived at a picture of a gruesome, pus-filled toe. The caption read:

Onychogryphosis: Progressive thickening of the nail plate is seen mainly in the elderly.

Shanti was watching a Looney Tunes Evening Easter Special. Chimerical Bugs was playing the Easter Rabbit, no less, depositing gifts of eggs and flowers to a mixed cast of characters, allies and foes alike.

No one fought; Daffy and Wile E. Coyote were conciliatory and well-behaved. Tweety Bird was her sagely sanguine self and, alarmingly, even Sylvester was exemplary – a model of good mental health – in his relations with her.

Shanti was exultant; it was a great thrill, it seemed, to have the ensemble at work in this way.

I asked her whether *she'd* like to play bulrush, but she was so consumed by the cartoons that she didn't even blink.

'Let's go to your place,' I suggested to Quentin.

He shrugged and, taking this as my cue, I grabbed his hand and walked out of the doleful house.

'I don't want any dinner!' I yelled to Mum as I slammed the screen door.

'Come back and change out of your pinafore!' she clacked.

'Quick!' I told him and we dashed like fugitives toward the Soyer's house.

I relished my visits to their house, a restored Federation, one of the loveliest on our street. In the summer, the scent of the jasmine and honeysuckle by the letterbox articulated the longing of my heart's own aloneness. Before the Soyers moved in, I would wait at the bus stop, admiring the sun as it struck the intricate lead-light panelling, yearning to skip school and take refuge in the rooms within. I had wanted for some time to find out what the light was like as it flooded through to the other side of those myriad-hued windows. Inside, the walls were adorned with fine paintings, the mantles with enchanting curios which seemed to scream out to my small touch.

I felt older, emboldened, suddenly large as Alice as I now walked the long hallway.

'My son, my son!' Mr. Soyer exclaimed with exaggerated relief when he saw us entering. 'You've returned! And he's brought with him the virtuoso violinist.'

I thought he was saying 'virtuous violinist' and so took the compliment without a second thought. Even these dear people, though we were still strangers, could discern my nobility, I thought, quietly vindicated.

Mr. Soyer now swept Quentin into his arms and planted a kiss on his dull cheek. Quentin succumbed shyly. In the midst of the embrace, though, I observed Mr. Soyer becoming uneasy, exerting a sudden reserve, as if remembering not to damage the fragile child.

'Like a glass of Ribena?' Mrs. Soyer asked, reaching into a kitchen cupboard for glasses.

Mr. Soyer came behind her and gripped her waist.

'Oh, stop it Ted,' she said coyly.

She turned to me, 'Would you like some creme wafers, too?'

'Oh no,' I declined more for the sake of politeness than for candour. (*Creme wafers!*)

'As far as I see it,' she told me, handing me the rich, dark drink and recklessly tearing open a packet of wafers with her jaw, 'there's just one life, Mina, and we must live it without reserve.'

I took one of the delightful biscuits and rolled my tongue against the tangy fruit creme centre. Contentedly, my feelers lay down at ease.

Mr. Soyer was taking large sips from a jelly glass and began jiving for our pleasure to a jazz standard on the radio. He cajoled Mrs. Soyer into joining him and, watching them sway, I was slowly hypnotised. It is here, I mused: the Land of Milk and Honey.

Quentin, abashed, sat beside me, slotting the eyeball in and out of the socket.

When the standard was over, Mr. Soyer changed the record to a Bach sonata and they strode back to the table arm in arm, Mr. Soyer affecting soulful introspection, Mrs. Soyer flushed and giggling.

'Here,' Mr. Soyer said, lifting the box of creme wafers again to me and I greedily put my hand in.

'Oh,' Mrs. Soyer sighed, pulling her fingers through Quentin's lanky hair, kissing his small head, which in her hands seemed even smaller, 'I've been meaning to have your mum and dad over for dinner or drinks *or something*. Things have just been so hectic.'

My nodes sensed danger, perked up. If my parents came over, I thought, there was a great possibility that Mrs. Soyer might mention the Concentrating Camp to Dad.

'Oh,' Dad would say, annihilating my whole world, 'that sounds just the thing for Mina.'

My heart, now a great beast, was rubbing up against my ribs. I let the rest of the wafer melt on my tongue.

'Oh, they can't come,' I said.

Startled, Mr. and Mrs. Soyer looked at me.

These, I thought, *were the instantaneous effects I wanted to be producing!*

'She's very busy,' I informed them, imagining the sigh of the iron again, of her weekend escape. 'Busy and tired.'

I watched their sympathetic eyes, their fallen, affected faces. *I was a natural at whatever this art was I had fallen upon!*

'Oh,' I sighed, 'she's never home.' And now I said something I didn't even mean to disclose, so wretched did I feel with my own glum life. 'She hates us!'

'Oh, dear,' Mrs. Soyer said, moving away from Quentin, her own child, and moving to comfort me. Her bosom was plush, a divine place for my head, and my feelers fell melancholically against her soft skin. 'I don't think that can be right. Human beings don't hate one another.'

'It is,' I said, even more wretched with myself, 'She hates us.'

'Now tell me something,' Mr. Soyer said, 'Your Mum's a . . .'

'A palliative physician,' I recited as I had learnt to at school. We'd sat in a circle and had to name and explain our parents' respective professions. All the other children seemed to have to learn only easy nouns: nurse, teacher, solicitor, clerk, they'd recite. Amen Anthony had made everyone laugh by saying his father was a bank robber. Only I had had that convoluted mouthful to contend with. No wonder my spelling was only fair; you demand grandiloquence from a child and she is bound to suffer a developmental crisis. *Dyslexia, aphasia* – these are just technical terms for a lay affliction: fear of words. Shrugging is also a symptom.

'Whoa!' Mr. Soyer said, admiring the breadth of my knowledge.

I nodded gravely.

'Do you want to be a palliative physician, too?' he asked.

'Oh, no,' I told him. 'I'd rather die.'

We all laughed rapturously at the unexpected pun. Even Quentin giggled unknowingly. We couldn't stop. Mr. Soyer threw his head back like Quick Draw McGraw and his laughter thundered throughout the house.

We were laughing so hard, Quentin and I bursting into further fits at intervals, we barely heard when Mrs. Soyer, suppressing a smile, suddenly said, 'You laugh like that and you'll end up crying.'

'And . . .' I went on, with a renewed sobriety, wondering at what moment they might decide to let me stay for good, at what point Mr. Soyer might turn to me and say, 'Child, this is your mother,' and to Mrs. Soyer, 'Mother, this is your child.' 'We have to eat fish,' I added disdainfully.

Mr. Soyer took another gulp of brandy.

'*Oh,*' he said kindly, knowingly, '*fish.*'

Now he turned to Quentin. 'You know the problem with fish?' he said.

Quentin shrugged.

He meant to tickle him, but Quentin was squeamish. Mr. Soyer gripped him by the waist and raised him into the air. The blood rushed to Quentin's face and I could see that he was scowling.

Mrs. Soyer stood back and observed not with delight but with, I thought, a palpable fear.

Mr. Soyer was trying to lift Quentin on his shoulders, but Quentin kept on writhing. 'They always try to get away!' Mr. Soyer chuckled like Quick Draw McGraw.

'I want to get down!' Quentin suddenly squealed.

'Leave him alone, Ted!' Mrs. Soyer said.

Mr. Soyer kept chortling and I watched Quentin's small body sway dangerously above the solid weight of his father.

'Let me down!' Quentin cried, and I thought he might burst into tears as I myself had many times atop Dad's shoulders.

Mr. Soyer begrudgingly let Quentin down.

'You're hurting me!' he pleaded.

'Stop it, Ted,' Mrs. Soyer said.

'A grown boy, why, of course I'm not hurting him. I love him,' Mr. Soyer said, rolling him inside his big arms.

She clasped her hands firmly now, as if in prayer. 'Ted, I'm telling you, leave him alone. You'll hurt him.'

Quentin suddenly dropped to the floor.

No one spoke. Mr. Soyer looked like a big sad bear, upbraiding himself for having misjudged his own strength. I studied Quentin's puny, relieved form, the hue returning to his dim visage. I remembered reading of the first Passover in Exodus, the Angel of Death passing over the doors of the Israelites' dwellings, saving only the firstborn of those families that had, in accordance with instructions, marked their doors with the blood of a slaughtered lamb. I thought of the crude wooden epitaph over Christ's body: INRI. Could a Messiah truly die such a simple death? Why, *He* was a firstborn, an only son, and still He had not been spared. *And where was the carpenter Joseph throughout? Did his mortality somehow save him from despair?*

Blood, Frogs, Flies, the Death of Animals, Boils, Hail, Locusts – all that I could endure. But Darkness. *Darkness,* I mused: the final curse over Egypt, which seemed to cast its spectre even now, so many millennia later, in this silent kitchen, now in the eyes of Mrs. Soyer. We might never be free, we might never part the sea of certain sorrows, for they are carried with us from an early hour. 'We have only one life and we must live it without reserve,' she had told me, but that caption concealed a tumour of a slower, more savage reality.

'Stop it Ted!' Mrs. Soyer now pleaded. 'Stop it! You'll

hurt him,' she wept. 'You always push it too far. Didn't I say, didn't I say, you'll laugh like that and you'll end up crying?'

'Come on,' Quentin tapped me on the shoulder.

I got up from the table and quietly followed him upstairs.

'Look,' he said ushering me into a beautiful room I had not seen before.

All the walls were covered in maps.

There were maps of Europe, of the world, a great selection of road maps of Australia. Quentin had told me his father was a geography teacher, but these, I noted, were more; they were the cartographies of a fugitive, a man who, like my mother, was making plans. ('Don't spy,' she had said, but was that not what she herself spent her life doing, under the bright light of examination tables, with the aid of stethoscopes, thermometers, and other topographic appurtenances, losing and lodging herself in foreign bodies?)

'Look, I'll show you where my mum and dad come from.'

Quentin pulled me toward a map of Europe. Mrs. Soyer's family were from Poland. She was a little girl when she'd left; she'd left, Quentin said, because *her* mother and father were killed by Hitler. She had come by ship to take up with an uncle of hers who already lived in Australia. *Like poor Mother Mary*, I thought, *a stranger in somebody else's home!*

I now went to the window of this upstairs room and looked out. I could see the wide side wall, a dim light rising from the living room, of my own house. I wondered whether they remembered me in my absence. I felt very bad for having said Mum hated us. I no longer wanted to be moored to the earth, but to make a barque of my body and float between these many pastel continents.

'Show me where your mum and dad come from!' Quentin demanded.

Wearily, I moved to one of the maps that showed Asia and the Pacific, rested my hand on the saggy soft breast of India, and pointed him to two, almost imperceptible, marks.

I lay down in the centre of the room. Quentin extracted his eyeball and began rolling it again in the palm of his hand. I closed my eyes, pretending death. Was it rain I heard then or somebody weeping? I had heard such an echo not all that long ago from my own mother's mouth. Aunty Sylvia had just called to tell us that Nana had died. Mum was at the kitchen sink, smashing, until her wrists were bloody, the cheap glass bangles she'd bought during our last trip to India. While Dad had comforted her in the kitchen that day, I had quietly climbed onto the bathroom sink and taken mercurochrome from the first aid cabinet to apply to her wounds; when I had held the tube out to her, though, she had stared at me with the eyes of a stranger.

In this room in the Soyers' house, the night sky was bright, the stars so luminous that I was afraid to look at them in case I should go blind. And I remembered having felt the same trepidation the very night my mother, father and Nana had returned from Linking Road markets and, with those cheap glass bangles, brought home for Deepa, Shanti, and myself a kaleidoscope of such poor quality that within the week the crystals at the bottom shifted not in divine contours, but in a predictable series of shapeless, loose blurs.

No, it was not rain now. The distinctive, shallow breath of human mourning rose and cast itself on the ceiling like the penumbra of the banyan tree that I would sometimes see cast onto the ceiling of the very Bombay apartment in which my mother's broken childhood had occurred and from which Nana had now faded into the amorphous motifs of my own poor phantasmagoria.

In silence we listened to Mrs. Soyer crying. Now and again I believed I heard her say something, but I was now adrift, unable to anchor myself in their meaning.

'Oh, it's too much,' I deciphered. 'Too much.'

And just as the vessel of her thought threatened to capsize on these rough waters; as I got up and made my way across the unstable deck and whispered to Quentin that I had best be going home, I heard something else.

'I can't live like this anymore.'

I made my way down the endless stairs. I wanted to lay my head upon her saggy, soft breast again, to call her mother. I wondered whether they saw me passing, but, frightened for my own life, I opened the front door and fled homeward.

Mum was at the dining table reading from *Australian Family Physician*. Dad was snoring on the couch. I did not say good-night. I did not stop to kiss her cheek. For my disloyalty I felt sick, wanted to hang myself from a tree or raise my arms and die between two thieves.

Safely ensconced in my bedroom, I opened my violin case and lovingly caressed that sad child of strings.

'I can't live like this anymore.' I spread these words out in my heart, tried to spell them, apply to them a grammar, a punctuation. I sounded them out. I concentrated, focused entirely on the sounds, in a way that the authors of my report card had led the world to believe I was maladroit.

I put my fingers to the taut mane of the bow and then to the body; I ran them down the bridge and down farther, along the long, long strings. I must have made a sound, created a minute effect, because Shanti sat up, watched me for a few seconds, and then sank again into her reverie.

With all his strength, Quentin was trying to secure his feet on the ground, keep me suspended in the air, but the seesaw creaked stubbornly.

'They're getting divorced,' he said.

The whole park lay in stillness, save the wind, the autumnal Sydney wind, which ran up my legs giving me goose bumps.

I can't live like this anymore. A whole year had passed and yet I still recalled the precise tone and tune and timbre with which those words had been spoken.

I had heard them played over and over in my mind one day at the end of the summer.

Deepa was standing in the living room, peering through the curtain of the bay window. Daylight Saving had ended and so we had only the streetlights by which to see and survey the damage. Even for Deepa this was an improbable manoeuvre. Shanti was transfixed.

Quick Draw McGraw was saying, 'Well, I'll be . . .'

A door slammed.

'Are they really getting a separation?' Deepa at that moment asked nobody in particular.

I went to the front door and pressed my nose to the

mesh. I saw Mr. Soyer standing on the lawn with a suitcase at his feet, shaking his head before embracing Mrs. Soyer.

'Don't spy,' Mum said.

To watch fellow human waste, this was an impertinence of the highest order.

At dinner that night, Dad had said of Mrs. Soyer, 'She's a woman buried under the impossible wreckage of history.'

Wreckage? Buried? And suddenly these monumental words of his had made perfect syntactical sense.

I myself had felt wrecked when having to forgo the beloved dream of being a musical prodigy. During my examination recital that March, I had failed to hum a melody back to the examiner. It was a simple tune, all in a major key, but when I'd replayed it, it had come out strange and dissonant. The rest was also ruined, for even though my summer had been spent trying to concentrate on, apply patience to, the pieces I was meant to be mastering, in the middle of a prelude or rondo, my nodes would prick up, I would hear arguments next door, clamorous voices, sometimes thunder – Mr. Soyer's raucous laughter – that would always end in wild tears. And then I, too, would feel like sobbing for a great waste. This is exactly what I had done at the Sydney Conservatorium of Music – put my head down and sobbed – in the midst of that Australian Music Examination Board recital.

At school, too, I had gained the reputation of an *enfant terrible*. Lucy Malone, sometime confidante – and, by force of the inclement conditions of her own family situation, herself a Fair Weather Friend – had long ago left the school and gone to live with her grandparents in the country. At my wits end trying to make friends, be included in the many cliques, groups and clubs, I had, earlier in the term, brought a whole stack of Mum's old journals in my school bag and distributed them among my colleagues. Miss Baldwin had caught two boys during Reading Hour perusing a special edition on endometriosis and other gynaecological disorders and demanded to know which depraved child had been responsible for promulgating unseemly literature. Betrayal must be the very essence of the human condition. Judas was not extraordinary; my peers became informants within moments, had no qualms about inculpating me on the spot, and I was detained for three weeks after school.

I will henceforth cease being a silly distraction to myself and peers was the line Miss Baldwin had me write out.

'Dad,' I had therefore shouted in response to my father at the dining table that night of Mr. Soyer's departure, knowing myself what it felt to be inhumed beneath detritus, to be thoroughly ghettoised, 'I'm not going!'

'Not going where?' Deepa asked.

'I'm just not going!' I beat my small fists on the table.

'Where?' Dad said.

'To the Concentrating Camp!' I exclaimed.

'Thus spake Zarathustra,' Deepa sighed viciously.

That autumn, the autumn of my eighth year, I did not keep Lenten promises as I had so zealously in the past; I sympathised with the Apostle Thomas and was not disappointed to discover that the world was quite hopeless even on the Third Day. When Father Murphy slipped into Good Friday mode, I did not weep but had the impulse to slap him. When our third grade class made those falsified chicks in eggs at school, I deliberately peeled back too much of the shell so that the cotton-ball chick appeared vulnerable and exposed, a posture, I was sure, of critical verisimilitude.

'See what happens when I trust you with something,' Mum reproached me when she discovered my accident with the treasured rationed egg she'd reluctantly placed in a tea towel before me; a small portion of the innards I had managed to catch in the tumbler, but the rest had unconsciously slipped out and stained the tablecloth.

Interested in the spectacle, Shanti had come by and burst the inky yolk with her finger, thus exacerbating my fate.

Dad, too, came in from the garden, where he'd been pruning the dead roses.

Witness to my wretchedness, he said brightly, 'What about an omelette for lunch?'

Mum muttered something and left again, this time taking the whole carton of remaining eggs with her. She snatched the pruning shears from my father's hand on her way out. Again, Dad and I followed her to the sliding door, but this time she had disappeared; there was no sign of her mourning by the backyard mint and coriander beds. We went to the front and it was then that Dad grabbed my hand, for when next we saw her, we were greeted with a most macabre spectacle: Mum was standing in the garden, her gaze raised boldly to the sky, to the flamingo evening, the turbulent clouds. She was whistling a haunting ditty I had never heard before and some local birds had gathered at her bare feet.

On that seesaw with Quentin, I began to see my whole world held in precarious balance. I began to see, if only with a partial vision, that despair is seeded, gestated, and birthed and bears a slow and dull sensation like milk teeth falling away, like an unremitting illness. I stopped imagining what those unnamable patients endured, which limbs they held out to my flighty, absconding mother, which bodies she took in her arms and anointed. In that white, faintly blood-splattered smock she wore like a shroud, I knew now she was no sweet, mild-mannered Nightingale, no queen warbler.

'He's an alcoholic, you know,' Quentin had gone on to tell me on the seesaw.

In silence we walked the long block back and, as we drew toward our homes, I was not surprised to find Mum and Mrs. Soyer together in the front garden. Their arms were raised and, like a pair of refractory blue jays caged in an aviary, they were gesticulating wildly.

'What are they doing that for?' Quentin asked me.

'They feel bad', I told him.

'Bad for what?'

Unsure myself, though, I could now only shrug.

DEEPA

Deepa was impossible. She simply knew too much. Sibling rivalry between us was never even an issue, for how could I have competed with a child genius? Not only that, she was a sophisticate. In scholarship, indeed, in any given task, she performed with the quiet efficiency, the suave, if a little savage, excellence of the Roadrunner. She was both good and bright. So I found it hard to fathom when, that winter I was eight, I came home to find that she had been suspended from school.

There had been only one occasion when I had profited from her voracious intellectualism. Mostly, I was relegated to the shadows of her brilliance. And yet, I have to admit, I enjoyed it there where it was darker and where public scrutiny was less palpable.

She was changing schools while I was entering kindergarten. Prior to our meeting the principal and staff, they had decided that – our names being the unusual specimens they were – we would be prime candidates for the English Second Language instruction that the school offered. *ESL*. That was where we were led together in metaphorical chains, against our actual pleas ('But we were born *here* – '), the first day of our arrival at St. Sophia's.

Woebegone, bored faces of the one Chinese, two Greek, and one Polish student in the school greeted us. I myself was secretly relieved to have been ushered to that hide-out, happily prepared not to ever have to associate with my fellow kindergarteners, ready to make myself at home in that haven of the linguistically condescended. '*We-just-want-to-make-su-re-that-your-rea-ding-and-wri-ting-and-spea-king-skills-are-up-to-a-good-stan-dard*,' Sister Marguerite, the ESL teacher, patiently enunciated for our benefit that fateful day.

She then deployed a series of cards with spare nouns inscribed on them. CAT, ROD, BABY, LAMB, HOLE, they read.

'Now, take your time, dear, It's not a problem if you can't say any of these,' she told Deepa.

Deepa was furious. I knew because, like Dad's, her cheeks puffed up when she was about to blow. I had never seen her so incensed. She grabbed me by the hand and, without a word, pulled me to the door.

'Really, I am not going to dignify your own spiritual and mental retardation by answering these questions,' she announced to a startled Sister Marguerite.

I smiled sheepishly, apologetically, at those poor ESL prisoners who would remain immured while we ourselves were acquitted five minutes into the interrogation.

'Who ever doubted that Joseph K. was a figment of a realist imagination?' Deepa lamented as we walked side by side down the long hallway.

We sauntered in silence to the kindergarten classroom. Upon arrival, Deepa peered inside and shook her head, deploring the simple stupidity of the scene that once again greeted us. One boy was screaming as his mother left him, weeping bitterly. The desperate kindergarten teacher, Miss Langston, was unsuccessfully placating him; urine trickled down his skinny legs. Other brats screamed and ran in unmeaningful circles, like young pups chasing their own tails.

'You'll be all right,' Deepa, spunky warrior, then said, leaving me at the classroom door, offering me her condolences. 'If anything happens, you'll find me in second class, room B-twelve.'

She handed me a piece of paper with the address of this higher grade marked on it.

I nodded, feigning bravery, and then proceeded alone into the civic unrest of my first, kindergarten year.

As the years moved on, though, it became plain that I was not her intellectual equal. Certain unbridgeable chasms stood between us. She could, for instance, do Rubik's with her eyes closed. When she played Scrabble she was so prodigious that she ensured that constructions like QUIXOTIC fell unfailingly across triple word score squares. She was, during any given Monopoly game, the proprietor of both Mayfair *and* Park Lane. While I drew mindless designs on the edges of the pages of the *Reader's Digest* IQ test for which Dad had sent away, she had completed and worked out her score – at six, a perfect 180 – and proceeded to ethnographically appraise the examination with reference to Eysenck's critical study 'Intellect and Intelligence Quotient,' recently published in the *Journal of American Psychology*.

When I was one and contentedly napping in my crib,

she had come to me, roused me from my slumber, and put before me this very puzzle:

> *This story is based on fact. It happened to a man in Sweden at around the turn of the century. It is extremely unlikely that it could happen nowadays. The man had been poor but at the time of the trial he was wealthy. He was physically and mentally normal, and was not a criminal. The teeth he had had removed were normal human teeth with no particular value. However, he was judged to have injured a third part by having those teeth out. Why?*

She was more than a keen strategist, however; she was, in every sense, an organic kind of intellectual. At three – when I would not yet have grappled with the Holy Trinity (three-persons-in-one is a daunting thesis even for the most enlightened child) – she had read the complete works of St. Thomas Aquinas and become a considered atheist. She moved into Hegel, Schopenhauer and Kierkegaard at four and five, only to resolve that it was fiction that had the truest philosophical content. She began with the English classics – Defoe, Austen, the Brontë sisters – and having discovered the modern novel for Joyce she had a particular fetish fell upon poetry with an insatiable appetite. It was no surprise to all of us at home that she was conversant with the French Existentialists by the third grade. Unsatisfied with translation, she taught herself French when she was but nine years old with the aid of a set of cassettes Dad had bought her for her birthday. She walked around the house murmuring stanzas from Baudelaire, Mallarmé, quoting lengthy passages from

Remembrance of Things Past. All this while other children her age were occupying themselves with dolls and train sets, while I myself pursued a pet rock collection and toyed with Quentin's eye.

One might be interested to know how such a child accessed these grown-up resources, and that, too, is a story that confirms her stature as a unique human being.

I was standing beside her at the loans desk of the Rain Hill Library when it all began. In my arms were a selection from the *Ramona* series by Beverly Cleary. I had felt some compassion for that young protagonist when I had read the first of them, *Ramona the Pest*. The title alone had seemed to sum up my existential crisis.

Deepa had selected her one precious book, *The Myth of Sisyphus*, and we were waiting in line. The Rain Hill librarian, a woman we had never much liked for her pedantry, peered imperiously down at us. It was, after all, hard to see us, since we were only just taller than the desk itself.

She quickly flicked through the book and then examined the spine.

'This is from the adult nonfiction section I'm afraid you can't borrow it,' she told Deepa.

Deepa, patient as Road Runner, always bypassing disaster with her firm faith in instrumental reason and that simple expression of her mettle, *Beep Beep*, startled all those in the queue behind us by saying, 'Indeed, I realise this. However, as the children's section has such a paucity of good titles, and as I have already read the majority of them, I was hoping you would use your discretion and thus make this one exception.'

Was she a freak, a midget, an adult in the body of a

child? The librarian composed herself and glared at us both. She reminded me with her pale, doughy complexion, her eyes as cold as glass, of a person who had never seen the sun. I felt a certain sympathy for her, stuck as she was in the cloistered rooms of that establishment, surrounded by all small gods – Shakespeare, Pushkin, Pasternak – and she herself their petty functionary. Fame was oh-so-remote from her station!

'Oh, no,' she said, incredulously. 'Do you think we just go about making exceptions like that for any little girl. We must be meticulous. Meticulous!'

She seemed to address this final part to the audience of borrowers who were showing benevolent interest in the unfolding drama.

'Well,' Deepa went on, 'I was hoping you would have at least a quota of *imagination*. But I can see I was gravely mistaken.'

Now the librarian lowered her glasses, as if carefully contriving her reprisal. I was terrified. *Did Deepa always have to carry things to such lengths?* She had said the I-word, a word that was bound to irk any human being, not least a mere bureaucrat whose most inspiring daily task consisted of sticking new loans cards inside the jackets of books.

'Look,' I wanted to tell Deepa, 'don't worry, just let Dad get it for you on his card.'

Dad borrowed library books on any number of unrelated subjects, but they would all languish unread in the car until such time as they were overdue. 'Oh, dear!' he would say self-deprecatingly, dropping them one by one down the shoot (*The Oxford Book of Australian Botany, The Cambridge Companion to Louis Althusser,* and, more curiously of late, titles that bore a consistent avian theme such as *The Penguin Book of Australian Birds* and *Birds: From the Black Forest to Brazil*) 'You girls will know more than me by the time you've left primary school.'

He helped us out with the spare space on his card when we had a school project and wanted access to a greater number of resources. Of course, I was never so diligent with such assignments; it was Deepa who used that space on his card.

'Oh, Deepa,' I said now, swallowing a large lump that had come into my throat, tugging her shirt, 'come on, just get something else.'

Of course, valiant Deepa would not concede defeat so soon.

'You should read Dostoyevsky,' I heard her suddenly say to the librarian. 'And you haven't heard the last of this – you'll be hearing from my parents' solicitors.'

'My, my aren't we the little know-it-all!' the librarian called after her.

She did it every time, reduced perfectly mature adults to the level of small children. I was waiting for the librarian to stick her thumbs in her ears, waggle her fingers, and stick her tongue out also, but by now Deepa was dourly dragging me out the large revolving doors of the library.

Many letters and phone calls later, the local council wrote to inform her that the complaint she had registered against the library – requesting that the prejudicial loans clauses ought to be reformed in keeping with the liberalism of the age – had been successful. She was, they were honoured to inform her, entitled to adult lending privileges.

'We are the philosophers, scholars, and academics of the future,' Deepa had ceremoniously written to Mayor Lynch; and, capitalising on the forthcoming election fever in Rain Hill, 'I will be happy to express my profound admiration for your leadership, and for a second candidacy to my fourth class peers, if you would assist me in this small matter. Yours faithfully, etc., Deepa Pereira.'

I found her that same afternoon as I had never seen her, utterly vindicated. She was curled up on a beanbag, surrounded by an enormous assortment of senior books.

In her arms she lovingly caressed the *Myth* and at points took the book to her chest and gave out a great self-indulgent sigh.

As I entered, she waved the letter at me, ecstatic.

'What's going on?' I asked.

'I got adult rights, dill-brain,' she confidently pronounced.

But it was also about this time of triumph that things at school began to get difficult for Deepa. Her fourth grade teacher, Mrs. Douglas, had surmised at the end of her report card that winter:

Deepa's development is well beyond that of a student of her age. Her grasp of numerical problems is exceptional, her reading and literacy skills unparalleled by any other of her peers. She is a delight to teach. However, Deepa needs to spend more time cultivating friendships and learning to display patience and humility with her classmates.

'What would that incompetent, poorly read excuse for a pedagogue know?' Deepa had exclaimed the evening my perturbed parents circumambulated the dining table, fretting over these comments.

Shanti was engrossed in other affairs. Wile E. Coyote was rolling a huge boulder to the edge of a steep cliff, anticipating Roadrunner's passage. Only for a second did the wise bird stop before moving smoothly on. '*Beep! Beep!*' she signalled.

Dad suggested that perhaps Deepa ought to be more sensitive to the deficiencies of other students.

'What are you saying, Daddy?' Deepa retorted.

'That miserable wench asked poor Adam Reed to come to the front of the class and spell *anemone*. He spelt it correctly. I mean, this is fourth grade. How would anybody not know how to spell *anemone*? "*Oh, no*," Mrs. Douglas said, tragically adding a second *E* to the end of the word. "Anemon*ee*," she corrected Adam. "Mrs. Douglas," I said, "I believe anemone is spelled with one *E*." She turned to me, would you believe, and gave me the nastiest most un-Christian look. "Deepa," she said, her sinewy arms reaching back toward the board, cunningly smudging the final *E* away with her hand behind her, "kindly put your hand up and wait your turn to be asked to speak if you have something to contribute." I mean, no wonder the country's in a mess!'

Deepa was visibly moved by the travesty of alphabetical justice practised on Adam. For a moment I thought I saw reflected in her eyes the zeal and gusto of the human rights activists one saw on television; the amnesty workers, fighting indefatigably for the rights of fellow man; the tireless eco-liberationists who would bind themselves to the trunks of trees for a single principle.

'Dear Mayor Lynch,' I imagined she would soon be

writing on Adam's behalf, 'I am part of a delegate campaigning for the rights of a person – a colleague of mine – whom I believe to be a prisoner of conscience at St. Sophia's, Rain Hill.'

Coyote, now wondering how she, stalwart bird, had escaped death, went down the cliff to look. The road was barren. Dumbfounded, he looked up. At that moment the boulder fell, crushing him. Shanti keeled about laughing.

Dad listened to Deepa and could not fault her logic. For a while, the equation that his eldest daughter was offering seemed no less than a stroke of genius: The country was in the political doldrums for no other reason than the . . . He scratched his head, appealing for her further counsel.

'It's revenge, don't you see it, Daddy!' Deepa, exhilarated, qualified.

Coyote was now scheming again. *Was it not he, burnt, crushed, and brutalised, who was truly impregnable?* I wondered. He had taken some sticks of dynamite and laid them on the road where Roadrunner would soon be advancing.

'Revenge?' Dad and Mum both repeated slowly, looking at each other.

Would they be entranced by what she was conjuring, I wondered, *submit to her oratorical charm?*

'Why, yes. She got me back for the anemone remark with this mention of lack of humility. Oh, but what is humility if not submission, submission if not cowardice!' Deepa keened.

Mum was tiring of this.

'Deepa,' she said, 'I know Mrs. Douglas might be wrong, but maybe you should at least try to make friends with someone your own age. You can't live your whole life as a bookworm.'

Coyote was bald when I next looked up at the television. The dynamite he'd industriously laid had backfired. The bird was still at large, and I guessed that it would somehow always be this way.

Deepa was destroyed, utterly disappointed with them. And I, too, wondered when they might be satisfied. If she, straight-A, bookish sister of mine, was being charged with misanthropy, what would they say of my own capacious, if so far furtive, neuroses. *God, forbid, what therapy might they suggest for idiosyncrasies so voluminous!* And Mum, humming in the garden, the birds about her feet, was she herself a model of social aplomb?

They began citing names then, surnames of children in Deepa's class, all of which Deepa reviled. I saw they did not hesitate, were quick to resolve a problem, but failed miserably only to identify, mull over the origins of, the cause. They began to display the resolve of mind of parents seeking matrimonials, knowing the bounty of their dowry, refining their choice, seeking a horoscope for the most auspicious match.

Dad suddenly plucked a name from memory.

'Jacinta Tyler!' he said. 'Why, she's a lovely girl.'

Mum apparently agreed, although I detected some reservation on her side; her brow was knit, her forehead furrowed. Had she sensed then the disaster to which they were wedding themselves, suggesting this girl as a possible *copine* for my sister? All this done, would we soon be looking on as Deepa and her betrothed walked through the saptapadi together, as the fire god, Agni, smouldered, as grains of rice were hurled into the flames?

The name itself sent a shiver down my spine. *Lovely* was not the adjective I would have selected to describe that girl whom I had seen running wild in the school playground. But then, poor Dad did not have much time to closely read either books or personality types.

'Humility and patience': this seemed to be the function my parents assigned to Jacinta Tyler's place in Deepa's life. 'She will teach her humility and patience,' my father said, like a Brahmin priest alluding to the sacred *Laws of Manu*.

And thus, on such noble pretexts, Jacinta Tyler, an influence for which they would forever reproach themselves, entered our lives.

She was the youngest and only girl of nine siblings. It was rumoured that Mrs. Tyler had continued to conceive because the children were so mischievous they kept stealing and hiding her diaphragm, and because they were too poor to keep replacing it. Mr. Tyler held a senior post in the NSW Ambulance Service and he was something of a legend at the school, for once a year he would come to assembly and give a lecture on first aid. Afterward, all the children stood in the playground watching while some fourth-graders were allowed to go and test the siren in the awe-inspiring vehicle.

Indeed, he could often be heard screaming from the backyard of his own house, doing battle with the cicadas and the lawn mowers, 'Whichever child has turned the siren on is going, believe me, to be given a thrashing!'

At this, the relevant child would sneak out, turn the ambulance siren off and sneak back in. He was never quick enough to catch the culprit. Fifteen minutes later another child would run into the ambulance, set the siren off, until Mr. Tyler ran out, this time with a cricket bat, but, alas, again too late.

Some years older than his wife, by the time Jacinta was born Mr. Tyler was weary and geriatric. The responsibility for discipline had therefore lain on the shoulders of Mrs. Tyler, and hers was a soft and yielding upper arm; her tenderness was exceeded only by her patience. Jacinta was doted on but casually neglected. Her straight, mousy hair was seldom brushed and was cut every month or so to get rid of the knots that would, as a consequence, amass around her scalp. She possessed the alert eyes of the frequently preyed upon, the dark quick eyes of nocturnal beasts; even her unruly bangs gave her this aspect. In a cycle of what seemed dialectical recursion, she was tormented by her brothers at home and forever running *after* the boys at school.

She entered our lives one Friday. The three of us were walking home from school together – Jacinta, Deepa, and myself. I'd suspected the reckless girl had accepted the invitation only to be fed by us. I know it was an uncharitable view of the state of affairs, but, as it turned out, it was a prophetic one, for her appetite knew no bounds. Chocolate cake, fairy bread, ice cream, and creaming soda: Mum had been prepared for the union as any doting mother secures with sweetmeats the best match for her beloved child, even moving aside the shoes and the bathroom appliances, which had by now secured a permanent place in the refrigerator.

I scuffed the tips of my shoes on the concrete as they, a glorious duet, a phalanx of camaraderie, paraded in front of me. Invincible as the Roadrunner, Deepa had perfected the art of friendship. When I thought that they were deliberately trying to outpace me with their speed, I did not submit to these childish tactics but kept dispassionately to my own gait. At one point Jacinta turned to me and, if I had yet some doubt, confirmed every despicable thought against her favour.

'What are *you* staring at?' she said.

I looked into her vicious eyes, which seemed to say, 'Kill or be killed.' I did not labour over an answer.

My main problem with Jacinta Tyler was her failure to extend her sympathies to my own plight of infamy and neglect. Her humour was not just not funny but dangerous.

'Come here,' she would command. 'I want to tell you something.'

Warily, I would give my lobe to her, waiting hopelessly to be put in her confidence.

'*Ahhhh!*' she would scream, almost shattering my eardrum, and then turn to Deepa, who, in spite of all her alleged maturity, would also roll about lampooning me.

Jacinta's idea of a prank was to jump on the bed mattresses in the house until the foam and springs burst through the cloth and, when there was nothing more to destroy, pee on her wreckage; and finally, owing to Mum's look of dismay when she came back from work to find the house demolished, she would cry that she wanted to go home.

'What are *you* staring at?' she again had the gall to ask me in my own home, when I once caught her pocketing three of Mum's rings and an amber necklace from the dresser.

Dad would come home, inspect the damage to the house after she had been over and shake his head. 'Juvenile delinquent,' I knew he wanted to conclude of Jacinta's machinations, but he continued – both of them did – to defer judgement, delude themselves that the persistent presence of this child was in Deepa's best social interest. The lesson however seemed to invert itself; it was they who, through Jacinta Tyler, were apprehending the advantages of Humility and Patience. Oh, how I felt for them, foolish as they were! *How*, they must have wondered, *had her own parents not only spawned but brooked Jacinta?*

The answer to such a question became clear when Dad drove her home. Jacinta would then become instantaneously demure; in the company of brothers, her whole aspect would transform and she would almost seem a different and altogether placid girl.

'Oh, Jacinta's home! Jacinta, Jacinta, Jacinta! The only one of my children who didn't turn out to be a terror!' Mrs. Tyler would say, greeting them at the door. 'You're lucky you only have girls,' she would then, taking him into her confidence, tell Dad.

This wholesome notion of their daughter was tempered by what the Tylers didn't know. And looking about at the stained walls, the broken toys, the stack of unwashed dishes, and food crushed into the fibre of the carpet, my father could not bear to destroy the illusion the Tylers maintained about their youngest child. Not even, that is, when Jacinta came to our house and collaborated with Deepa in playing a wicked, wicked trick.

They said that they were going swimming, that after they swam they were going to eat ice blocks and then maybe go to the park on their bicycles. I had my suspicions. Strife had to be a part of the plan, or else there was something amiss. I was watching from the back, sentient, sawing away at a piece of wood with the miniature saw Dad had given me. They were in the pool, plotting.

Now and then Jacinta threw me one of her malevolent glances and shouted, 'What are *you* staring at?'

There was a splash.

'Ahhh!' cried Jacinta, 'Deepa, Deepa! Help, someone, help! Deepa's drowning!'

I then looked up to see my sister floating, face down on the surface of the water, so still, so practised, why, in such a superb performance!

Feigning panic, Jacinta herself began to try and drag Deepa from the deep end of the pool.

'Well,' she shouted, turning to me, 'aren't you going to call an ambulance?'

I stared at her then, inimical, unmoved. Again, I did not even gratify her with an answer.

'Oh dear,' she said, not even wavering, 'I better do it myself.'

She was no suitor, no charmer, she, an incarnation of Kali, goddess of destruction, wreaking havoc on our lives and then dancing barefoot on the violated sacrificed corpses.

She climbed out of the pool, soaking; her bangs were plastered to her forehead, concealing her eyes like those of a feral animal.

Dripping, she ran through the back door and expertly to the telephone. She dialled 000, told the operator our address, spelled out our name, did everything.

Not long after, I heard the siren of an ambulance.

Two officers bearing medical kits burst through the house and, with Jacinta's own instructions, followed the trail of falsified tragedy to the back.

'Hey, isn't that one of the Tyler kids?' I heard one of them ask the other as they passed me on the patio, still sawing away.

'It is, it's the Tyler kid again!' the other whispered back.

They then stepped over the body, and from where I was sitting, I detected them exchanging knowing glances.

Deepa's cunning face suddenly came alive now, a small smile broke across her mouth, though she almost lost consciousness again when she saw one of the officers hovering over her, preparing himself for cardiopulmonary resuscitation.

'I think it's too late. I think she's one for the morgue,' he said gravely, winking at the other officer, lifting Deepa, who was now fully conscious, into his arms.

'No!' Deepa screamed, jerking herself up. 'No, let me down, please! It was *her* idea not mine!' she cried.

Jacinta was licking her sunburnt lips, relishing the bittersweet aftertaste of her junket. Still soppy, she disappeared passed me into the house so that when the officers now turned to make out her shape, all that was left of her was a shallow puddle of pool water.

By now Mum had arrived home from work and it was evident that a cruel joke, the cruelest joke, had been played. Having seen the ambulance parked in the driveway, she had run to the back and arrived, like a *Sati*, preparing to hurl herself into the water with one sacrificial dive.

'I'm so very, very sorry,' she told the ambulance officers as they let Deepa, kicking and screaming and bawling her eyes out, to her feet. 'I can't imagine what they thought they would achieve.'

'Don't worry, Missus, believe me this is not the first time we've been called out on account of the Tyler kids. Mind you, it's usually the boys that are the brats. I'd say you better watch out for that girl. She's a menace.'

Mum remained as dignified as possible, which is to say that, after asking me to see the ambulance officers to the door, she went to the kettle, made a cup of tea, enthroned herself on a dining chair, and, nestling her head in her arms, cried and keened and started up some strange, fowllike burbling noises.

She was like this when Dad arrived home.

Solemnly, Dad drove Jacinta back to the Tylers'. Her house was not five minutes from ours, but she fell into a deep slumber on the way home.

Upon arrival, Mrs. Tyler watched my father carry Jacinta in through the garden, once again crooning her daughter's name, 'Jacinta, my Jacinta!' and to Dad: 'You're lucky you only have girls, you know.'

Secrets so weighty can be kept only so long. My parents' threshold of tolerance was high, but not so high that they did not despair for having encouraged the union. They blamed themselves, I could see it, and no measure of kindness or time seemed to allay the guilt that bedevilled them. *How could they have been so blind?* they beat their breasts searchingly. And Deepa herself, was she, too, intrinsically evil, only masquerading as a precocious but genuinely sweet genius? Did they know their own daughter? To where had the bright, good, if a little supercilious, child they had known disappeared?

I imagined them cerebrating all this as Deepa arrived home one evening and as they again anxiously circumambulated the dining table.

I was playing my violin in my bedroom, but even 'Claire de Lune' seemed an elegy too facile for the proportions of this tragedy. I heard the car door slam and my feelers rose, receptive to the contemporary crisis; I stopped the bow midway through, crushed my chin into the chin rest, waiting for a sign.

Shanti, again the most reticent of us all, continued to be amazed by the transaction of Coyote and Roadrunner. *When would she learn*, I wondered, *that the scenario was never going to change; the bird had to win out, for these were the politics of the wilderness*. There was no reason to be had; reason, whatever tattered remains there were left of it, was behind us now.

In Goa, I would often beg Dad to come walking with me in the mountains that surrounded the village. I loved those lush mountains, the voluptuous silence in which each element and sound was amplified: the brook, a croaking frog, gipsies' children playing and crying out beneath the spray of the natural spring. Deepa saw neither beauty nor adventure in the excursion, and Shanti, too, was never very interested in accompanying us. There was one evening, cooler than usual for December, when I had put on my cardigan and shoes and waited for hours rocking back and forth on the porch chair for Dad to take me. Dark, turbulent clouds were encircling above me and after an eternity Dad called out to say he was ready. The Angelus was tolling. We walked a little but no sooner had we made our way across the tiny cemetery at the foot of the mountains and a little way up past the dilapidated bridge than Dad was squeezing my hand and putting his finger to his lip to silence me. He lifted me into his arms and, without a word of explanation, began leading me back the way we'd come. It was only as I craned my neck over his shoulder that in the distance I suddenly saw the figure of a mangy, gnarling dog – more a wolf than a dog – its ire so stultifying that even the Angelus bells stopped ringing in my ears. There was what looked like shaving cream coming out of its mouth. Dad carried me inside a derelict chapel and told me not to move or speak; I could feel his pulse riding through and knocking my own. After some time, he carried me down the slope of the mountain. We emerged onto the village streets; the twilight was now soft and warm and I kept on wondering how the spectacle of the distempered dog might feature in a good anecdote for the evening.

I sat at the table in the kitchen, clearing out the sweet young flesh of the coconut Dad had, as if in consolation, bought for me at the village market. I had just begun relating my fantastic tale about the foaming mutt to Deepa, Shanti, and the servant boy, Tomas, when Deepa looked up from the fish croquets she was folding.

'That wasn't shaving cream you saw,' she had undercut me, self-important as a member of the Pasteur Institute.

I remembered this hubris now as she sat at our own dining table. School Camp was supposed to have strengthened her, helped her to solidify friendships, to learn the importance of consensus and solidarity. Fourth grade was supposed to have been a epoch of privilege conferred not taken. There she sat, her jeans black, her once-beautiful, kempt hair now dirty and scrambled. There were traces of brown – bloodstains – all over her flannel shirt. She trembled. Her face was grubbied with tears and with, it was true, the viscera of the slaughtered. She was ragged and distracted as the student Raskolnikov, or was it poor, put-upon Tom whom she now most resembled?

They'd called my parents to come and collect her early from the Hawkesbury River.

'Grievous harm,' they'd said of my sister's influence at Camp Confidence.

Only one name had been mentioned – Jacinta Tyler – to qualify what had happened, and my parents were in the car, driving the long length of the Pacific Highway. Unlike the quality of that road, though, they themselves were hardly serene.

Deepa nervously squeaked the rubber soles of her sneakers together.

'What were you doing?' Dad now questioned her.

'Nothing, I swear, it was the others – '

'Suspended! Suspended!' Mum wailed and thrashed and flapped.

Dad tried to comfort her, but it was useless. She had made a nest of her arms now and was once more burbling incoherently. *How had a perfectly divine child turned into a murderer?* Even Satan was a beautiful angel until the last hour before his falling, my grandfather had once sagely advised me.

Dr. Spock – *Ben* – had written, *'Better to admit crossness. A child is happier around parents who aren't afraid to admit their anger, because then he can be more comfortable about his own.'*

'I'm going to ask you one last time,' Dad now roared at Deepa. His face was bloated like a popper fish. 'What happened?'

'It's all your fault!' Deepa suddenly shouted.

'Our fault?' Dad and Mum slowly repeated, looking at each other.

'Yes! You made me befriend her, did you not? You made me! What did you think, that she would provide distraction, entertainment for me? She's just a stupid little girl, and she was happy to be my friend if it meant she could copy my homework.'

On and on she went in this fashion, bemoaning and ululating, a haunting jeremiad of parental injury.

'Oh, I never meant for it to turn out this way. Oh, so vile! So dark and comfortless! All I wanted was to read and improve myself, but it was never enough for you!'

I was struck by her eloquence; even at this time of chaos she was composed and articulate. Moreover, I could not fault her logic. Why, even I had been the inadvertent victim of the pressure put on my sister! Genius came easy to her. *But to me?*

Ben had written: '*Since all children are quite different, no parent can feel just the same about any two of them, either in the sense of enjoying their special charms or being displeased by their special faults.*'

'Mum,' Deepa had recently counterpointed Spockian wisdom, quoting aloud from the Klein essay she was reading,

' "a small child which fulfils all the requirements of its upbringing and does not let itself be dominated by its life of fantasy and instinct, which is in fact, to all appearances completely adapted to reality and, more-over, shows little sign of anxiety – such a child would not only be precocious and quite devoid of charm, but would be abnormal in the fullest sense of the word."'

The rest did not matter. It was that she had only tried to please them. *How could she, only ten years old, have known it would have ended in so gruesome a way?*

I listened from the banister, my jaw still lodged against the chin rest of my violin, feeling something – not quite compassion – for her.

Had she known Jacinta Tyler would have had such an impression on the boys at the camp? Had she believed the boys would follow Jacinta in the middle of the night from their tents, beyond the limits of the campsite? Had Deepa not run after them, entreating them to stop, when, under Jacinta's leadership, they had climbed over and grabbed the koalas from the protected wildlife enclosure, when they had handled them and, accepting Jacinta's maniacal dare, begun to stab them with the blunted blades of their imitation Swiss Army knives? Had she not cried out as they laughed like lunatics in the moonlight, tying the cadavers of the koalas with fishing wire to the nearby trees; red blood wood, stringy bark, scribbly gum? Had she, Deepa, not fallen to her knees at the site of the carnage, and as they, her classmates, had without remorse, run back to their tents in the cool darkness? Had she not wondered how children – the precursors of adults – could be so brutal? Had she not sobbed through the night in her mildewed sleeping bag for the souls of those innocent marsupials whose only charge in life was to suckle gum leaves, to mate and to carry their young on their backs?

FALSE
CONSCIOUSNESS

They refused to let me be a Brownie, though I got down on my knees and even pleaded that I'd pay my own way into that secret club of which anyone who was anyone in third grade was a member.

It began one evening, late, in the kitchen.

'No!' Mum clacked, crying from the scent of frying onion and fresh chili. She was seasoning the minced beef before setting out some pastry in which to fold samosas.

'Yes!' I entreated, encircling her with eight-year-old hope and hostility.

I was a patient child, patient and infinitely considerate. And for my forbearance all I received from my mother was spurning and negation. I wanted at that moment to be at war with her. What, I wanted to implore, were violin lessons, poetry, and good food if I didn't have a single confidante with whom to share a vision of myself and of the glorious world?

'Suffer the little children,' I whispered, my back turned from her.

'*What* did you say?'

Could she really have heard me? Yes, there was no doubt about it. Mum was a sonic panopticon.

I turned about and without compunction repeated the Biblical maxim (after all, it was she who'd taught it to me): 'Suffer the little children,' but this time the words were enveloped by the calamity of filial insolence. My feelers fell in shame.

She turned toward me and, swinging the spoon midair, splattering and staining her floral blouse with gravy, didactically squawked, '*Who* am I? Who am I?'

She was hard pressed to offer a comeback when, instead of dutifully reciting that she was Mum, I called her by her full name.

'Dolores Maria Adelina Pereira,' I said with a smirk.

I could not help myself. I had wanted to challenge the idiocy of her authorial reasoning for some time, and besides, I basked in the romance of that name. I could tell she had not been prepared, for she stomped into the bathroom and must have there determined that the only way to teach me a lesson, reform my 'smart aleck ways' (*Who on earth was Alec?*), was culinarily, and therefore I was given on my plate for dinner that night not those delicious pyramidal feats that seemed to be works of the highest oragamic workmanship, which she had spent the evening preparing, but a piece of leftover lamb without marrow and stale rice and some desperate-looking lady-fingers, which she knew – she must have known it – frightened me because of the literalist set of associations my eight-year-old mind attached to them.

Yet, it was not the first time that she'd exacted dietary reprisals.

'Think of all the poor babas in India, going without

food, then you're sure to finish those pieces of cauli-flower.'

'If they're so hungry why don't you send it international post, heh?'

This was a not uncommon dinnertime exchange.

One recent evening, after a particularly virulent alter-cation, Mum had not just confiscated the meal, but put me, like Sylvester, out of the house.

'You all right there?' Mrs. Rabe inquired when she saw me, like a robber, trying to bend the grille of the front door.

'She's locked me out!' I had appealed to our kind senior neighbour.

'Well, that's not very good. Just don't do any-thing drastic,' Mrs. Rabe sniggered, before strolling calmly on.

However, the form her present taste-bud totalitarianism took was even more severe.

Shanti felt sorry for me and tried to sneak me one of her samosas under the dining table. But not only did Mum have eyes at the back of her head, she seemed to be as omnipotent as the Holy Spirit.

She grabbed the samosa as it was in transit between our young hands and plunked it back onto Shanti's plate.

'If the Mouth wants to enjoy the privileges of all the children her age, she'll have to be more respectful.'

The Mouth! That cruel, cruel cognomen that, for rea-sons of a happy appetite and a tendency toward menda-city, had for some weeks now been employed as a means of maternal torture!

*   *   *

'Daddy,' I asked my father that night when he was putting me to bed, 'why can't I be a Brownie?'

'You are brownie,' he laughed, 'you don't need to join any club to be brownie. Look,' he said, pulling my chin and stroking my hair with delight, 'you're brownie all over.'

Hysteria had not helped me earlier that evening. Now I was my sweet, sagacious self.

'*A* Brownie,' I said, underlining the noumenal nature of the word. '*Be* serious,' I told my father.

'Mina, why do you want to be a Brownie? Of all the clubs in the world, of all the people you want to befriend, why the Brownies?'

Did he still not get it, and if he did, why this dogged opposition to the Girl Guides Association of Australia? I wondered.

Staring at his long eyelashes as he patiently waited for a justification, I said, 'Well, you know, they are all friends, and go camping together and have special names for each other. Everyone else – '

'*Who* is everyone else?'

That dreaded interrogation We had been through this before, roller skates, stamp collections, and Royal Easter Show bags were all out of the question, not only because they were objects of no particular intellectual or spiritual beauty, but because, in the end, according to my father, they standardised the imagination. He had warned me many times about the perils of copying fools, and I had remained silent, unable to admit the way I really felt about it, that is, if I had to be a fool to fit in, then so be it.

I didn't say it. I didn't tell him how, in the darkness of Amy Perkins's bedroom earlier in the month, under the pretence of a birthday party dare, I had taken off my plum pinafore and run into the garden, where the family dog, who seemed utterly surprised by my presence, had bit me on the hindquarters. Indeed, I hadn't even mentioned the dog bite to anyone at the time, such was my staying power. I'd waited to cry privately in the bathroom *after* they had laughed and venerated me for my courage. In that bathroom, hearing them rolling around, cackling at my misfortune, I had suspected that my own invitation to that party had been earned on account of my brazenness, my mere exhibition value, known privately to me by another name: loneliness.

Dad was waiting for a response from me, so I started with a detailed account of 'everyone else,' the pre-eminent members of the third grade, name by name, until I came to people such as myself – Felicity Summers and Chloe Withers, the ordinary and the despised, the ostracised, who were soon going to be initiated, too.

But I saw the furrow in his forehead and the doomed destination of this colloquy.

'If Felicity Summers and Chloe Withers threw themselves down a well would you, too?'

I appreciated the philosophical principle of this trajectory, but the well, to me, was a ludicrous, absolutely incongruous – and not to mention provincial – analogy for a predicament as unique as mine. *Where*, I wondered, did *they come upon these primitive references?*

'What well?' I asked him.

'Let's say, Grandmama's well.'

I had thought many times about that well and whether I'd be rescued were I to fall into it. In my grandmother's house, out the back, near the rice sacks and the massive

grinding stone, there was a deep and ancient well, oper-
ated at one time by Hindu rice farmers but now quite
redundant in an abode of taps and tanks and running
water. Sometimes I would torment Apu by sitting on the
edge of the well to watch her prepare the water over coals
for my bath. She was deaf, and when attempting to keep
one eye on the fire and one eye on my safety, she often
went cross-eyed in the process. She would come to me
when I'd pretended to have lost my balance, slap me on
the thigh, and then squeeze me into the enormous melon-
like breasts of hers. Her real name, I was once startled to
discover, was Karena. She was called Apu because in
Konkani, *apu* means deaf. That I might have been calling
her *Deaf! Deaf!* all this time – even though she could not
hear me – seemed so cruel.

Dad was evidently not impressed with my reasoning. I
needed to try another tack and so told him of the stories I
had heard at show-and-tell of the Brownies, of their
marvellous-sounding rites and tribal ceremonies, jambor-
ees (I had said this wonderful word to myself over and
over upon hearing it), of the scarlet bandannas and the
singing of that stirring anthem to girlhood.

Ging-Gang-Gooly-Gooly-Wash-Wash

How gripping the aura of the uniforms with the small
embroidered four-leaf clover and the socks and matching
beret! How I longed to be there, as the girls at school
remarked about the campfires and the dancing and the
shepherd's pie and the ghost stories related in front of the
fire and . . .

But still he did not seem impressed.

Even Quentin had abandoned me, I pointed out to him. On Friday evenings he'd go to join the fraternity of boys his age as they prowled about the Rain Hill Cub Scouts Headquarters, preparing, I supposed, for their impending manhood.

'Isn't it enough that you are Daddy's daughter and Mummy's daughter and the sister of your sisters and Miss Anderson's pupil?'

'Yes, yes, yes!' I told him, suddenly exasperated. 'But don't you see, I want to be a *member!*'

I wanted desperately to be a member, and I resented that they were not empathic enough to grant me this one wish. I began to believe that they had reservations of an ideological nature against the Brownies, privately harboured reasons that they were not fully divulging. *Why was it*, I wondered, *that every time I mentioned the Brownies, my parents talked of the corrupting influences of group dynamics, the conspiracy of crowds?*

It was a Friday evening. Deepa was reading Hasek, and I was moping about the house when all the other children of the world seemed to have been delivered to God. I wistfully hummed their borrowed anthem as if it were a Song of Myself, my own glorious incantation:

Ging-Gang-Gooly-Gooly-Wash-Wash
Ging-Gang-Goo
Ging-Gang-Goo
Ging-Gang-Gooly-Gooly-Wash-Wash

On hearing me, Deepa looked up from her book.

It was clear that, however deep our bond, however

proximate the substance of the deoxyribose nucleic acid from which we had been fashioned – the configuration of our very chromosomes – socially, there could be no sorority between us. I had been penitent for my own offences against her, but she seemed unable to atone for hers; the stealing of my Golden Books, the foul names she had called me, the time she'd climbed in my cot when I was only four months old and cut a hole in my pacifier so that there was no satisfaction left in suckling the violated rubber teat of it.

To no avail, I had attempted to share more than a blood bond with her.

'Look!' I had recently sought her attention while standing within the frame of her bedroom door, my arms outstretched, pressing my weight against the jamb.

It was a technique some girls at school had been perfecting. You held yourself like that for some moments and then let go; in the time the muscles would take to contract, the body would experience a levitational sensation.

'You do this for a minute and you'll feel like you're flying,' I told her.

'So what? You do that in public and you'll look like a moron.'

As though *she* could talk, she who had, only weeks before, humiliated herself in front of the anonymous stranger who'd stood beside her in church as Father Murphy had beseeched the congregation to offer one another the Sign of Peace.

'What does any of this really matter, comrade?' she had contrived, shaking the hand of the stunned parishioner, while everyone else obsequiously obeyed the simple consonance of 'Peace be with you'.

Now she glared at me as I continued to hum that shibboleth, that nonsensical ode to my lost girlhood:

Ging-Gang-Gooly-Gooly-Wash-Wash
Ging-Gang Goo

'You realise,' she quipped, 'the Romans stole that song from the Gaelic when they conquered Galloway. The Brownies are undergoing a serious bout of false consciousness if they think any of what they do, play, or say is original.'

Consciousness. Would I have even been able to spell that word and, more to the point, would it bear away my eight-year-old longing for amity, even if I was able to use it correctly in a sentence? Could there be an authentic consciousness and could any truer, purer wisdom alter the simple reality that at school on Monday my peers would be greeting each other with handshakes, secret signs, that they would be winking at one another, making gestures of mutual understanding while Miss Anderson had her head turned to the blackboard, that they would be joined in a beautiful and mysterious unity while I would be again forlorn and alien, able to neither fathom their furtive indices nor decipher their elaborate codes? I had read the Universal Declaration of Human Rights, I had seen the clauses relating to the rights of the child, and here in my own home, I was having my sovereignty violated. Was there no form of redress available unto me?

'I can't feel anything, Mina!' Chloe was saying.

'Neither can I,' said Felicity.

I'd bribed them. I'd told them that I had a neighbour

who could dislodge his eyeball from his socket and that if they came over to my house after school they'd be able to have a feel of it. I had not considered it a dishonourable bid; I preferred to think the whole scheme a kind of scholarly investigation. I needed information. If I was not going to be admitted as a member, I would find out exactly what I was forfeiting.

But the car was not in the Soyers' driveway. As it had turned out, Quentin had not yet arrived back from school.

'Mina,' Chloe protested, 'is this some kind of trick?'

I shook my head.

'Oh, no,' I assured them. 'You've just got to raise your arms a little longer.'

The three of us, in our school tunics, as if mounted at Golgotha, had our arms extended against the frames of the doors of my parents' room, Deepa's bedroom, and the bathroom, respectively.

'But it hurts!' Chloe cried.

'Just twenty seconds more,' I told her.

We waited out these twenty in silence.

'Okay, time's up,' I said.

Relieved, they dropped their leaden arms to their sides.

I closed my eyes and felt my body rise off the ground like a seraph. I wouldn't have forgone that feeling, however false, for any kind of elevation of my consciousness.

But, tragically, it was cut short.

'Mina, I still can't feel anything,' Chloe grumbled.

'Me, neither!' Felicity chimed.

I opened my eyes. They were not impressed and grimaced at me with a scorn equal to Deepa's.

Had I, Mina Pereira – their look implied – tried to *delude* them?

'Oh, well, I guess it only works with some people,' said I, the distinguished doorjamb flyer.

I ran to the bay window to see if Quentin might have arrived, but still the Soyers' driveway was a void.

Now what would I do? Disrobe and run naked for their perverse diversion?

'I want to pet your dog!' I heard Chloe whine.

Oh, God, how could I have brought such a fate upon myself? *Dog?* The closest I had really come to a domesticated creature was that Bata shoebox under my bed with the pet rock inside it, and even that I had not taken seriously enough to endow it a name.

I waited, still, looking out the window, pretending I had not heard her hefty solicitation. If I could not make them fly, how indeed was I to make a dog appear from thin air?

Then I heard them, their school shoes shuffling across the linoleum in the kitchen as they came to find me, still aggrieved by their aerodynamic anticlimax.

'Mina,' Felicity said, 'can't we pet your dog?'

Again with that behest! I turned around and saw their innocent pale freckled faces. Maybe I could circumvent the truth by breaking it to them kindly. Surely they, the ordinary and despised of the form, the quiet prodigies of the third grade, would understand how I had been led to that error of judgment, that disingenuous aberration. It was a noble impulse that had led me to that lie: I had wanted to be liked and admired. Was that so reprehensible?

I shook my head, 'I'm afraid not.'

The words were somebody else's, but they accurately confirmed my state of mind. First, I was terrified; second, they could not fondle any canine in my house.

Chloe, the duller, more petulant of the pair groaned, 'But you said you got a dog for your birthday in show-and-tell!'

It was true. Oh, how I had forgotten that three-month-old falsehood that I'd delivered to the class. Was it my fault the school provided stages, pedagogically sanctioned forums, for children to learn the arts of hyperbole and ostentation? Not just show-and-tell, but the sepulchral solemnity of the Church confessional had been for some time a great burden to me. Was it not a natural psychological response, when put before an audience, any audience, to perform and improvise?

'On Saturday it was my birthday and my parents bought me a puppy, which we called Digger,' I had told my third grade peers that fateful Monday morning.

'Forgive me, Father, for I have sinned,' I had, in the same vein, explained to Father Murphy. 'I selfishly punctured the tyres of the family car and my sisters' bikes with a nail.'

'Oh, and for what selfish motive was that, child?'

'So they would never be able to leave me, Father.'

The latter was not entirely a lie; I had entertained the notion many a time, and, as for the former, if I had not felt so inadequate among my peers for having been deprived of an authentic pet (Magic Monkeys would not suffice), perhaps I would not have been led to that particular prevarication.

Chloe was nonplussed and Felicity was likely to turn on me, too.

I turned again and looked desperately through the window.

Quentin, prodigal neighbour, brother of mine, where

was he when I really needed him? Oh, I should never have come to depend on him; it was a fault, a fault! I saw right through the revolution, I could, only eight years-old, rip the tenets of dialectical materialism to tatters if I had to. We are creatures of our own interests, always ready to jeopardise collective prosperity for the sake of personal gain, be divisive, engage in internecine warfare.

'Look,' I said, trying to change the subject and cut to my own agenda, 'why don't you tell me what happened at the retreat on the weekend?'

There'd been a retreat, something like a glorified school camp, I imagined. I knew because the whole week at school the girls had been talking about it. One girl, Belinda Clarke, had been silenced by the others when she stepped up for show-and-tell on the verge of disclosing the details of what had transpired.

Chloe and Felicity now looked at each other searchingly.

'Oh, come on, Quentin will be home soon, and then you'll say you can't tell me in front of a boy.' I had discerned that much; the nebulous boundaries between the genders that had already been developing in the playground had now, with the advent of Brownies and Cubs, been accentuated.

They stared pregnantly at each other.

'Well . . .' Felicity was about to continue, but Chloe lurched forward. 'You can't tell. It's against the rules. Sorry, Mina.'

I looked to an alliance with wise, sensible Felicity, but she too deprecated, 'Sorry, we're sworn to secrecy. They'll kick us out.'

'But I'm not going to tell anyone,' I opined.

They were firm and resolute, stood before me pityingly, shaking their heads, spurning and negating me. It was the same old routine.

They had obviously forgotten about the dog, so thrilled with themselves over their exclusionary keeping of confidence. I detected, however, that there was an element of pressure to which they were forced to submit, that the potential for excommunication was heavier on their nerdy backs than on those of the other, well-loved third grade girls.

'Look,' I said, 'I'll tell you something you would never, ever have dreamed – a secret – if you tell me just a little about what happened at the camp.'

Felicity smiled wryly. She may have been the brighter, but she was also more gullible.

I was holding the curtain of the window over my head like a veil, aspiring belatedly to the candour and purity of a nun.

Chloe grabbed Felicity by the hand as if exhorting her.

'This isn't another stupid trick, Mina Pereira?'

Just then the Soyers' car swung up the curb and into the driveway.

'Trick?' I repeated the word, flabbergasted. 'You'll see the false eye in just a moment,' I promised like any improvising con artist, made good with the few lucky ruses I had like any shabby circus magician.

'Well, it better be good, otherwise we're not saying anything. Right, Felicity?'

Felicity nodded dreamily. Her focus was actually beyond us, out the window, for it was she who had been, was most enchanted by, more eagerly accepted, my proposition about Quentin's manoeuvrable eye.

'Well?' Chloe said long-sufferingly.

'Are you ready for this?' I asked.

They nodded in unison, exemplars of the consensual harmony of clan, kinship, and Brownie Order.

'Ever wondered why I've got these things?' I said, indicating my nodes.

Again they nodded, complicit.

'Ever thought, "Hey, Mina looks nothing like Deepa"?'

They pondered this for a second and again together nodded their heads in affirmation, slowly spellbound by the subterfugal darkness into which I was leading them.

'Ever wondered why they treat me so badly here, why they insult me?' (This one grievance was my own and they didn't nod so much as sympathise, like the well-bred, sensitive girls they were, recalling perhaps their own domestic hardships.)

They waited. They knew it was going to be a weighty revelation.

'I was adopted,' I said, and stood back to observe while, as if I'd prompted a latent suspension, they moved beyond their current consciousness, rose from the ground and floated in the dining room.

Mina the Mouth. *The Mouth*. Against every wish of mine, against my bleating and my pleas and cries of protest, this was the epithet, so lacking in maternal tenderness, that was bestowed on me and fixed hereafter, the same way I had once, desperate for some solid, unassailable companionship when I was eight years old, fixed my affections to a rock. Like a bad wind, the rumour of my adoption had spread at school and come full circle. Parent-Teacher Night had enabled Miss Anderson the proper opportunity to express her 'surprise at not having been previously informed that Mina was adopted', to explain to Mum that it came as even more of a shock, since she had always seen 'such a striking resemblance between Deepa and Mina', although, 'it was clear that, of the two, Mina was the more highly strung'.

I thought it a rather telling paradox that the punishment that ensued from my malefaction involved a further act of dispossession. I was ordered to on the one hand confess my crime to Father Murphy; on the other, I was not to have any friends over for a month.

The first I could endure.

'Forgive me, Father, for I have sinned,' I whispered to sweet, merciful Father Murphy. He had become distracted in his old age; I wondered whether the rumours I'd heard about his plundering the Sacristy's reserves of Holy Wine were true. His breath, even through the mesh that divided us, was caustic. I gave him the bad news.

'And why on earth would you have told that falsehood?'

'Oh, Father,' I had cried, looking into his rheumy, inebriated eyes, 'because it sounded so true, I didn't mean to, but it sounded so true!' He let me mull over the sin for a second and then said, 'Is that all, child?'

'Oh, Father,' I cried again, 'I had wanted to be a member!'

'But a member of what, child?' he softly tried me.

'The Brownies!' I chanted.

The truth was that by then I had thoroughly abandoned the hope of being, given over entirely the desire to become, an associate of any organisational dynamic. Barring friends from the house, the second course of chastisement, was even easier to bear, for I had resolved myself to an inner state of consciousness that involved embracing what I believed to be a more bona fide public stature: that of the child-loner. I prepared myself for social failure in a way that made Deepa's earlier forays with Jacinta Tyler seem like child's play. Relinquishing the rock as a false companion, I remained loyal to Quentin. He had come grovelling back to me months after having realised the fraud of the Rain Hill Cub Scouts' credo:

Be prepared!

Even the artificial eye had not charmed them, earned him respect or Cub Points. The worst had come when, one evening after the predictable session of misogyny, brutality, and emasculation, a group of bullies who maintained a hegemony in the organisation led poor Quentin, his hands tied behind his back, to the bathroom, gouged the eye, and flushed it down the toilet.

'Poor thing,' I said, when he told me. 'Just like Gloucester.'

'Like who?'

'Like Gloucester.'

'Anyway, are we still friends?' he asked.

'Of course.'

Friends I'd agree to; it had a certain noncommittal, ambiguous ring to it. But comrades, cronies, companions, soul mates – none of these terms could I any longer suffer. Granted, he was a boy, but with my reputation for deception and delusion – or, as Chloe Withers would later charge me, compulsive lying – Quentin Soyer would have to do.

I was utterly alone. The Brownies had instigated a revolution, but it was revolution of The Self. I felt pared back, sloughed off, as though I had an alter ego who loomed above me where and when I walked alone, though I could never see her face. If she had been less mercurial, I would likely have embraced my own shadow. Every experience turned on the same psychic pivot, every shock struck the same epicentre: myself. I wanted to feel, breathe, and live alone and only for myself, solid as a rock. I wanted to be, I reckoned, inviolable.

Deepa rarely knocked before entering, but now she was standing at the door of my bedroom.

She had witnessed Mum's wrath as it had come down on me, seen me slapped and sent to bed starved; she had watched while, as if in a dance I would come to perform regularly in my lifetime, my feelers had fallen in disgrace.

'I thought you might like this,' she said, handing me a book, a grand gesture indeed, for she was generally known for her bibliophilic stealth and selfishness. I inspected the title: It was her personal copy of *Psychopathology of Everyday Life*.

'I've marked the pertinent chapters. You can ignore my notes in the margin.'

This was her precious manual, a text which she had read and reread by the age of seven alongside the collected works, thoroughly deconstructing the whole penis-envy thesis. I opened it. She had carefully drawn my attention to one of the final chapters, entitled 'Errors.' The first mark she'd made read:

What I find, therefore, both in grosser disturbances of speech and in those more subtle ones which can still be subsumed under the heading of 'slips of the tongue', is the influence of thoughts that lie outside the intended speech which determines the occurrence of the slip and provides an adequate explanation of the mistake.

Now Deepa was smiling a ludicrous smile. She reminded me, during these rare displays of affection, of sympathy, of – dare I say it – sorority, of my father. ('You're brownie,' he had said. 'You are brownie.')

She remained in my doorway. Her arms were suspended, her palms set flat against the frame. She had her eyes closed and seemed to be concentrating with all her might.

I read on:

We speak of 'being in error' rather than 'remembering wrongly' where we wish to emphasise the characteristic of objective reality in the psychical material which we are trying to reproduce. The occurrence of an error is a quite general indication that the mental activity in question has had to struggle with a disturbing influence of some sort.

'I feel it, I feel it!' she exclaimed midway through.

Her arms were at her side now and she had shut her eyes, a significant development for that child-sceptic.

Her body swayed, suggesting the muscles had really been tested.

Should I have believed that she could feel what I had? Should I have believed that together we could fly? Was it something in the blood, a primitive propensity, written in the very nuclei of our cells? No doubt it was a sign of promise, but by then there was too much that had separated and divided us, too much time had passed for promises of amity, alliance, or even benevolence.

'Mina, did you hear me?' She had opened her eyes now. 'I felt it.'

'Good for you,' I said brutally and flung the book at her.

HOMEWORK

We knew not why Mum was packing suitcases. Not just two-day affairs, but huge thirty-kilo vessels. We were not *going* anywhere. It was still spring; the summer vacation, when we would be going to India, was indeed many weeks away. She managed to keep this operation clandestine a whole season. But then one evening after school when I was playing cops-and-robbers with Shanti and I'd tried to hide under their bed – I was always forced by that six-year-old heavyweight sister of mine to be, of course, the thief; it was an arrangement made at her insistence that play should resemble our actual social roles – I'd found the suitcases obstructing my passage.

Thinking them empty, I kicked and beat them with my legs, but found that they would not budge. I dragged one of them out into the light, undid the latches and discovered, to my amazement, a stockpile of provisions: packets upon packets of dry foods; tinned cheese; meats, fruit, cereals and preserves; long-life and powdered milk.

'You're supposed to be *hiding*,' Shanti said reproachfully when she found me, sitting with the leather lid flipped up, examining the contents.

The gold foil of a box of chocolate eclairs winked at me. 'Want some?' I asked her.

Shanti shrugged. 'If you say *you* opened them.'

'Okay,' I acquiesced, not just thief but recidivist.

Accountability wasn't a problem so long as I had someone with whom to share the actual transgression, for that, as all delinquents know, is where the real pleasure lies. I quickly tore the packet open and filled my mouth. The caramel centres were cool and tough. For some moments we sat in silence, our jaws bound by taffy. When finally my tongue was free, I convinced Shanti to help me carry the other artefacts to the dining table for Mum and Dad's later inspection.

'But, Mama, what's it all for?'

She had returned from work, was now marching back and forth, restoring the stash of food to the suitcases, which we'd left strewn, as pirates having plundered the treasures and leaving behind the worthless chest, on their bedroom floor.

I followed her.

She pulled the two other suitcases out from under the bed (together there were three) and now, as if everything could finally be brought into the light, open and aired – indeed, with some measure of relief – Mum lined the luggage along the passageway to their bedroom.

Dad sat down at the table and held his head in hands.

'What's wrong, Daddy?' I asked.

'This is madness, madness!' he called out after her as she stormed from living room to bedroom carrying a five-kilo sack of rice in her hands.

'But, Mama, what's it all for?' I pleaded, trying to keep up with her on these interchambre jaunts.

'State of Emergency!' she suddenly said.

'Emergency?' Deepa looked up inquiringly from *Finnegan's Wake*.

'The Crisis.' She swooped past. 'We know not the Day or the Hour.'

At these words, Dad again dropped his face into his hands.

'What's wrong, Daddy?' I asked him.

'This is madness!' he said, now striking his fists on the table. 'Plain madness. What do you want to do, live like a refugee?'

I took it he wasn't addressing me.

He had often told us of the Indo-Chinese refugees whose lives were held in his own tender but somewhat clumsy hands. They were locked in cold suburban detention centres. Like animals or murderers. Sometimes, I knew, he'd be advocating on their behalf for weeks, for months. Clemency was never certain.

'Boat people!' Deepa had said in the car, when once he had taken us to a meet the Lahoun children, two children of our ages, who had fled Laos without their parents. He'd lost their case; they were to be deported.

'They're not boat people,' Dad had corrected, trying to change lanes. 'They're human beings, children, just normal children, okay?' The vehicle in the other lane would neither slow nor speed up and pass. 'Damn it,' I heard him say under his breath.

'Hello,' I had said, feeling foolish before the girl my age to whom I was introduced. I handed her a gift, a pair of flannel pyjamas that Dad had stopped to purchase at Woolworths.

I had wondered if it would be too warm for such attire in equatorial Laos, but did not make my query known.

The gaunt, sad face suddenly smiled and the hand reached shyly for my feelers.

'Oh, don't worry about those,' I'd said.

And that's when I had noticed that she had no digits at the end of that outstretched limb.

Now I went to the bathroom and brushed my teeth, rinsed and gargled away the sickly aftertaste of caramel. My stomach ached from the eclairs. And not just that: My head was feeling heavy. Maybe, I contentedly mused, I was *really* coming down with something! I turned the tap on full blast. *Was this what it meant to live like a refugee?* I reflected, fitting my mimetic digits into my hand to see what it would look like under the mirage of the water jet.

I recalled how in Goa, Dad had once taken us to see the exposition of the body of the venerable Patron Saint Francis Xavier at the Bon Jesus Chapel, a cadaver said to have been so sacred it would not deteriorate with age. I didn't care much for the sight of his eyes, still as pebbles; the flaccid skin crumbling on his cheeks and hands; no, my attention had been drawn to the missionary saint's left hand, where, as everybody was aware, his index finger was missing. Local legend had it that a devout Catholic woman, having made the pilgrimage from Puna after being abandoned by her Hindu lover, was so overcome by the figure of the saint that she had feverishly taken Xavier's hand to her mouth and severed the digit with her jaw. Police caught up with her later in the day at the restaurant of Panjim's famous Hotel Fidalgo. She was sipping a lime soda. The delicate dead organ was found in a secret compartment of her handbag: black and blue, but no blood on the wad of tissue in which it had been gingerly wrapped.

But this fancy was interrupted as I now heard Dad saying something.

'I'm telling you,' he said soberly, 'you need to see someone.'

My feelers rocked and resonated. *See someone?* Where was she going? And why on earth did she need all that baggage to see anybody?

'See who?' I said coming out of the bathroom.

'See *whom*,' Deepa priggishly corrected.

There was no answer to my question, though, nothing but that volatile Tower of Babel towering above me, swinging and swirling, stirring up my terror and crashing down upon me.

They, Dad and Mum, were moving rapidly from Portuguese to Konkani to English and back again.

'Where are you going?' I asked Mum as she lifted the last suitcase into the hallway.

'Don't you have homework to do?'

'See whom?' I said, returning to the living room, to my patient, solicitous father.

He was still holding his disconsolate, heavy head in his hands. He looked up.

'Don't you have homework, Mina?'

And thus I was banished to my quarters, a place I didn't mind so much for it was here, alone, that I had contrived some of my best schemes, conducted my most formidable investigations, made my requisite plans. How, for instance, to dexterously skip school, a mode of action that I was coming to depend on increasingly. In the third drawer of my desk, I kept a record on a few pages on computer paper of the ailments from which I could plausibly be suffering; one column noting symptoms, the other registering the date, and the third the corresponding malady of my last school absence. The value of this document could not be overestimated, for although domestic embargo on friends had been lifted, my predicament of *anomie* had in no way abated.

Chloe Withers had put it succinctly when she turned to me while we had our heads bowed together at the bubblers recently. My fountain was defective, suffering an erratic spitting effect; I was being cautious, but still it blew in my face and very slightly splayed and sprayed Chloe beside me.

'Mina Pereira,' she inveighed, the collar of her uniform just slightly drenched, 'You did that on purpose!'

'I didn't. It's busted, see – '

But it was too late for apologies, sympathies or explanations, much less amity. I had not provided her – it was regrettable – with that dog.

'You did it on purpose, you stupid liar!'

I settled into the chair, got comfortable at my desk, and switched on the reading lamp. When I had finished sharpening all the pencils I possessed into perfect points, I took out my social studies project book and ruled margins with a red biro for about forty pages. *We know not the Day or the Hour.* Yes, it was a truism, one needed to keep at least something of oneself in reserve. Who knew when I would be caught out, Mrs. Douglas (yes, the very one!) asking us to copy notes from the board, and me without a margin on my page to embody the knowledge, my crude cursive made even more crude: lawless.

Does not complete work on time. Leaves assignments to

the last minute. It was one week since Mrs. Douglas had betrayed to my parents via my social studies progress report the indolent lurking inside my young body. No doubt, it was for this reason that they now believed they possessed the liberty to usher me away, to suspect at any given moment that I was – to use the word Deepa spitefully invoked in relation to my activities – 'procrastinating.' *What kind of ninny did they take me for?* This debased perception – inaccurate, let me say right now – had its advantages for them. I had discerned that any moment of tension or scandal would now be expediently turned into an occasion for exclusion and ostracism, for me to be directed to my room on the pretext of 'uncompleted homework'.

It was not just Mrs. Douglas, though, who was responsible for the tarnishing of my reputation for industry; Ms. King, my beloved violin teacher, had also turned from me in these last weeks. *Her* means were even more unconscionable than those of my fourth grade professor.

One Saturday, Dad was waiting in the car to pick me up from my violin lesson. My lesson would proceed in this same dependable fashion: I'd try to spend as much time as possible with Ms. King on my musicianship, make lengthy technical queries, and thus forestall the agony of actually having to play those wretched pieces.

'Mina, did you practise at all this week?' she might lower her wire frame glasses and gently inquire only at the end of the lesson.

'Oh, yes,' I'd tell her. 'But I had a bit of difficulty with the tempo of the serenade. Could you perhaps play it for me again, Ms. King?'

Here she would smile knowingly, sigh, and take her own bow in her hand; then, revelling in the face of profound admiration that I had over the years cultivated specifically for my transactions with her, she'd play that serenade beautifully.

On this particular Saturday, though, we played our roles the same way; I paid her the tuition fee and then proceeded to the front door, where, instead of waving good-bye to me, entreating me to 'practise hard,' she began accompanying me down the sandstone porch steps toward my waiting father. I thought perhaps she was simply going to greet him, but seeing her approach, Dad genially rolled down the window.

'I thought you might like to come in for a cup of coffee.' This was the phrase that I had etched into my mind, the clincher.

Canny Dad eyed me as we followed Ms. King back into her studio.

'What would you like, Mina?'

'Oh, I'll have a cup of coffee, too,' I affected with my most convincing grown-up voice. 'Look, Dad!' I said, reaching for Ms. King's quaint metronome, which lay on a shelf in her studio, a souvenir (I could use this word any time in a sentence now) from Budapest.

'Don't touch that, Mina,' he said gruffly.

I sank sulkily into a chair. When Ms. King returned she asked if she might speak to Dad alone.

I exited and paced up and down her hallway with my coffee. To my misfortune, the walls of the studio had been soundproofed, a fact that had so far served me well, in that nobody but Ms. King could know the impoverishment of my weekly performance.

I could not drink that foul bitter beverage after all and so went to pour it down the sink.

I played with Ms. King's little ginger cat until, after what seemed hours, the door to the studio opened again and I was summoned inside.

'Mina,' Ms. King said, handing back to Dad the ten-dollar note I had earlier given her. 'I can't take your dad's money anymore. It's not fair.'

They were supposed to have been kind to me ever since the crushing experience of that examination recital during which I'd broken into sobs; I should have had work pressures alleviated!

Instead, she continued, 'I really can't teach you anything if you turn up here every week without practising, understand?'

I looked at Dad's brusque, blank, devastated expression.

Oh, yeah, I understood! And then there were those hideous words, the sort one offers to the utterly depraved (and what's more they were not even directed to me – *to me!* – the truly injured party).

'Don't get me wrong. She's good. Very good. She plays with an inner talent, an instinctive drive. It's just at some point in life one needs much more than talent and feeling to carry oneself.'

More than feeling and talent! Oh, if they all had the collective compassion to read my alleged sloth for what it was. Procrastination had become the external designation for a secret inner impulse I had these last months been suffering: The Death Drive had taken over and not even Dr. Freud could be of assistance. Oh, I could slavishly obey commands, fill the necessary quota of my life with homework and violin practise, but would these tasks truly prepare me for the forthcoming apocalypse, which now – after all my intimations about doom – Mum had finally heeded. That – and not fainéance – was the source of my present deferral.

Social studies was tedious, had for me become an irrelevancy; where we – with our young lives running out – should have been instructed in the real allegories of modern human historiography, the eschatology with which I had to placate myself lay, trite and meaningless, at the top of my page. What else was there to do but avoid such a topic:

What contribution did John Macarthur make to the sheep-farming industry of Australia?

When I had completed the margins, then, I reflected on some of the projects I had throughout the year undertaken. Burke and Wills; Blaxland, Lawson, and Wentworth; Abel Tasman; John King – pioneers of this great continent (or so we had learned in school), intrepid journeymen. Leaving was how they had made a living. From what firm inner mettle they must have been constituted! Did the prospect of starvation not daunt them, I wondered, thinking of the trouble I had in leaving the house to endure an occasion as psychologically benign as a school excursion?

How many permission slips – could I even count them on my able-bodied fingers? – had I 'accidentally' forgotten to give my parents to sign: the Australian Museum, Botanical Gardens, Arnott's Biscuit Factory. It was not that the idea of dinosaur fossils, flora, or sweet dough didn't arouse my curiosity, it was something else, something to do with what happened when you let children into the real world for a day: Things, I had discovered, were often more brutal than in the playground. I had therefore attempted to avert the terror as far as possible, make like a mollusc, refrain from leaving the house.

I had learnt my lesson when in second grade we had been taken on an excursion for a tour of the Sydney Opera House, that mutant carapace that rises at the harbour. There was I, lost on those billion steps, minding my own business, eating my soggy lunch (I always told her to leave the tomato *separate* – 'I'll cut it myself' – but she never *did* comply; 'Can I trust you with a knife when I can't even trust you with a simple appliance like a toaster,' she would say, referring to an incident which I would rather have forgotten).

The boys had milled around me – Amen Anthony, Adrian Simpson.

'Hey, Mina, see that ramp there?' Adrian said.

I turned and saw an abandoned workman's ramp.

'Yeah.'

'You think Amen and I could get up there?'

'Oh, yeah, of course you could.' And indeed, it would be possible to climb that ramp and get to the scaly, tiled Opera House roof.

'Why don't you try first, then we'll come up?'

I put my soggy sandwich into my lunchbox and took a sip of lime cordial from my drink bottle for strength. I admired the boys their masculinity, their lunchtimes were consumed with really productive activities and I felt privileged to have been inducted into their circle.

First, I ensured that nobody was watching. The girls

were running up and down the steps like fools. Miss Baldwin had her head turned and her arms over her eyes trying to stave off the glare of the sun; she'd struck up conversation with the ridiculous-looking man in red coat-tails who'd been allocated as our guide for the day. Now and again she'd look up and say, 'Be careful not to get in the way of anyone coming up,' and the girls would euphoniously sing, 'Okay, Miss.'

'Okay,' I agreed.

The task could not take so long, and with what else was I going to occupy myself during that long lunch hour, anyway? Wearing myself out on the steps?

Amen and Adrian held the ramp while I pulled myself up onto it.

The distance from the end of the ramp to the edge of the first tile was not so high, it was just a matter of reaching for it.

'Got it?' the boys asked.

'Not yet.'

'Hurry up. Someone will catch us!'

I groped for the edge of the roof and was relieved when I finally caught hold. I was on my tiptoes.

'Got it?' they again called.

'I think so.'

When I got to the top I climbed over the edge.

No sooner had I made it, though, than I looked down to find they'd moved the ramp away.

'Hey, that's not funny! Put it back!' I bellowed.

But they were oblivious to my cries. They were chortling among themselves while I had risked my lives for them.

At that moment I looked down, and my life suddenly seemed to fall out of my stomach. From that height, the girls had turned into small, uniformed ants marching in a serious but essentially motley kind of parade. Below me, the boys were tiny as Tom Thumb, and the ships and ferries docked in the harbour bobbed like toy boats. I tried to find a way down but the tiles, covered in dust and grime, were slippery. I tried to keep my balance, but I could feel myself sliding on the incline. At one point, I did slip and would have died, I'm sure, if not for the fact that I'd firmly gripped the narrow eaves with my able-bodied fingers. My small legs dangled perilously over the edge of the roof.

'Put it back!' I intoned. But it was useless.

Amen and Adrian had moved out of sight: I'd been set up.

There were only tourists below and, upon hearing my cries, one of them looked up. She was pointing me out and nudging the man beside her as if to confirm her eyes were not playing tricks on her.

By this time I was saying my Hail Marys.

'Help! Help!' I, a small smudge in the sky, barely able to hang on to the guttering of the Opera House roof, screamed.

Others gathered around and, as if to heighten my terror, covered their horrified mouths with their hands.

Seeing the spectacle, the girls from school had left the steps and run over.

'It's Mina, it's Mina!' they screamed whereupon Miss Baldwin came running to the disaster zone.

'Oh, God!' I heard her call. 'Don't you move, Mina. Can you hear me? I'm just getting someone! Do you hear?'

'Yes!' I called out meekly, wondering at what point my small fingers – strong but tiny – would betray me.

The heat was beating down on me and my palms were perspiring. I knew that I couldn't hold on for much longer.

Soon enough, though, a rescue team arrived, led by the guide in coattails. A ladder was extended. An ambulance and fire engine pulled up at the forecourt to the building just as a stocky man in a singlet and stubbies grabbed my small form.

'You're all right, then. I've got you, I've got you,' he said soothingly as he carried me down the rungs of the ladder. 'That was a close call,' he confided.

'Yes,' I had sniffled, at which moment my vigilant, frightened feelers, hitherto frozen like straws, lay down.

No, indeed! What purpose was there in teaching a student something she had no use for, revising a lesson she had inscribed on the very matter of her mind? The Death Drive for me was primal. The routes and frontiers opened by our national explorers seemed menial when compared to some of my own expeditions toward the hereafter. I was comfortable with my life at home and now hoped, sitting at my desk, staring into oblivion, that somehow the world would end before I would have to put pen to paper and enter into a discourse, a final memoir, about a man whose greatest exploit, whose cause for notoriety – the introduction of sheep to the Australian landscape – might, had it occurred at a later time, been a matter for the Royal Society for the Prevention of Cruelty to Animals, not for the annals of national history.

There was good reason why I had been not only tardy with my previous work, but that when I'd finally completed it, death had become a not inconsiderable ontological preoccupation. Barbarity and cruelty, to put it bluntly, was a sociological narrative with which I had become helplessly comfortable. I had not thought myself a solipsist for simply having noted how the invariably disastrous outcomes of these epic stories confirmed my own nine-year-old *weltanschauung*; this had merely seemed a conceit of every social historian, from Thucydides to Dr Seuss. Why, I had reasonably wondered, at the end of my assignment on Burke and Wills, had Mrs. Douglas written,

> *This is very imaginative, Mina, but you need to spend more time focusing on the actual details of their expedition. Please note: Burke was an Englishman. He did not – under any circumstances before God – indulge in cannibalism.*

Details? Expedition? Two men on donkeys venturing to cross the continent from the Nullarbor to the Gulf of Carpentaria. What more could I have said? Was it not a pilgrimage doomed from the outset? Thinking this, I had naturally engrossed myself in the particulars of their dying, carrion of Burke feeding on Wills's dehydrated flesh; the aged dromedaries exiled from Arabia, their humps slumped in the unrelenting heat of Alice Springs:

> *Wills died. His body was parched and emaciated, not even good for animal fodder, but in the weeks ahead Burke would gain strength by feeding on the rotting meat of it.*

I had taken the liberty of embellishing similar fates and scenarios for Lawson, King, and Tasman respectively.

These were works of hard literary slog; I had needed time to come up with plots so intricate. *And what were the rewards for my, if a little dilatory, dedication and perfection?*

Similar comments appeared at the end of my other assignments. Toward the end, Mrs. Douglas had been blunt:

> *Late again. If you cannot keep to the facts, I'll have to make you redo these.*

'Morbid streak,' Mrs. Douglas, before her outright report-card perfidy, had recently attributed to me in passing at a school awards night.

Deepa had brought her library bag so she'd have a receptacle large enough to contain the public recognition of her brilliance.

'Obsession with death,' Mrs. Douglas had said of my character flaws.

Uttered to them as cursory remarks, she could not have known that Mum and Dad had also observed certain necrophilic tendencies in me; the way, for instance, I had presided over the currawong chick that had fallen out of the she-oak and died earlier that spring; how I had placed it in a tea towel and slept with it a whole week before Mum, making my bed one morning, had found its smelly cadaver buried beneath my doona.

Could this, I wished to tell them, as one recent afternoon they had led me into the dark office of a certain locally renowned child psychologist, Dr. Blaby, not all be traced back to my own near-death experience, all the way back to second grade, to that day on the Opera House roof, an incident, which at the time, they'd callously dismissed, ascribed to supposed delinquency?

Thinking on all this as I now sat at my desk, I recognised that I had heard that oracular phrase before: *to see someone*. This had been the very vague way they'd intimated that they thought I should also 'see someone.'

'Do you think about death very often, Mina?'

'Oh, yes,' I said, unwittingly owning up to my morbidity. 'All the time.'

'How old are you, Mina?' (*Dear physician, if only you knew the great weight of history that was carried on my narrow shoulder from birth!*)

'Nine.'

'Nine!' an overenthusiastic Dr. Blaby had repeated to me, confounded, the flowers of his own happiness – three mentally stable children – beaming from the photo frames on his desk.

'You should be living life, Mina. Why are you worrying over death?'

Then I had frankly told him about my antennae, how I felt with those protuberances on my head like my mother burdened by her stethoscope, the figurative dial in my case extended to the heart of every living creature I came upon.

Dr. Blaby sent me away with some lessons to do: Every time I thought of death, I was to remind myself of the gift of my own life.

To my parents he solicited, 'It'll pass. It's probably just a phase she's going through.'

History, dear therapist, is repetitive catastrophe! I had wanted to shout in the aftermath of that session as my relieved parents drove me home. *Any phase, like the moon's own implacable mood, repeats itself.*

I looked again at the ugly cursive lettering of that week's project, due in fact the following day:

What contribution did John Macarthur make to the sheep-farming industry of Australia?

Now my feelers ached. There was no reprieve from the weight of my life. Could I even bear to consider those poor dim animals, herded and diseased, carried against their moronic wills to this brutal savage land? I had done the research, spent hours in the library admiring the more modest pioneering spirit of an altogether different man, Melville Dewey, who had, with one principle, ordered all there was possible to know about the world. *Oh, if only my life could fall into such an easy inventory!* I would think as I walked the aisles of the school and public libraries, dizzy with the absolute harmony of the decimal point system.

Safely tucked under the pillow of my bed was the copy of *Anne Frank's Diary* I had earlier in the term stolen from the school library. It was a crime for which I had felt no remorse. That intimate chronicle had come to be a text as indispensable to me as a guidebook in the unmappable territory of my life.

I got up from my desk now and reached under my pillow for it.

I took out the hula hoop that was resting against my bed head and swung that hoop around my thin waist like a professional while reading. *The Emergency. The Crisis.*

How the Franks had become refugees without even leaving a single dwelling, their daily lives concealed behind a bookshelf. They had not risked their lives in a boat battered by rain and pirates across the Indian Ocean, but they were captives of another kind; never moving, neither seeing nor nearing land.

My nodes were throbbing. I let the hoop fall to the ground and dropped to my knees.

I emerged from my bedroom.

'See *whom*?' I begged Dad.

'See whom what, darling?' he asked.

'Who should Mama see?' I insisted.

'Have you finished your project yet, Mina?'

I groaned. 'I'm not feeling so good, I think I'm coming down with something.'

Dad put his hand to my forehead.

Please, dear God! I prayed, trying to conserve all my body heat, like a person in the last desperate stages of hypothermia.

'Well, you do seem to have a fever.'

The television was on. *Oh, little sister, what a simple life you lead!* She was watching Speedy Gonzsalez running from the gringo cat:

Arriva, Arriva!
Andare, Andare!

At least Speedy, I thought, had a conspicuous reason for his runaway existence; everyone could see, not least the bulldog, that that cat was a menace to society. How many mouse-types could Warner Bros. come up with, how many redemptive finales, before a five-year-old child would stop believing, demand from animation a certain moral equivocality?

My dear father had gone to seek the thermometer.

Now, I thought, *they would truly measure my anguish and once and for all know that I was no malingerer!*

He shook it and then, raising my arm, tucked it in under my T-shirt sleeve. From the corner of my eye I could see the suitcases were still in the passageway.

'Daddy,' I said as the mercury made the gauge rise, 'where's she going?'

'I wish I knew, Baba,' was my father's reply.

And now my antennae, as if they were cords leading to his own throbbing heart, deafened me with their stethoscopic reading.

'Do I have to go to school tomorrow?' I asked in my weakest voice.

'Not if you're not well in the morning.'

Liberation!

Psychosomatia; Hypochondria: names for an existential condition that lays itself bare only in dream. I woke trembling in the middle of that night, overtaken by a real chill. The phantasm of my nightmare stood before me as a human figure. So immanent was its form that I had the urge to wake Shanti, but she breathed deeply: the stupor of the truly at peace. I opened my eyes to find the roses on the wallpaper dancing. My head was swimming. Beyond the window I could see the night skidded with stars, the stars slipping outside their designated stations, coloured, sloppily, outside the lines. I had dreamt of a man in a swagger hat, of Macarthur, of his importing and exporting merino sheep from Spain; I had dreamt of cargo, of ships bursting with sheep and of stevedores waiting far away, waiting for a ship that never crosses the equator because it meets with an accident; I had dreamt of a ship capsizing, of sheep densely struggling one on top of the other; I had dreamt of their bleating in useless protest and their drowning. And now again the roses swirled on the walls, swung as though there were a hungry wind rushing between them, but a wind that ran only in two dimensions.

Still shaking, I rose from my bed and walked the long dark passageway to my parents' bedroom, counting the one, two, three suitcases still there.

See whom? Whom was she going to see?

I crouched by the door. As I suspected, they were awake, nighttime being the best time for their domestic convention.

'God, I want to die, I want to die!'

The window was open. It was her voice I heard but at a distance.

'Get down from there. You have to stop this. Go and see someone . . .'

I peered beyond the door and saw my father in his pyjamas, whispering his address to her from the window-sill.

I took one step forward and heard her cry again in the low, slow voice of an owl, 'God, I want to die. God, I want to die!'

It was now that I made out her figure. On the nature strip just beyond their bedroom, my mother was hugging the trunk of the very same large she-oak from which the currawong chick had, earlier that spring, fallen and died.

*　　　*　　　*

The next morning found me slumped at the table, barely able to carry the spoonful of Weet-bix that lay before me to my mouth.

'Hypochondriac,' Deepa said accusingly.

I 'accidentally' kicked her under the table.

'Ouch! That hurt, you idiot!'

Mum glared at me from the kitchen.

'What's the matter now? Go and change into your uniform, Mina!'

'I can't go to school!'

'Liar,' Deepa interjected.

'Really, ask Dad. I'm sick!'

'Ask her whether she's finished her project,' Deepa muttered.

I moaned and dropped my spoon into the milk, carefully splashing Deepa.

'You did that on purpose. Mum – she splattered me on purpose.'

'Go to your room, Mina.'

My room, haven, sanctuary!

I went there and got under the covers, reaching my hand for my precious Dutch friend.

Moments later I was discovered by the Gestapo: Mum opened the door.

'You better watch out if you haven't finished that project by tonight.'

I drew the doona over my head and closed my eyes.

'It's not just you who wants to die,' I heard myself utter after she'd departed.

I could go if she was going. I, too, had once packed three bags, stolen some crumpets from the fridge and a frozen chicken from the freezer, and left it all behind my bedroom door, ready for my getaway.

'Where are you going?' Shanti had asked as I'd randomly stuffed clothes into my bag – sneakers, skivvies, garments I would no doubt need in the wilderness.

Indeed, I knew better than anybody of those fugitive plans. *Next time I'll make you sorry!* I had often thought when they'd bad-mouthed me or been unnecessarily punitive, resolving that *that* would be the opportune moment for my escape.

I'd tried, on legion occasions with Quentin, to run away from home, but had never been very successful; he would cry halfway down the street and I myself would give in a little farther, always returning with a lump in my throat after having got as far as the sorrowful street corner where old Mrs. Rabe would invariably greet me and say with final, kind wisdom, 'Say hello to your mum and dad for me'; always returning, our legs quivering, after having come face-to-face with the barking Alsatian that belonged to the angry Russian man at the end of the street. I knew all along it was not the Russian's fault. His attitude was attributable to two facts: It was the time of the Cold War and it was the time of Deepa's Tremendous Personality, her illustrious Imagination.

One day at the end of a happier October, Deepa had had the bright idea of celebrating Halloween. Since we knew it was getting too warm for anything but bathing suits and shorts, we had abandoned the elaborate costumes and simply walked in our everyday garments between our neighbours' dwellings, begging for sweets. Quentin had been there when Mr. Moscow – as we came to refer to him – had leapt on us with an anti-capitalist, anti-American invective. The Alsatian had lain loyal throughout, growling and gnashing his teeth, his eyes on our plastic bag of soft, stale lollies, which we, frightened for our lives, had subsequently dropped in our haste home.

At times you just have to go along with your death wish while seeming to comply with the outside order. Hypochondriacs, as those who are well know, suffer a heightened sense of life, not death; life, the awareness of whose loss is our greatest weakness.

I sat at my desk, convalescing that day off school (the eighth that term, Mrs. Douglas would not fail to note in my report card) and obediently wrote some vacuous lines about John Macarthur and what a fine pioneer and farmer he was, what remarkable contributions he made to the continent, and of his wife, Elizabeth, and the legacy of a fine wool industry.

I then took the pen to the fresh, white page and drew a figure of a merino sheep, although it looked regrettably more like a cat. I took cotton wool from the cabinet in the bathroom and fixed it to the body, feigning three dimensions (for the sheep would forever be in profile on the page, I thought, with half a body, one eye, an incomplete livingness).

Deepa inspected the project lying on the dining table when she arrived home from school, took one look at the artwork on the cover, and scoffed.

'Feeling better?' she sardonically remarked.

But I'd resolved to do more than become the vigilant, monastic student they wanted that day I was absent from school. I'd resolved to relinquish forever my outward delinquency and become the ascetic they wanted, reconstituting old social narratives, saving everybody but my-self from the brutal reality of our collective eschatology.

'God, I want to die,' I had heard her roll from the she-oak, a perfect, practised tune. If she could live a double life – mother and sanctuary-seeker – so I reasonably could, too.

Quentin and I often rode our bicycles by a sign out the front of the Local Presbytarian Church.

'Look,' Quentin would excitedly point it out to me each time:

Jesus Is Coming!

One evening, after riding by the sign, he'd come over and found the suitcases in the passageway to Mum and Dad's bedroom; ready when that Day and Hour finally dawned.

'What are they for?'

'Oh, my father is going away on *another* business trip.'

What else might I have explained to him about the Second Coming? What could I have said of Christ's late epiphany? Those words I'd really heard by their bedroom door – from she in the she-oak and he with his heart impaled at the ledge – to one who from a tender age knew intimately what it was to harbour and conceal an escapee parent also?

Dad took to holding his head in his hands a lot after this. He held his head in his hands when the Rain Hill Council trucks came by one weekend. Having heard their saws and the din of the trucks starting up, Mum had darted from the kitchen to the nature strip, again clutching the trunk of the she-oak, obstructing and holding off the workers with the bread knife still in her hand.

Deepa, Shanti, and myself were huddled by the bay window, three pair of alert eyes.

'We have instructions to cut it back, this is council property, Missus!' we could hear one of them appealing.

'It's a dying tree. To save it we've got to pulp about half of it!' another reasoned in vain.

'How would you like it if I made a pulp of you?' she threatened, waving the knife in their direction.

Dad finally intervened. He grappled with her and grabbed the serrated weapon; he apologised to the astonished group of council workers, and then managed, with much resistance on her part, to lead Mum inside, whereupon, he went directly to the dining table and slowly lowered his head into his hands.

Not only his head, but Dad's entire body became dense. As Mum began embracing the arboreal trunks of our nature strip and garden – the she-oak, the banksia, and bottlebrush – Dad went down, sank, literally retreated beneath the house.

Innumerable below-ground electrical connections and insulations he would find needed attention on weekends.

'Daddy?' Shanti and I would, on our hands and knees, creep and seek and call to him between the floorboards.

Two thuds would then be heard from him, meaning, 'Com-ing!'

We were children who became quickly proficient in a complex mode of subterranean Morse Code and, when we saw him emerge, mired in the dust and grime and tar beneath the house, we believed that he was no hypogean god but an occasional miner drilling a monumental lacuna that began and ended with her.

'Just going to see if things are all right down there with the foundations,' he would say each weekend of the state of more than electrical wiring, lowering himself into the manhole below our home.

Deep down he went because, deep down, having seen a manic desperation in my mother's packing of suitcases, my father must have known that refugees of her kind seldom have a fixed destination: only departure is the single historical necessity.

The luggage remained like a litany of sorrows, obstacles of their love, lined against the walkway to their bedroom all the rest of our days.

By the time we had use for it, by the time we had to escape to save ourselves – no, even sooner – by the time she would split herself, become like those stars in my mind, by the time my mother took flight, I would have become as inconspicuous and wraithlike as the ghosts I saw and that kept me awake, which made of me a permanent somnambulist.

OLD SYDNEY TOWN

The spring, then, when I was ten, I came to a startling realisation: My father was an apostate. Granted, his treasonous ventures were small. Domestic, even. He did not have the patience for jail sentences and therefore lacked the political integrity of the world's true freedom fighters. Of the one woman with whom he spent his life – out of resignation, I'd divined, rather than real passion – he now shrugged and said, 'I chose her,' meaning 'I chose her, I must live with her. I must die and go to the grave with her.'

He was neither heroic nor charismatic in the given sense of these terms and managed to perform his many acts of insurgency by way of fortune rather than tactical intent. He fled on a few occasions, all times when ambushed by this aforementioned woman – my mother. His revolution was slow. Without the microscopic vision of the past that is hindsight, one might even be so cynical as to say that such a man is a paltry figure, a man of little significance.

I – though it is true I'd be partial to such a thing – admired him. From the moment of my birth, he equipped me with tirades for slandering governments, schooled me

in political theories to topple the most tyrannical admin-
istrations. Moreover, for him, there appeared to be no
contradiction between this anarchic pedagogy and his
craven collusion with teachers' socialisation strategies.

'School,' he would thus repeat for my mollification
when I'd been teased in the playground for one reason
or another, when I might have been depressed about an
unfair entry in my report card, 'is an ideological apparatus
of the state – *don't submit*!'

Stalemates between myself and Mum had been reached
over dinner because of the rigour of Dad's instruction in
tactics of subversion.

'You're eating those peas!' Mum would warble as I
would carefully excise the peas from the pilau, pile them
on the side of my plate and eat the simple, wholesome
basmati rice.

'Oh, no, I'm not!' I might answer back, inciting insur-
rection at the dining table.

Looking back, I guess that she held me in antipathy for
the very first thing I ever spoke and for the fact that it was
under Dad's tutelage that I learned to speak it. She took it
to heart, a conspiracy begot by my father, that I did not
gurgle 'Mama'; that I did not grab her hand and holler
some infant gibberish that she could take into her own
entitlement. No. In a tone both unambiguous and una-
pologetic, the first fractious words I ever uttered, shot in
my mother's direction, tearing apart forever the tender
maternal quality of her relation, shattering irreparably the
natural bonds betwixt mother and daughter: *Free Goa!*
Before I could walk, before I could fire and then slink
away from the face of utter agony that was her retaliation,
these were the seditious words I spoke: *Free Goa!*

If I recall it correctly, it had been Dad who had instructed me in the virtues of fair play and humility.

We were at the baby health clinic.

I was shaking violently while receiving inoculations against the regular childhood afflictions. The nurse administering to me handled her polio injections like personal chastisements. Mum had slapped me, only strengthening the force of my resistance. My feelers were swinging like shrubs receiving a cyclonic battering.

'Cowardice,' Dad announced out of the blue, 'might very well be a form of hope.'

He was an upstart. Other babies sat up and took notice of him.

'What are you trying to do, turn her into a poltroon at one?' Mum shouted above the cacophony of cries that, taking their lead from Dad's words, had followed.

Before we knew it, a riot had broken out. Mothers with their breasts exposed frantically attempted to pacify the reluctant inoculates. A maelstrom of babies' tears threatened to engulf the clinic and we were asked to leave.

MOB VIOLENCE ERUPTS IN RAIN HILL BABY HEALTH CARE CENTRE! the story in the local paper had been headed the following week, with a flattering photograph of Dad, the alleged malcontent, accompanying the article.

In another reincarnation I was sure Dad would have been a Sardaji; he sympathised dearly with the extremist insubordination of the Sikh nationalist struggle and often remarked that a fight for a separate state in the Punjab was a struggle only second to his agenda to free Goa. When he was feeling particularly ineffectual in his political conscious, he would wrap a tea towel turban-style around his head and brandish a kitchen knife in his hand as if it were a sacred kris.

'Look, Baba, who am I?' he would test us in this warrior pose.

'Joshan Singh,' we would together recite the name of the ancient Sikh warlord.

Overhearing this, Mum, who ridiculed his anticolonialism, would irk him by shouting, 'There are invasions and *invasions*!'

What she, of course, was trying to do was remind Dad that a national resistance movement cannot be founded, as it had been in Goa, on the effort of a few college boys flicking rubber bands at an encroaching Indian Army.

Dad would glumly retire to the garage at such times, where, among other things, he had restored and set up an old printing press; authored, edited, and published a triannual periodical on Goan liberation. (He was saddened to concede that successive appeals for support to the Australia Council had been miserably rejected.)

'India,' I heard him declare recently while we were standing in a lengthy queue at the checkouts of Woolworths, 'is a figment of the Western imagination, a metonymical artifice!'

This was no worse than the occasion when, during the last school break, he had taken the day off work and told Mum he was taking us to the Blue Mountains. I waited in vain for the Three Sisters, for the glorious azure peaks, for four hours later we were not encountering Katoomba but had crossed the state and were entering the doors of Parliament House in Canberra.

Aboriginal activists and women's rights lobbyists were handing pamphlets to visitors and tourists. Dad consulted with them and, a few minutes later, returned to the boot of the car to fetch a placard he kept in there with the words FREE GOA scrawled in capital lettering.

'Just in case,' he would say of this redundant accoutrement, 'just in case,' anticipating an unexpected moment for publicity triumph.

We spent the next few hours rallying in the forecourt of Federal Parliament, three young girls and a spirited patriarch.

Later in the day, at the sitting of the House of Representatives – the entire purpose of our escapade I would realise only too late – during question time, the familiar voice of a small brown man was heard shouting to the Prime Minister from the public gallery, 'And Goa, what is to be done with Goa?'

Now, when I was ten, some twenty-five years after Nehru had occupied Goa with no resistance save those few boys from Bambolim College flicking rubber bands in the direction of the advancing Indian army ('nationalist propaganda,' he would say when Mum over and over used this fact of history against him; 'lies'; 'all balls'), Dad was still devising a plan to reconquer his homeland. And it wasn't just the Sikhs from whom he took his lead; he borrowed anthems from the Tamil Tigers of Elam, the Inkartha Freedom Fighters; the Basques and the Sinn Fein were separatists whose aspirations and minor histories my father reconstituted into a private education. Reading José Martí or Aimé Césaire could make Dad weep. *The Wretched of the Earth* lay in the bookshelf beside the family copy of the *Good News Bible*. While fathers of my colleagues accompanied *their* children to weekend cricket and football matches, Dad would secretly school me in the treachery of the Indian state, the superiority of my Goan Soul.

'Invasion!' he would lament of his former home, 'Annexation!'

'There are invasions and *invasions*,' Mum would rebuke again, and it couldn't have had a more corrosive effect had she broken his skin and applied chili powder to the bloody wound.

'Where are you from?' To this question he had drummed into me to answer, 'Goa'; should I be further interrogated – worse, should I be accused of pedantry – I was to explain that since Goa was illegally confiscated by the Indian state, my allegiance was technically not Indian but Portuguese.

When, in the third grade, we had had to stand up at assembly and each student say their name and present to the school a flag they'd made of their native land (multiculturalism had just, only just, made it to St. Sophia's), Dad refused to allow me to brandish the evocative spinning wheel bound by amber and green familiar to Miss Anderson.

In this way, he caused a great deal of controversy and me much heartache.

'Subcontinental history is problematic, to say the least,' I'd muttered like an eight-year-old fool before the whole school and held up to the bored student body the unusual specimen of a Lusitanian flag.

One of the most tender moments I recall having shared with Dad occurred one recent Thursday.

'Got her, the bitch!' he cheered and applauded as live CNN footage showed the slain body of Indira Gandhi being carried on a stretcher from the Golden Temple.

A small war transpired, my mother weeping for the end of dynasty, Dad acclaiming the same demise with jubilation.

'India, I thought, was supposed to be a secular democracy,' he said when she suggested his behaviour was tantamount to sacrilege.

'You worship your gods and I'll worship mine,' my mother truculantly retorted, clutching the scapular she wore around her neck; on one side was a picture of Mary Queen of Heaven, on the other the dark, diabolical features of Indira Gandhi, Mamaji of a Nation.

'Indira,' Dad thus begun to derisively address her from his own cavernous refuge, but even that did not move her, since she took to accepting it as an endearment of the highest import.

There was no blood in the partition of our own house. When she was present at all these days, Mum despotically occupied all rooms at once; he, in dissident fashion, refused to be territorial.

'Daddy!' Shanti and I would now, before searching anywhere else, crawl on our knees and call and seek our father through the dense medium of floorboards.

Some days it seemed that he might have retreated indefinitely underground – that is, beneath the house – though in time it had become plain that he was not here plotting a *putsch* or even monitoring electrical connections, so much as hiding from her.

The house was in a permanent state of disorder with goods that seemed week by week to mysteriously appear and burgeon: food, linens, second-hand clothes, appliances that we already possessed or of which we would never have need. Mum would now accumulate, care lovingly for and hoard away, among other things, motel minutiae, aeroplane trinkets, restaurant sachets of salt and sugar, objects made of Styrofoam, plastic Chinese food containers, the empty, plastic sacks of bread.

Resourceful, austere, it may have been, but, as Dad pointed out, we ourselves had no outstanding debts with the World Bank or International Monetary Fund.

'State of Emergency!' she would declare again if we so much as demonstrated curiosity in these neurotic developments.

She now took flight over the smallest altercations or irritations with us. Where previously she would have retired to the kitchen, clanged a couple of pots together and subjected whoever was at fault to a round of culinary reprisals, we would now hear the door slam and look out the bay window to find her sulking by the boughs of the oleander, the frangipani and poplar trees, whistling her dirgelike ditties to the birds whom she had taken to feeding nuts and pepitas and who'd come in strange kinship to crowd about her feet.

None of us spoke of her absence, though these disappearances were often hours long. It was only one morning as Shanti and I had followed her into the garden that I had become seriously perturbed. From where we were standing, Mum was not scattering seed to the birds or clutching the trunk of the she-oak, but, it seemed, scraping her thighs against the bark as she struggled, like a gangling child, to mount it.

For weeks I said nothing about this incident, tried to put it out of mind, but one evening as I was riding my bicycle by Clearwater Park with Quentin, I came upon an even more alarming spectacle.

Quentin was scared of the bird attacks common around early September, and I, too, had my fears since a small parrot peck at Taronga Zoo had left my left feeler swollen and agitated for days.

I was scanning the trees for paranoid magpies and almost fell off my seat when, in the distance, I caught sight of the figure of a grown woman contentedly roosting in a great gum, calling and cawing, imitating and entering into the twilight confabulations of the mindless galahs and temerarious cockatoos. She was in the tree.

'I've found a shortcut!' I, upon identifying Mum, lied to distract Quentin.

'That didn't seem like a shortcut to me,' Quentin, his cheeks flushed, the calves of his legs throbbing, panted, when, hours later, we arrived home and he almost fainted from exertion.

Perhaps I had feared believing it then, perhaps we all failed to align the signs of her ascent, but indeed I could no longer doubt what was going through Mum's mind when, one afternoon this same spring, I put my hand to the back of the pantry and, among other articles of refuse – empty cigarette packets, chocolate bar wrappers – retrieved a small stack of netted twigs and leaves.

I knocked on the door of the manhole in order to show Dad my important finding.

At first he reassured me that Mum must have had a reason for this.

'Home crafts. Good idea. It'll help take her mind off things,' he said, inspecting the nest.

But as the weeks went by and we began to find a whole

stash of these odd sculptures about the place – hidden behind the fireplace grille, stored in the dryer, under piles of her unopened mail – Dad, instead of speaking of the therapeutic value of domestic leisure activities, wearily dropped his head into his hands or quickly disappeared underground. Thereby, my own suspicion was, if only tacitly, confirmed: From those spring branches she was climbing like a kid, my mother had taken to stealing the freshly composed eyries of whatever species of bird she could find.

Dad did not resist but began to bear her misery in silence. He left her alone, for, after all, she wished to be left alone. Mum's estrangement from us was now all the more pronounced and, in stealing the nests of innocent September fledglings, I had to wonder whether she thought she was recuperating for herself the very thing that had long ago fallen away: those eggs that once arrived and departed with solid regularity inside her very body. Her face acquired small lines, traces of waste; she aged not by years but in days and hours before my grieving eyes.

Dad began, that year I was ten, to speak permanently in the subjunctive, always speculating change, never referring to it as a tangible imperative.

'If the world were lighter, I, girls, would be a happier man,' he would sigh at certain times before placing the miner's lamp he had recently purchased on his head and silently disappearing into the manhole.

There were times when he would file Deepa, Shanti, and myself into the car and drive only one block away from the house, taking us to the milk bar for 'an ice-cream'. Sometimes he'd have a look of such hopelessness on his face, it would bring me to tears. When I began to cry, Shanti would also cry. And he, unable to console us, to receive a response when asking us, 'Sweetheart, what's wrong?' would develop a waxy sheen in his own eyes. Once, so unaware of his own sorrow, he turned the windscreen wipers on. It was a warm dry evening – not a trace of rain – but to him it was easier to blame his blurry vision on the vagary of the Sydney sky than on the water damming in his own sockets.

I began to detest the taste of Bubble O'Bills. The thought of a Cornetto would turn my stomach, and when I meditated on the potent citrus of Streets Calypsos, I would weep to recall the delicious ice candies sold by the ice candy wallahs, which we'd furtively eat by the beach at Benaulim, never certain that the frozen water was not going to give us cholera.

And yet, his determination did not wane. This spring he redirected his resistance to our private education. Where we would learn in school of the plight of the poor convicts, taken in chains to the barren continent of Australia, he would fill that history with tales about the unpublicised murder of people, dark like us. On the day at school that Shanti and I had recently to dress ourselves as famous Australians, he insisted we go as Trugininni twins, naked and with spears he'd spent an entire weekend carving by hand in the garage.

He explained in no uncertain terms that the history of the very land on which we were living was founded in blood and that it was not because the people that lived here were either weaker or more stupid than the dough-faced conquerors who came, but simply that they were poorer; and their poverty was due not to lack of enterprise or laziness or godlessness at all, but because these people didn't have the meanness of spirit to go to the continent of Africa and turn the bodies of many Africans into fast money, selling them to the sweet free cause of Sugar, Cotton, and Cocoa. And with this money to make guns with which to empty the world of its people; and when that endeavour itself became futile, imposing upon them a loveless God, writing books in the metropolitan academies about a strangeness that to their own depraved souls, had seemed devoid of beauty. And when, because they had enslaved and permanently exiled the native inhabitants of those places they had conquered, they found themselves without enough cheap labour to build railways and bridges, when they discovered that among their own dough-faced kin they felt homesick and all alone, they dragged people of coffee-coloured skin from India, from China, to build these things, to populate and indenture.

We all knew where Deepa's litigious streak originated. When he was nineteen, my father had filed a claim in the newly appointed World Court of the United Nations, attempting to upturn that pact by which the Iberian empires had – four hundred years before – divided the world between themselves along the border of Brazil: the Treaty of Tordesillas. Even now, miles away in Sydney, Australia, we were still receiving documents in the mail signed in the hand of the Secretary General, detailing the technical problems involved in settling this arduous case.

There were other places, besides the milk bar and Federal Parliament, to which we were taken. Frequently, he would take us for field trips to our own metropolis, to, for example, that infamous landing site of the nation's founder at Botany on Sydney's eastern outskirts, an industrial waste dump, where now one hears the arrival of planes, the departure of planes, a thunderous coming and going with that aching that makes one sad to be alone on the earth without wings. He would take us to Sydney harbour; I'd have to turn my back on the Opera House, the huge figure she cut over the inlet. Through the streets of those at once hideous and glorious edifices of colonialism, the Rocks, we would walk – my father, Deepa, Shanti, and myself – in silent remembrance for the dead. We would look contemptuously at the tourists who marvelled at how beautiful and young the city was; and then we would stop at Bennelong, where lie the shops containing the artefacts of those whose ancestors had been slaughtered in order to make room for the shops containing the artefacts of those whose ancestors had been slaughtered.

'Look,' Dad would gravely say.

One seditious day about this time he told Mum that he was taking us to the beach. The beach is an innocent place and I believed it to be so; I had fond memories of the beaches of Coogee and Bondi, where Dad would bury himself for hours in sand, enduring sunstroke in order to maintain the farce that he really could not get himself out without our archaeological assistance.

For hours we'd ignore him. For hours I'd sit at the sea's edge building artless sand castles with Shanti as an even more artless auxiliary. My aquatic insouciance was yet to come; I'd stand forlorn at the shore, watching Deepa far out, prancing like a young mermaid, the weed dragging at my feet.

'Really!' he would say at the end of the day as we ran back and began emptying the sand from the crotches of our bathing costumes. 'Help me, Baba, I can't get out!'

Mum would go on reading from one of her medical journals, pretending imperviousness. Each time his deception was lost on us; each time we'd gullibly comply; each time we'd dutifully disinter Dad with three miniature spades, Mum watching from the corner of her eye and with a smile she could no longer suppress at the edge of her mouth. He would emerge, shaking the sand from his body as if had been entrapped beneath solid concrete, simulating relief for his life, praising us as children whose loyalties had been tested, but were doubtless in the right place. *Next time*, we thought, *next time we won't go for this*.

But on the occasion about which I speak, we did not in fact go to the beach.

'Quentin and me . . .' I had begun to say, but stopped as Dad pulled the car to the side of the road on our journey southwest.

'Australia,' he began, 'was founded by convicts. These people, being poor and displaced, did not know how to speak proper English.'

At the end of his harangue he paused and began my sentence again for me: 'Quentin and I . . .'

These were rudimentary lessons he was teaching us. Someday soon he would be correcting the legitimacy of our euphemisms, admonishing us for the inaccuracy of our metaphors.

There is a place not far from Sydney that is a great monument to terror. It is called Old Sydney Town. It is old only in the same way that every recapitulation of the past is an inventory in fact of the ordinary cruelty of our own present time. In Old Sydney Town, one can see men being flogged, chain gangs, and governors' young wives dressed in period costume – whalebone corsets, bonnets, and boots – weary with the heat, fainting for the perverse pleasure of the crowd. One can hear cannons being fired (though they advise that you block your ears to mute the sound of the explosion). That these young girls and geriatric men who wake in early-morning hours for their shifts, donning themselves daily in the garb of a different era, are only playing parts that they may, at will, abandon on the bus, or as soon as they walk into the doors of their homes, was a thought that did not cross my mind as Dad parked the car and led us by our hands into the awe-inspiring archway. That a penal colony was the extent of this continent's cursed illegitimacy I did not believe.

We had arrived at Old Sydney Town, Dad wearing a tracksuit, and we three overalls, skivvies, and sneakers. I can't say we were well-equipped for attack, but at least our clothes served us somewhat as a camouflage. The town was ill-prepared for us. Innocence – such a false philanthropic interest in the culture of settlement life – pervaded the place. Japanese tourists did not fail in documenting this landscape that proved not only the barbarity of the nation's conception but a vile desire to relive it, reconstruct it in all its disavowals. (We, I carefully noted, were the only dark-skinned people here; we, the descendants of another continent entirely.)

Together we ate a lunch of fish and chips in a nearby kiosk and surveyed the souvenir shop. Then we headed for action.

The first objects of sabotage were the guillotine pieces Dad, for fun, put his head and hands through the manacles.

'You want to take a photograph? This is the way Mum would like to keep me permanently!' he called.

We giggled, and would have stopped giggling and moved on to the next attraction had Dad not tried to perform another trick: He could not get his hands out.

'Sure, Dad,' Deepa called. *'Sure!'*

We had to be cynical, He was known to play such abominable stunts just to test our allegiances.

My feelers suddenly aroused, though, I could sense something like genuine alarm in his face as he struggled, twisting his wrists this way and that, wresting his limbs away from the vast bracelet of wood that was the guillotine piece. I ran to him and tried to help him to no avail. Cynicism gave way to concern on the parts of Deepa and Shanti, but even collaboratively, yanking his hands, virtually breaking the arms of our hapless father in several places, we could not free him.

At this stage, a number of Japanese tourists had come by and, finding Dad's pitiful predicament more amusing than any other attraction, began capturing him with their own Nikons.

Dad – I looked on horrified – obligingly smiled for them.

Soon there were other enraptured spectators crowding round.

'Aren't we going to do something?' I asked with a certain desperateness, for there was something odious about the face of Dad in a guillotine pose.

But he himself evidently found it all very amusing. Now he was nonchalantly chatting in broken English with an elderly Japanese man about the politics of Japanese war history.

Deepa, who was inclined to find such things humiliating to her smooth thirteen-year-old reputation, hid among a crowd of people near to where the flogging was taking place.

'Sufferin' suckertash!' I could not find sympathy with Shanti, either; the pathetic smile and imitative cartoon discourse of a child whose knowledge of the world would come, I believed, only with the grace of time.

A man wearing the formal attire of an officer in the colony – an actor – had by now come by the spectacle. He clapped his hands, attempting to bring the crowd that had gathered to order and demanded an explanation, which Dad, in plain words, gave him.

It was only at this moment that it struck me that this man was merely a thesp, his garments the tools of his modest trade, and yet, he quite believed it within his power to take Dad's fate in his hands.

And Dad, assuming the role of the prisoner, the petty criminal again – unbelievably – obliged. 'If you could get me out of here, I would be very grateful.'

I watched, burying my face into my hands, my antennae picking up this ancient exchange of ritual submission and subjugation, that in the course of its repetition, its play, embeds itself in the consciousness.

Now the elder Japanese man who had befriended him began running to Dad's defence, punching and prodding the officer, until the officer grabbed him by his collar, called him a 'bloody nip' and, for authoritative emphasis, told the pugnacious geriatric 'slope' to 'go back to your own country!'

The irony of the situation was not lost on me and I think I decided at this moment on the futility of Dad's revolution; it had to be by other means.

I put my small arms around Shanti.

Again she mouthed glabrous Daffy's exasperated expletive, more amused by the occasion than able to see in it the profound violence of Historical Memory.

The would-be officer had radioed for help and was now giving orders to two young men, Asian men, dressed in workman's clothes, smuggled it seemed from the island of the Old Sydney Town storage and repairs shed; they were smiling blithely at Dad's state and in their hands were axes and other such instruments that suggested to me irreparable damage to his limbs.

When I saw these things I ran to Dad's pockets. I thought quickly and felt around inside them for some change. I went up to one of the vacuous young maids and asked where I might find the nearest public telephone booth. She pointed in a vague direction. I dialled our home telephone number.

Mum answered, but just as I screamed down the line, 'Mama, you have to come quickly! They're going to kill Dad' a familiar voice called me, a voice full of glee, and I turned and suddenly made out the figure of Deepa strapped to the nearby whipping post, about to receive a flogging.

Mum was begging that I tell her what on earth I was talking about, which beach we were at, but I was struck dumb by what I saw. Deepa was now voluntarily being tied to the post, and a man dressed in the same martial garb asked if she would like to cry something out in penitence for her villainy.

'Look, Mina. Look at me!' she called. 'Come and take a photo, quick!'

I watched, further bewildered, as the flogger – on closer observation, a frail-looking man whose costume seemed a little too big for his frame – proceeded to apathetically pound Deepa's small body. I watched, astonished, as the rope slowly splattered a gory scarlet over the smock Deepa had been dressed in. All through this, Deepa could not help but draw attention to herself, I was confounded less by the simulacrum of this image than by the fact that Deepa was herself hysterical with mirth. On hearing her squeals of pleasure at each lashing received, the crowds, too, began to snicker among themselves.

The poor officer was losing face, I could sense his credibility fast diminishing; the authority he ought to have commanded was fast reduced to ridicule. He grew, in these few minutes, to hate Deepa, I could see the antipathy. He despised her, just a child, for giving away the secret, which had never charmed or really convinced a single spectator.

'Hey, Mina, look, look at me, look at me!'

'Mama?' I said, 'Ma? Are you still there?'

But the line was dead.

'Mina, over here! Look at me!'

Now fed up with Deepa, the flogger was storming away, abandoning forever his duty, and I supposed from the look on his face that he may well have been walking directly to the administration office to sign for his resignation.

Deepa was left, tied to the whipping post, guffawing.

The crowds, in riotous fits of laughter, screamed, 'Encore, encore!'

Shanti was now pulling at my skivvy sleeve.

I turned back to where Dad had been trapped and saw the Asian workmen release and unburden him of the great weight of timber in which he had been held.

The guillotine attraction, axed in several places, now lay in splintered pieces on ground.

The rescue operation had attracted what seemed thousands of onlookers. A journalist, accompanied by a crew from a major television network, was holding a dictaphone to Dad's face.

'Well, sir, can you tell us how this happened?'

'In 1788,' my father began, 'a group of pasty-faced criminals were brought here under the charge of some even pastier-faced officials . . .'

'No, sir,' the young reporter was saying, 'I mean today, How did you get yourself in this bind today?'

Realising he was on camera, having apparently recovered from the trauma, Dad reached for the opportunity for which he had been waiting all his life.

'Free Goa! *Goa libre!* Free Goa! *Goa libre!*' he suddenly chanted, beaming at the eight million potential viewers who may have seen him on commercial news that night.

There was little room for us in the car this day. I had to hold Shanti, who was getting to be quite big – bigger than I – on my lap. The elderly Japanese man, Mr. Kirishigo, and his family sat huddled in the backseat of the Toyota. They were flanked by Philip and Andrew Tran, two Vietnamese brothers to whom Dad, ever grateful for his life, had offered something close to sanctuary in return.

In the aftermath of his ordeal they had mentioned to him that they were only employed at the godforsaken Old

Sydney Town while awaiting their bridging visas. They were, in fact, U.S.-trained mechanical and chemical engineers. Dad, wasting no time at all, had told them of his 'connections' and pledged that he would be only too glad to help speed up the processing of their applications at the Department of Immigration and Ethnic Affairs.

I was giddy and it was not from Dad's driving but from the horror of all I had witnessed in those hours and, most particularly, the thought that Mum had been left dangling on the end of the phone line believing Dad was going to be murdered at Bondi Beach.

Deepa's skivvy was stained with fake blood and now, watching her, ever-loquacious, nattering away with Mrs Kirishigo, I was reminded of a none-too-distant occasion when she had been inculpated in a crime against another national icon. Had Dad's countercolonial peccadilloes rubbed off on her in such a macabre way as to have produced that bout of savagery? *Had all his revolutionary training tainted her sense of what might reasonably justify atrocity?*

Wearily, I looked out through the car window and again determined that there had to be a less debilitating path to political transformation. I saw the leaves of the native trees swimming and shimmering and, in my head, sought allegiance with only the melancholy lines of a divided modernism:

All changed, changed utterly
A terrible beauty is born

'Not Indian, *Goan*,' Dad painstakingly explained to an excitable Mr. Kirishigo.

I was fatigued by this panegyric, and just as I thought I might regurgitate on the youngest Kirishigo child's lap – such was the extent that I had exerted myself, smiling and simulating that I knew anything at all about the nature of the past – Dad reversed into our driveway in Rain Hill.

As I opened the car door and ran to the rose bushes, emptying myself of all the terror I'd stored that day, I saw Mum rush into to the garden.

Seeing her there, weary and old as God, I wanted to cry:

Too long a sacrifice
Can make a stone of the heart.
O, when may it suffice?

I wanted her to take me in her arms and give me succour, to murmur my name, lull my wild limbs into a mellifluous slumber.

She took one look at the parade of internationalists Dad had hospitably invited back to the house for tea and biscuits, and coldly returned inside.

'There are invasions and *invasions!*' she crowed icily, making the very roses that stood before my bilious face freeze and fall off.

Shaken, I struggled to the door behind everyone.

'My wife,' I heard Dad declare to the Tran brothers and the Kirishigos, pointing in the direction of Mum's retreat, 'doesn't like me so much.'

LONG DIVISION

W hen you are a child, long division can be inter-
minable. I had stopped counting the number of
times Mum whispered to me, 'I want to die, I want to die!'
had stopped wondering how many times her life could
have gone into more substantial operations, when Death
finally came to claim her.

This is when we had been warned in class, 'Long division is
what we'll be doing the next few chapters, so I advise you,
girls, to come and see me if you're not going to be here, or to
borrow the notes from your colleagues.'

Sweet, dear, doting Mr. Heaney, so prepared for battle
with our young minds! But to marvel at how smaller units
of value may slip and split into and between those much
larger, division must take you by surprise, usher you alone
into unfamiliar mathematical territory. I myself did not
marvel; I had been vigilant, receptive, a witness from the
very beginning when sadness had seemed massive and
insurmountable. To me, then, splitting and spilling seemed
quite natural.

She began to split routinely. Not with the suitcases but
with the handicap of her own heart.

'I'm leaving,' she'd simply announce, slamming the front door.

It always seemed she would say this when it was raining, when the evening had come upon us early and what was left of the day was ruined with no hope at the end of it.

'I'm leaving,' she said, as she put on her raincoat, the red raincoat that was falling apart at the seams and as a result made her sodden return seem all the more spectacular.

On this occasion, she was waiting, I believe, for someone to summon her back, to beg mercy, but when no-one responded she was all the more resolute. I didn't look up from my work, scholar that I was, hermit that I had slowly become; I did not look up offering her the satisfaction of my filial vulnerability and say, as the words fought with my will and welled in silent, ungovernable form in my eyes, 'Mama, don't go!' I had other concerns – *Was I to live my life forever in appeal for her?* I wondered – and so returned to the bigger event that now confronted me:

Jenny has seven dollars and sixty cents and would like to buy some hair ribbon. How many metres may she buy if ribbon is eighty cents per metre?

Shanti was glued to the television, now unfased by these episodes that had acquired a domestic place in her seven-year-old consciousness.

That terribly unrealistic encounter between two dogs, a father dog and a son dog, was playing itself out. From the corner of my eye I could see the father dog patting the son dog on the shoulder and saying, 'I love you very much,

Auggie boy' and the son dog responding on cue, 'Dad, dear Dad, you're the best dad any boy could ask for.'

I could not answer the question about Jenny and the ribbon, for though I despised her, my mind took flight with that thin, mean body of hers. I got up from the table and carried my pencil to the door. As I stood there, listening austerely through the rain, past the small, dull sounds of the nocturnal insects, stretching my antennae until I reached the pure sonorous echo of the rustling of the plastic of her raincoat, lulling myself to the clicking of her slippers, the splattering of the rain on the con- crete, I stabbed the pencil into the palm of my hand and begged Jesus' forgiveness for not having pleaded with her to stay.

When there was nothing left in that darkness with which to comfort myself, I searched for the sounds of cars; the faster they drove, the more they screeched, the wilder my grief became.

Dad, all grubby and tar-smudged, had at this moment come up to prepare dinner and now said something like this: 'She's pretty visible in that red, she'll be quite visible to traffic, won't she?'

And I did not say anything but wondered whether this was the kind of question an adult asked for reassurance or because he truly wanted to know what I thought the chances were of Mum being killed by a car.

I listened till her footsteps were too far, the small splashes distant in the darkness, wondering how it was possible to rescue such a person from her misery.

'Why are you sad?' I had by now asked many times, mostly late at night when she would take to locking herself in the bathroom and I, like an interlocutor in the dark, would hear from behind the door her impenetrable, in-consolable grief.

'God, I want to die!' she, to my startled ears, once directly responded from the other side.

Dad had dragged me and Deepa out of bed in the middle of the night the day before my major maths test. Mr. Heaney had written:

> Mina seems distracted in class. She frequently makes unnecessary errors. I am hoping her score will improve in the forthcoming exam.

Mum was slumped in her bed and in her hand was a bottle of sleeping pills.

'Mummy's very unhappy,' Dad told us.

Poor Dad, always trying to explain things as if explaining would erase their self-evidence.

'Why are you sad, Mama?'

These are questions, I had begun to learn, for which one has no answer, they are problems with no set formulae. Mass sorrow cannot be alleviated by subjecting it to something smaller than itself, because one is left then only with a series of disconnected fears.

I turned my attention back to Jenny's more modest dilemma but, try as I did, could not concentrate.

Dad was now in the kitchen. I watched him.

His were the hands of a man that were clumsy but tender in their responsibility. When we were smaller and he used to bathe us, he would take special care with our infant digits and toes, terrified that they might come off in his hands. Now he was preparing the frozen Woolworth's burgers that had become synonymous with the caprice of her moroseness.

'How many would you like?' he asked Shanti.

'None!'

Auggie boy,

I heard the improbable father dog declare at that moment,

you're the best boy any father could ask for.

Watching him, I wondered whether my anxieties had not begun much earlier with my encounter with times tables, for my journey with multiplication had coincided with Mum's being taken away in April to a 'beautiful house' somewhere in the 'bush' to recover from the 'illness'.

'Multiplication,' Mr. Heaney had then informed us, 'is like poetry; to incorporate it you must commit it to memory.'

I, however, had had more patience for poetry than for multiplication. I was gazing out the window of the classroom, repeating the words of the final, apocalyptic stanza, '*This is the way the world ends, this is the way the world ends . . .*' when Mr. Heaney came to whisper something in my ear. But the beautiful melodic notes of his Irish accent could barely rouse me from my stupor.

'You're daydreaming, aren't you? Now could you please answer the question?'

This had been the question: 'Cathy has six hens and each hen produces six more chickens. How many chickens will there be altogether?'

Forty-two was the correct answer, but was it wrong to have wondered whether the roosters who sired the chickens were included in the equation?

'No.' The Irish no, particularly about issues mathematical, was emphatic.

'But, Mr. – '

'Miss,' he had said rather curtly, 'those hens sat on those eggs all day. Don't you go inquiring about the role of the roosters. Were the roosters there when the hens were hungry, when their backsides were sore?'

I took over and told Dad to go and have a bath, for I thought he wanted to throw his hope on the griddle.

The ice on the burgers numbed my fingers, but I then realised that life had not assigned us time for the thawing of such things. FORK-SPLIT BURGERS IN ORDER TO THAW, the box instructed. We fried them frozen and hoped they would revive.

I imagined where she might be now – the park, the middle of any street, walking on the road, waiting for someone to summon her back, elicit her compassion. I could hardly bear contemplating what neighbours and strangers strolling through Clearwater Park these August evenings said when they saw the spectacle of Mum mounting those large public arbours, indeed, giving new meaning to the expression, 'her head is in the clouds'. *It must be cold out there*, I thought, and remembered the fervour with which Mum had recently related to Shanti, Deepa, and myself the sad tale of St. Catherine of Sienna, who chose to walk barefoot on coals rather than denounce God.

'What happened?' I had demanded as she came to the sanctimonious end of the narrative.

'Well,' she'd said with a sudden cruelty, 'what do you *think* happened?'

Her slippers had holes in the bottom of them. We had bought her a new pair for her birthday, but she would not wear them.

'I'll put them away for later,' she had told us as she reached into the refrigerator, at the back of which she had by now also methodically folded and shelved a woollen jacket Dad had given her for Christmas; a small bottle of perfume that Aunty Beatrice had brought her back as a gift from Switzerland; the fancy hair dryer Uncle Vincent had given her from the company he was working for; various packets of chocolates, unopened and, like those inside the suitcases, probably perishing in the boxes.

'I'll put them away for later!'

I was impatient for later, had begun to hold it suspect. Later had become as imminent as death and I was no longer willing to defer it.

'Whatever she has done,' Dad tried to console us when she had been hospitalised earlier this winter for something he and Aunty Sylvia, who came to mind us, found difficult to explain, 'you must remember that she loves you very much.'

I was memorising the nines when I had heard a mute whimpering; I had gone into the garden, where I had discovered Mrs. Rabe's grandchildren petrified in the driveway, the skid marks of the bright blue rubber stoppers of their roller skates long jagged lines behind them.

When they saw me they did not say anything but silently gestured toward the roof of the house.

A vertiginous déjà vu then overcame me as I shifted my gaze and saw Mum scaling her own height; near to where some pigeons and mynas were imperiously inspecting her, she was perched on the eaves, awkwardly reaching for her balance, sobbing and burbling and saying she wanted to get down. In her hand she was clutching what I thought was a carton of low-cholesterol supermarket eggs.

Hours later, when the ambulance came to take her, Dad again held his head in his hands.

Again Mum returned from hospital with a host of stolen goods, bejewelled with the same old identity bracelet; this time, though, not one of us was beguiled.

Manic depressive. I had heard these words only once, uttered from Uncle Vincent's lips. Late at night not long after she had been taken to hospital, Dad was crying; I had never heard him cry so disconsolately before.

He was weeping and Uncle Vincent had said something as he took my father into his arms, something like, 'You cannot bear the responsibility of a manic depressive, it will bring you down.'

My cheek, pressed deep against the wood of the banister, ached as I imagined a great weight collapsing on Dad.

'Whatever she has done, you must always remember that she has done it with genuine affection.'

These were the indefatigable hands of a man that gestured always to the greater strength of things, affirming the superstructure of our lives, but whose face frequently bore an expression that belied him, that seemed to say he no longer wanted to live beneath that strength.

'Oh, well, think I'll attend to the mess I left down there,' he would invariably excuse himself after making us dinner, pointing toward his nether-sanctuary; 'It's a mighty task recircuiting a home, and you girls are lucky I'm not bad with a drill.'

When he emerged from what now sounded like a

formidable quarrying operation, Dad was forever qualifying what we saw with words like these: 'Your mother feels defeated.'

Auggie boy, will you do your dad a big favour?
Sure, Dad, anything for you, Daddy mine, the best dad in the whole world

Defeat. I knew this word, for it was words that I had amassed inside me, been wired in this world for. Maths, admittedly, I had difficulty with, but the vocabulary of bitterness had bloomed inside me.

'Oh, child!': This I had assiduously apprehended was her code for 'I wish you had perished inside me.'

'I can't take this anymore!': This I knew meant, 'I am waiting for the right moment, only it seems never to come, to surprise you with pain. I will make you suffer.' 'You just never listen!': These words might mean, depending on the inflection, 'Things would be better if you did not ask questions', or 'Leave me alone, leave me alone, I want to be alone!'

At moments of my own scholastic defeat, I now willed her to die and longed to find myself in the situation of Meursault, who had been sentenced to death for not having demonstrated the proper quantity of grief at his mother's funeral. This way, I thought, I might not be defeated by truth but use it to some greater metaphysical purpose. It was not just her death I wanted to endure but the agony of a trial, an horrendous juridical fiasco, in which, unlike St. Catherine, I would do the denouncing and yet bring about my own end anyway. But the more I envisaged myself the Stranger, the more deeply I felt bound to the condition of her estrangement and the more I, too, wanted to flee.

Mina seems distracted in class. She frequently makes unnecessary errors. I am hoping her score will improve in the forthcoming exam.

I remembered long ago feeling this same estrangement and desire to flee from the man and the woman whose scooter had crashed into the pillar at our Hindu neighbours' house in Goa. No one else had heard their howls but I that morning. I had slipped out in my nightie, passed the porch, and found them lying limp and disfigured against the concrete slabs.

Hearing my own screams, Mum and Dad ran out, and villagers, too, began crowding around.

I could have told them all that I knew this couple were dead on impact, but I did not say anything. I could have announced, then and there, my feelers stiff as pins, that I knew they were already gone.

Karena led me inside while the adults began attending to the mess of blood, in vain ferrying trays of ice from my grandmother's refrigerator to the bodies and, as I looked back, I saw Mum moving their smashed figures, trying to determine whether either of them, so very young, was conscious.

'Look' I'd wanted to shout at her, 'they're dead! Can't you tell already? They're dead!'

Karena then carried me into the kitchen, and, dear thing, in trying to comfort me, fed me vast quantities of an array of foods I was known to enjoy: first, a glass of rose milk made with steamed buffalo's milk; then some sweetened molasses; and finally, three stale Angel's Ribs.

Why were they surprised when I spent the whole day vomiting?

'Did they die? Did they die' I had groggily interrogated each sympathetic relation who came to my bedside to check on me. 'Did they die? Did they die?' I had hollowly cried, for no one answered me except my grandmother, who, in the midst of her own oneiric soliloquy, cursing the name of my dead grandfather, once replied, 'But who, Baba?'

'She's better now, She was sad before, but I think things are all right,' I was apologising to Felicity as we entered the house, my hands, my face, my whole being trembling. It had been some time before I had harnessed the courage to allow even Quentin over since Mum's return from the 'beautiful house' in the 'bush'.

Felicity must have sensed this because she said, 'Don't worry. Plenty of people get upset. My mum gets upset all the time. Dad tells her not to mope and that just puts her in a bad mood. We can't seem to escape her.'

But I knew these were paltry reassurances from the girl whose concentration was so focused she routinely received the award for mathematical excellence. *Escape, oh if only she knew!*

As I opened the front door I wished that there would be something interesting to eat as at Felicity's, where there were always meringues or pikelets or the glorious Full-o-Fruit biscuits whose abundance seemed an extension of Mrs. Summers' bountiful affection.

I would take in these expressions of Felicity's life with

deep pity for myself, envying the rhythm and movement of the exchanges between mother and daughter, the vying for the mother's attention between siblings, and the effort on the mother's part to maintain interest in the staggered tales of which teacher did what at school and which child got into trouble and what embarrassing things had been said, but it was an effort – and this is what pained me most – that Mrs. Summers delighted in. I would observe her with a small and sudden nakedness in my soul, the wide-eyed interest never diminishing, preempting with her brilliant hazel eyes the small joys her children had brought home to share with her.

Now and again she might sigh and smile and gently chide one of the children, saying, 'Oh, Felicity' or 'Oh, Nicola,' though each child knew the absolute unseriousness with which such admonishing took place.

Now we were moving inside the house. As we made our way toward the kitchen, I caught a glimpse of the suitcases in their positions against the corridor to my parents' bedroom, the house itself in a state of ruin that might otherwise have suggested Jacinta Tyler's presence had it not now been several years since the menace's involvement in our lives.

These words, 'You'll have to excuse the mess' – the entire grammar of humiliation – had been inherited directly from Dad.

I watched, perplexed, as Felicity scoffed and said, 'Mess? This isn't a mess at all!'

In the living room alone I could see Mum's unopened journals strewn in a haphazard way across the dining table, and the foul smell of stale curry and unwashed crockery almost caused me to swoon as I neared the kitchen sink.

Dad would now and again emerge from his endless electrical observations beneath the house with an eye toward putting things in order, but it was all that he could manage to drag the vacuum cleaner out and, seeking a spot where he might begin, instead lower his head into his hands and quietly weep.

An odd, unpleasant smell pervaded as one passed by the suitcases in which the State of Emergency provisions were now putrescent, and even their queen bed discharged the scent of decay. It was that sweet fetid scent of decomposition that only the living-dead emanate. Not just the sheets and blankets, but vast mounds of Mum's clothes, unlaundered for months, stank from behind the door. And she – it has to be said – was also reeking.

Malodorous Mum did, very reluctantly, take a shower, and we knew because after these occasional ablutions her face would be bloated, her skin red and irritated; for some hours she herself would be on edge, as happens when a peahen falls against its nature into a puddle of rain, sopping and deranging its plume.

A Sydney Water Board specialist had been prevailed upon one Saturday morning when one of our pipes had burst, and I had been particularly bewildered to overhear him discoursing with Dad about the problematic drainage circuits in the house, speculating about the source of the blockages we had recently been experiencing in the shower recess.

'Feathers!' I overheard him explaining.

'Feathers!' Dad had repeated exasperated.

'Feathers,' I heard Mr. Plumber say again, 'It's a great mystery to me how it was that bird feathers got stuck in those drains!'

Dad had not said anything about it, but then, as I had been discovering for myself, it was only one of many secrets he was keeping.

'What are you doing down here?' we had in simultaneity, daughter and father, asked each other when, not long after this episode with the plumber, I'd caught him in the middle of the night in his cavernous haunt.

Lying awake to strange scuttling noises beneath the house, I had trembled to think that rats might have made a final infestation, their siege beginning below ground. When I could no longer bear the racket, I'd slipped on a jumper, pressed my feet into slippers, and gone to confirm, only to find the latch undone on the manhole.

The door was pushed back and, before I knew it, a bright miner's lamp was beaming light on my sleepless eyes. It was Dad, in his pyjamas.

'What's all that?' I'd said, seeing a mattress and a small fold-away table, assembled as in those fantastical tales of beavers and moles and other fossorial creatures whose domestic behaviours are anthropomorphised in order that we might understand why they choose to live in darkness.

Dad shrugged shyly and then wincingly said, 'Just thought I'd go down and see how the insulation bats were doing.'

'At three o'clock in the morning?' I'd scolded him, he who now, like a shy myopic beaver, could only hang his head, betraying to me that indeed he had much more than a fibreglass underworld on his mind.

'I thought there might have been rats, that's all' I'd said, before closing the door and leaving him to himself again.

The truth was that Dad now made his bed each night by burrowing in and out of the clean earth below the house, where, with the aid of some heavy-duty camping equipment – sleeping bag, small portable cooking stove (our suspicions were confirmed when such items began to mysteriously amass themselves on Bank Card bills) – he had secured indefinite lodgement, away from the stench and corruption of Mum.

Late at night he might yawn and stretch his arms and say, 'Oops, think I left the pliers down there,' before slinking down and not returning until morning.

'We haven't had a chance to clean up since Mum's been away,' I now deprecated, directing Felicity's attention away from a burgled nest that was protruding from beneath a *Medical Examiner*.

But Felicity was not at all interested in what I had to say; I could have begun to tell her, 'My mother is a manic depressive', and she would probably have not been perturbed, for at that moment she had discovered the Rubik's Cube lying abandoned on the dining table. The Rubik's Cube that only Deepa had mastered.

'Mum!' I screamed in order to warn her that suicidal behaviour would not be tolerated, since I had a guest. 'Mama!'

No answer.

The scenes that came to me now – of her in the bathroom or locked in the laundry with the gas pipe on, or breathless and blue, hugging the pillow in my own bed, or with blood perhaps running from her wrists or some other frail part of her body – came lucidly, almost as if on a script I had read and reread.

'Time me!' I turned to face Felicity; she was gleaming with the unabashed pride of a prodigy. In less than a minute, silent, unmoved by the surrounding mess of days, weeks, months of our shame, she completed the Rubik's puzzle. Each square perfectly constituted by her masterful hands into a face of uniform colour. I myself had been daunted by that puzzle and felt very ashamed for having recently, during a childish aberration, peeled the adhesive stickers and diligently rearranged them so that Deepa thought I was as clever as she.

Felicity was now bored with the puzzle and put it away saying, 'You know they say you can do Rubik's if you are good at math – do you think there is a *correlation*?'

In fact, the only relationship, devoid of sophistication, I could really figure was this: The barren house reminded me of the possibility that she might be dead in any one of its rooms.

Opening the fridge with that dread, I surreptitiously pulled from among the strange collection of perishables – shoes, hair dryer and perfume – a loaf of bread. Mildew mottled the surface of it.

'I'm sorry,' I told Felicity, 'Is toasted bread with honey all right?'

'Oh I love B.B.H.,' she squealed and I patiently waited for her to enlighten me, as she generally did, about this particular acronym. 'Mum makes us bread, butter, and honey sometimes when we get fed up with biscuits. Do you have sprinkles, too?'

'Are you kidding?' I wanted to say to her, to temper

some of this zeal. 'The only colour in this house is what you'll find on the underside of stale food.'

'Mama!'

Still no answer.

'Can you hold on a minute? I just want to go and check something.'

'I thought you said your mother was home?'

'Yeah, I thought so. Maybe I'll go out the back and check.'

I went to the back, my heart beating, pounding, my antennae in anguish.

I pushed the laundry door ajar as if waiting for a monster or some grotesque creature to roar and bark. She was not there.

I returned inside and went to her bedroom, waiting for the same dragon to now yelp or bellow in pain. No sign of her. The blinds were darkened as though she were home.

I went to my own room and, before I knew it, the mathematical genius, Felicity, was accompanying me.

'What are you doing?'

I pushed the door forward, waiting now for this ogre to pounce and gorge us.

'I'm looking for Mum.'

The creature had escaped. Silence, that dreaded, unaccommodating room of sorrow, was all that was left.

My friendship with Felicity had since that day slowly cancelled itself. Unabashed, and the genius that she was, she'd offered me her estimation of myself one day when I candidly admitted to having copied the answers to the previous night's math homework from the back of the book: 'You're weird.'

The gulf between us, though, I suspect came less because of this episode with the invisible fiend in the house than because I had proved myself a dunce at long division. Geniuses cannot bear to patronise the base for too long; it is beyond their vocation; that is, it is beyond the scope of the precise talent upon which they are called forth in this world to concentrate their attention. (Mum had recently said, 'Felicity doesn't come over anymore. You should call her over.' I was mortified.)

Brigette has five litres of lemonade. How many friends will she have if she does not know how to do her sums? Long division; I was impatient with it, doomed therefore to perform poorly in the face of it.

'Mina' – the melodious Irish whisper again in my ear – 'is there something the matter, dear, something I might be able to help you with?'

Again I was looking beyond the classroom through the window and repeating these lines to myself, *'This is the way the world ends, this is the way the world ends . . .'*

And even he, patient and virtuous professor that he was, could not rescue me from my doom, for the day before our final-term test, the school principal came into our class and announced, 'Mr. Heaney will not be coming back to school, I'm afraid,' and then – as if to explain the particular quality of our loss – added, 'ever. His mother has fallen very ill, and he's decided to return to his native Ireland.'

There forever without a guide through the days of my long division. The terror of this journey's imminence was heightened by my sudden knowledge that I, distracted and companionless, was a native of nothing: zero. Nothing went into me and I too seemed irreducible in my gigantic lonesomeness, except perhaps in that primitive place that was now forever alien to me, and where, without our even knowing, we divide ourselves so painlessly. I looked again through the window.

'Multiplication,' he had told us, 'is like poetry; to incorporate it you must commit it to memory.'

In fact, he had been wrong again; the process had to be reversed, for life itself, which thrashes against you and reminds you of its hopelessness, is only ever an elixir in its aftermath. It was my father who, in these dark hours of waiting for her, had provided me with the adage for my whole life.

'Everything,' he had said, all grimy as he climbed out of his subterranean haunt, 'that you anticipate and live your life for brings you sorrow and loss; joy is the remainder, what is carried over.'

She emerged from the night, brought the night in with her. I despised her but now could not arrest the swell of grief from unleashing itself upon her. The problem of Jenny and the ribbon had not yet been resolved. Indeed, the burnt burger I had eaten was churning inside my stomach and I thought I might vomit. Her clothes were soaked and I heard the wind rush in and make Shanti, still besotted with the anthropomorphic dogs, shudder. Dad arrived from the bathroom also at this moment, bringing with him steam that was supposed, I thought, to have thawed his heart.

'Is she back, then? Is she back?'

He, too, was caught in the barren economy of 'later'.

She did not say anything but unbuttoned the red raincoat and took off her tattered, drenched slippers. She went to the fireplace.

I wondered if this was the guise of death as she stood there. Death was what filled the space between us, so hollow and indifferent.

I put my head down. I wanted at this moment to be reconciled to something, deeply, vehemently. I wanted to open the door and stand between the wind and the fire and vivify my senses. Perhaps I even wanted to run into the storm and wait for someone to summon me back. On the page my own rain flowed and poured across the empty interrogation:

> *Jenny has seven dollars and sixty cents and would like to buy some hair ribbon. How many metres may she buy if ribbon is eighty cents per metre?*

SHYNESS

There then came a slow, sweltering summer when she felt it necessary to enlighten me about something, something about which she supposed I had no idea. The previous night Deepa had announced at the dinner table that her ninth grade English teacher, Ms. Reynolds, was a lesbian.

My parents had looked at each other perplexed.

I had sought to ease their discomfort by picking two peas from my plate and placing one in each nostril.

This was a mistake; I'd not only earned the ire of them both – Mum said, 'You think that food is a prop, heh! Always performing, always acting the fool,' and then proceeded to rob me of the rest of my dinner (ladyfingers, crab curry, peas pilau); Dad told me to go and get rid of the peas – but, when I'd gone to the bathroom to extract them, I realised that in my earnestness I had perhaps pushed them in too far. They were intractable.

I returned to the table, snorting and sniffing, the peas buried impossibly somewhere in my sinal passage.

Even Shanti was desultory, unable to humour me.

Deepa now looked over at me, scornful; I had deprived her once again of her great moment.

'I bet you don't even know what a lesbian is!' she suddenly turned on me.

Again Dad and Mum looked at each other; this time they entered into a discussion in Konkani.

'Well, do you?' she pushed me.

'Yes!' I suddenly said, raging, rising to the challenge, my antennae extended and belligerent as a pair of scimitars.

Who did she think she was, anyway, with this encyclopaedic preserve!

'I'm waiting . . !' she chimed.

I turned desperately to my parents; they were now moving between idioms, my father very calm, even smirking, my mother squawking and flapping, swallowing large mouthfuls of food.

'It's something sexy,' I blurted. 'Something like fucking.'

Where were these words coming from! How had I even made the crude association? Perhaps I had heard the words on television not so long ago; yes, that had to have been where. I had crept down in the middle of the night after having had my recently recurring nightmare in which someone unidentifiable died. I had woken, tears streaming down my face, and sought the gentle pacifier. I'd randomly switched on a channel to find this scene: a man was sitting on a bed where a blond woman with very large breasts lay naked. He turned to her, kissed her on the mouth, and said, 'You're very sexy.'

'You're very sexy,' I'd murmured to myself when the commercial break had come. 'You're *very* sexy.' I'd thought this seemed like a great compliment, something like a high IQ.

And the fucking? All that made perfect sense: at school that spring Amen Anthony had been suspended for a week and it was well known this was for his having presented as news for show-and-tell that his mother fucked his father; that he'd caught them that weekend when Sunday school had finished early. 'Fucking,' he'd said. Of course, I had by now in my innocent catechism also fallen upon the *Song of Songs* (Love Poem to the Lord: *I didn't buy that*), and there was the private research I had been surreptitiously conducting.

Deepa was now in hysterics and I felt my feelers straighten in defence mode.

'That's enough!' Mum screeched, trying to put an end to it.

'You know, Daddy,' Deepa went on, 'Oscar Wilde was a homosexual. He was incarcerated because of it just like the Hilton Bomber. Did you know that?'

Dad now looked at Mum helplessly. His role in her rehabilitation had been to 'mitigate unnecessary sources of angst and tension'. I guessed this was why he had left his subterranean hideout and was now behaving like an exiled prince, the ousted ambassador of a former uxorious kingdom.

'And Shakespeare, too. You know that poem "Shall I Compare Thee to a Summer's Day"? That was composed for a boy he did it with. That's what Ms. Reynolds said.'

Deepa now began quoting casual stanzas from 'The Garden of Eros' and I looked on incredulous at her confidence.

'There are the flowers which mourning Herakles
Strewed on the tomb of Hylas, columbine,
Its white doves all a-flutter where the breeze
Kissed them too harshly, the small celandine,
The yellow-kittled chorlister of eve
And lilac lady's-smock – but let them bloom
   alone and leave . . .'

'Don't leave your mouth open like that, you'll swallow a fly,' Dad said to me teasingly, trying for diplomacy in raillery.

He didn't realise I needed to get oxygen that way, what with the peas still lodged in my nostrils. I remembered having read somewhere that King Tutankhamen had his brain extracted through the nostrils. That was the method used prior to mummification; otherwise the corpse would go bad. I wondered whether the peas could find their way to my brain, then, based on the same principle. I imagined falling mysteriously dead in class one day, being vivisected at the morgue and the doctors finding the peas embedded in the brain matter.

'Oh,' they might then mourn me, 'she was not as slow as we thought. There was a precise *reason* for those cognitive idiosyncrasies we detected!'

Surely I would then be a legacy among my peers.

Deepa was still reciting from Wilde:

'And I will tell thee why the jacinth wears
Such dread embroidery of dolorous moan'

'Dolores!' Shanti screamed. 'She said you name, Mama, didn't she?'

'*And why the hapless nightingale forbears*
To sing her song at noon, but weeps alone
When the fleet swallow sleeps, and rich men feast,
And why the laurel trembles when she sees the
     lightening east . . .'

That night Deepa came into my bedroom, her white nightie illumining her like a lady phantom, a night sprite, a miniature Nefertiti. It was one of those dense summer nights, the crickets croaking in fits of love, when even the air lies in suspension. Shanti was snoring peacefully in the bed opposite. I feigned sleep, although by the time she had made her way into the room I was wide awake.

She stepped to my bedside and lightly tugged my right antenna.

'Hey, Miss Sexy,' she whispered.

I pretended to wake, rubbed my eyes to find a vision of my sister, metamorphosed in the night, smiling wildly, incandescent.

'Want to know what a lesbian is?'

'What?' I said grumpily.

'It's two women,' she said.

'What?'

'Two women – fucking.'

I turned over and closed my eyes and hoped she would leave me be.

'You didn't know that, did you, smarty pants?' she whispered.

I heard the door creak closed, her voice trail away, and I opened my eyes to see her moonlit shadow shrink from the wall.

Lo! while we spake the earth did turn away
Her visage from the God, and Hecate's boat
Rose silver-laden, till the jealous day
Blew all its torches out: I did note
The waning hours, to young Endymions
Time's palsied fingers count in vain his rosary
*   of suns!*

All *that* had transpired the previous night.

The following day found Mum and me sitting ill at ease together on the coffee-coloured sofa in the sunroom.

From here I could see Dad in the backyard, doing battle with an old mop and nightie of Mum's, habilitating a makeshift scarecrow on the burnt lawn.

The operation was not without reason, for our yard now possessed all the attributes of a professional avian wilderland. Theirs had at first been a subtle incursion; fledglings bashing into the windowpanes and cheeping from the fence in the spring. By the middle of the summer, though, we had found huge bleached cockatoos annexing the hedge and backyard pines; egrets who, like vast creatures escaped from a zoo, had also wandered from the small pond in Clearwater Park, their myriad-hued turds curling across the driveway. When the birds began keeping us awake at night with their claws scrabbling against the corrugated iron of the roof, Dad had decided on action, drawn up plans.

By now I had forgotten much of the previous night's drama, forgotten even about the peas, which had not shown any further sign of hazard – at least for the moment. There had been other developments. All week-end there had been news of fires. I was preoccupied with suffering of all kinds, but as I'd stood in front of the television watching people flee their homes in cars and in small boats; firemen evacuating peaceful outlying suburbs; trees scorched and hunched over like cripples; and finally, the image of a couple weeping as firefighters carried their young son, dead, on a stretcher from a burning house, I'd felt penetrated by intense sorrow. My feelers swung dangerously and, while watching the chaos of the outside world, I had had to raise my hand to my head to steady them.

'I'm telling you all this early so that it doesn't come as a surprise as it did for me,' Mum now began. 'You're growing up.'

At a distance I could hear the television. Shanti was watching the yellow-bellied, effeminate Snagglepus drawing Minxy and Jinxy into an obviously calamitous set of circumstances. 'Exit stage left,' I heard him call; 'exit stage right,' and I, too, wanted to make a dastardly departure.

The commercial break came and a news reporter suddenly said:

'More than four thousand firefighters are battling the state's fires today, of which half will remain uncontained by nightfall.'

The Forestry Fire Commissioner came on to say that,

'What worries me most is that the mood of the fire is unpredictable. Survival is always more tricky when the force of a blaze is erratic.'

I wanted suddenly to gather Shanti and even Deepa next to me, enclose them in my own arms, to collect everything, all of them, and escape from the house. I had done that – fled – once when I was alone after school; I'd stuck a piece of pita bread in the toaster and the whole apparatus had ignited. When I'd worked up the courage to come back inside, the toaster had melted on the bench top, but the flames were out.

'Always a performance, always a drama, can't you experience anything without escalating it to a crisis!' Mum had said when she'd returned from work that evening, coughing in hyperbolic fashion, muttering about carcinogens.

'Are you listening?' she said now. 'You miss one piece of this and you'll blame me for not having forewarned you.'

I nodded solemnly.

'As I was saying, you're growing up, and that means . . .'

I knew what she was going to say. *I knew it!* What *she* hadn't divined was that I myself had been referring to a red hardcover book called *The Joy of Sex* for some time. I knew pretty much what was going on, although, if I could have stopped it from happening to *me* I would have very much liked to.

It had all begun, I suppose, when Quentin had told me one day at the park that he would only do it once, just to try, that once was more than enough for him.

'Do what?' I had innocently asked.

I was at the top of the slide.

'You know,' he had said disarmingly, breaking some bark off a tree with his hands, 'sex.'

I had landed joylessly at the bottom, registering somewhat remorsefully that I had perhaps become too big for that two-metre sheet of inclined steel.

'Yeah, me, too,' I had confided quickly.

Then I'd run home angry, on a pretext I was sure he'd seen right through. I'd gone directly to consult the huge *Webster's Dictionary* by Dad's typewriter.

sex *secks n.* [Fr. *sexe* < L. *sexus*, a sex, < *seco*, to cut] The total physical and behavioural differences, properties, and characteristics by which the male and female are distinguished; either of the two groups, male and female, into which organisms are divided, esp. according to their distinct functions in the reproductive process; activities relating to or based on sexual attraction, sexual relations, or sexual reproduction; sexual intercourse. – *v.t.* To find out the sex of, as of chicks. – **sex up:** to stir or excite sexually; to make more sexually interesting, appealing or enticing, as a novel.

The tome weighed tortuously on me and, by the time I had got to the end of the passage, I'd thought I might swoon.

Next, I'd located that text whose whereabouts I had always known, but of which until that moment I had never had need to take serious notice: *The Joy of Sex*. I'd found it, its gold-embossed lettering glinting from its place on the bookshelf between an encyclopedia of Australian wildlife and a dictionary of Hindu mythology – out, they had misguidedly presumed, of harm's way. To me at that moment, the perils of ignorance had seemed far greater.

For some weeks, then, I began to pore over this text,

sneaking it into my bedroom, memorising the macabre coital pictography and the words that accompanied it:

When she is ready to be filled, the woman's vagina will be moist and elastic and the engorged penis might as soon just slip in.

The illustration showed two naked people sitting on the edge of a bed, the woman straddling the man, her face contorted into an attitude of pain, her head tilted slightly to one side. As I took in this image, I brought to mind my father's member; I'd seen it often enough as he'd walked from the bathroom in the nude searching for a towel. *Why, what a preposterous suggestion it was that that limp thing could be the antagonist of so profound a consequence!*

Confounded first up by the notion that this is how it all happened, I flipped through pages, resigning myself, a little bitterly, to the inexorable reality of it all. It became a wisdom of necessity. Some afternoons I took to snatching the book from the shelf and feverishly reading it by the door of the house until I heard the six o'clock bus climbing the street or the engine of Mum's car as it backed into the driveway, whereupon I would scurry back to replace it on the shelf.

If Quentin mentioned the *S* word again, I'd teach him a thing or two.

I moved about unsettled on the couch now, tracing my fingers along the even lines of corduroy.

'There are certain things you need to know. I don't want you finding it out from some crass classmate or from a toilet door,' Mum continued.

I now thought sympathetically of Amen Anthony; I considered his exile; I wondered whether it was not harsh to inculpate a person – a mere child – for stumbling upon his parents' afternoon proclivities. Indeed, it had been plain to me that Amen's bravado in the classroom during show-and-tell was only a front for the shock of the larger revelation.

I supposed the journey to his parents' bedroom after Sunday school to have been akin to one of those spurious Choose Your Own Adventure scenarios that everybody at school was reading: You found yourself on the path of a doomed denouement and, sure, you could turn back, but you could never experience the one true happy ending without knowing the several other twisted permutations which, by default, gave you your narrative orgasm. There had no doubt been a great cost to Amen's knowledge, even if he had not had the humility to have intimated it right out. (I privately derided those pseudo stories, was a conservative in matters of high culture; in art, as in life, I wanted a distinctive beginning, middle, and end, and I certainly would not have paid good money for those circuitous excuses for juvenile literature *even if* Mum had allowed me to subscribe.)

The smoke was now surrounding us. I could hear the timber of the house cry, crashing in the wake of a fire, the floorboards curling and falling within the flames' embrace. I recalled now what it must have been like for the twelve at Pentecost, the flames licking dangerously above their heads and the Holy Spirit imploring them to have courage.

'Exit stage left!' I wanted to timorously cry before shrinking.

She started with most rudimentary facts.

'When you bleed, you will be able to have a baby.'

We then moved on to wet dreams – *wet* dreams – a disturbing thought for me, the undercover insomniac, who already found sleep an excruciating effort. Happily, she said this was the male's domain.

Next she rose, went to the bookshelf, and paused; she pulled out a number of texts, among them *The Joy of Sex*.

Now my palpitations really began. *Would she notice the greasy fingerprints on the pages, the dog-eared dilapidation of the book?* My heart thudded.

She turned to the table of contents and then presented me with a page: a cross-section of the vagina. I, though, could hardly partake of her delight, appreciate the rich density of detail, the filigree nature of the work that she, physician that she was, appeared so instinctively to do; to my twelve-year-old eyes the vaginal section was abstracted, disembodied even, which is why I had not paid the illustration much heed in the first place.

I thought this was 'it', then, what they called, for reasons too literal for my esoteric logic, 'the facts of life'. It seemed an unmomentous revelation indeed, a poor anatomy, the words cursory: *hymen, labia minora, labia majora, clitoris, vaginal opening*. She circled these terms with her fingers, was speaking it seemed in tongues. The facts seemed such a naive analogy for, why, just a caricature of, the complex machinery of living to which I had, in my small time on earth, already borne witness. If these were the main events, I wanted another story.

'We had to bleed onto scraps of cloth, old saris, and then wash them ourselves,' she said.

Now I looked up at her and discovered that there was something strange and eerie, something like genuine joy, in my mother's eyes. Yes, she seemed almost enraptured providing me with this information. *For once my instruction was not a great labour to her!*

The fire suddenly seemed perilously close, the heat of it bearing down, about to engulf us. I moved my hand across the fabric of the couch and watched the perspiration on my palm leave small, dark impressions here and there.

'Life is pain,' she continued. 'Menses, childbirth, it all begins now – you're growing up.'

Again she said it! It was like a refrain. And had she not sighed, too, now that I recall it! I wanted, at that moment, to turn back to the page I knew, refer her to the man and woman on the edge of the bed, the woman with that anguished, aslant expression.

I felt now as I had earlier in the year at my confirmation. The archbishop had handed me a card with a new name on it, told me I was regarded as an adult now by the Church and in the eyes of God. I'd felt ensnared within a responsibility too weighty. I did not abide the symbolism of his next gesture. I did not take good council. When he had raised his hand, I had closed my eyes tight, scrunched my face, anticipating a great blow. Even when I opened them and found him smiling benignly before me, my cheek barely bruised by the assault, I still could not trust him (no doubt, I had not fully recovered from the hydrophobic trauma of that preliminary Holy Sacrament). I had spent the whole next week searching myself for the lavish gifts of the Holy Spirit now owing to me: neither knowledge nor wisdom, courage, faith, or understanding, fell into my lap, though. As for fear of God, I'd begun to live my whole life terrorised by one thing or another and did not know how to distinguish that particular configuration of dread.

I hadn't wanted to disappoint her. I'd sat, at moments wanting to leap from that scalding sofa, yet adeptly pretended ignorance throughout. The ordeal had been made more difficult because she was so strangely animated. It had dawned on me that this was not the mother who had deprived me of dinner only the night before; the mother who, months earlier, had made sudden and fast departures; the mother whose soul was scarred, who scaled the roof and took frequently to the trees. I had looked up at her only that once and seen a hysterical, lucid joy in her expression.

She's mad, I now thought. *She's mad*. There are whole communities being engulfed by fire as we speak and she is preoccupied with *this*.

And, as I sat there, my fingers circling aimlessly on the sofa, unable to bear the sight of her present incarnation, she said something I will never forget, something perverse and extraordinary.

'I want you to know,' she told me, 'I will always be your mother whatever happens, that you can tell me, ask me, anything.'

My feelers drooped, parched and lifeless. I saw Dad, burdened by the sun, desperately trying with gaffa tape to stick the neck of the nightdress to the handle of the broom and thus make the darned scarecrow stay upright. This renewed determination was as endearing and bungled as that of his former Old Sydney Town anarchy. I decided I had really to make my exit now; there was too much at stake in delay. I ran to my bedroom, the banister burning, the staircase in ruins, and smothered the last flames of myself with the doona.

* * *

Her words remain with me, haunt me because they remind me just how brutal the school holidays became, how I experienced my mother as if she herself were going through a second puberty: mood swings, premenstrual tension, the whole hormonal gamut.

No sooner had we had this exchange on the sofa than she began, for example, baffling me with new pet names. 'The Adolescent': this is how she began referring to me when in the company of Dad, who did not say anything but seemed as stunned as I by her sprightliness.

Her filial requests were neither different nor more daunting than those with which I had dealt all my life – 'Can you empty the garbage?' – except that now when making her demands, she frequently added by way of address, 'my young lady' or 'my grown woman'.

On Christmas Day she continued this fiasco with Aunty Sylvia and Uncle Vincent, and they, too, regarded me with a new and ludicrous awe. Not only that, but she volunteered recommendations, which is no doubt why my Christmas gifts this year included goods with which I had never before contended: face creams, sweet smelling soaps, a tacky satin nightie, and, from Aunty Beatrice – the worst present of all – a set of pink nylon underpants.

When I did not respond kindly to the gifts or the pronouncements ('My, how Mina's *maturing*'), Mum made her apologies on my behalf: 'She's shy about it, that's all,' she told my disgruntled relations. 'She's just shy.'

I was taken aback was all, and irritated by all this fuss. I was not by any means in denial but the celebrations were taking place without giving me time for preparation. I knew what was happening but, as I said, would have liked very much to have stopped it happening to *me*. Maybe I went too far when, not long after The Talk, she took me on a special expedition to Target to buy my first bra.

It was a Thursday night, shops were open late, and she had summoned me early before school to arrange that I go with her. I'd shrugged, unable to put up an argument; I did not want to be responsible for shattering her fragile recovery.

Quentin, however, came over just before we were about to leave.

'I thought we might go chase up all those balls down in the river.'

The river, barely a river at that time of year, was pregnant with lost golf balls. We had been arranging for this expedition all summer.

I was standing at the door, dressed in something that suggested prior engagement; sandals replacing my worn thongs, a skirt, a clean T-shirt. The fly screen mesh was between us and I caught his disappointment, the betrayed mien of the gaze in which he beheld me.

I pushed my face against the gauze, heard Mum patter past and catch a clear glimpse of us. I thought, *She has even arrived home early from work for the darned occasion!*

'Mina, all ready?' she called.

'Yes,' I responded meekly.

'Look,' I said to Quentin, 'maybe we can do that tomorrow evening. The balls won't be going anywhere'.

This irked him, I could tell; between us, immediate gratification was *the* unspoken principle.

'Where are you going, anyway?'

Deepa walked past. 'Oh, hi, Quentin!' she said enthusiastically.

'Hi, Deepa.'

I waited until she was safely gone.

'Oh, we have to buy some Christmas presents, you know, we've got all those poor relations over in India.'

'Oh,' he said, scratching his head. I could see him evoking a picture of our kin in his mind's eye: a clan of beggars huddled over an insipid kerosene flame in some depraved Bombay slum. Dad would have been very disappointed in me if he had been privy to my lie.

Still Quentin did not motion that he might leave.

'We'll be coming back quite late. It'll probably be dark by then,' I heavied.

Deepa pranced past again.

'Bye, Quentin!' she called affectedly.

'Bye, Deepa!'

'*That's* what I have to put up with,' I said.

'So are you all going, then?'

'Nope, just Mum and me.'

'But you always say you hate shopping.'

I pressed my face to the screen again; I could feel the wire imprint little squares upon my cheek. I saw Quentin on the other side, just a small, puny figure as docile and assailable as my father. There seemed in that instant to be no fundamental difference between us on any account.

'I do,' I said, 'this is just for Mum's sake, *understand*?'

He nodded gravely and then drew away from the door, his hands deep in his pockets, his head bowed.

Then he turned back.

'Hey, do you think Deepa might want to come with me?' he asked with renewed exuberance.

I was horrified. *This was the greater betrayal!*

'Deepa!' I screamed. 'Deepa!' And then I began to

discern certain discrepancies; me in my skirt, my delicate brown legs with the first light field of black hair; Quentin with his scrawny legs, his knees a mosaic of scabs.

I slapped a mosquito somewhere on my lower thigh and enjoyed the masochistic thrill of it.

'I've got to go in now, I'm being bitten,' I said and walked haughtily inside.

As if an affirmation of my mother's high spirits, the entire length and breadth of Target was draped in decorations for the festive season. SPOIL YOURSELF, one sign entreated. CHRISTMAS COMES BUT ONCE A YEAR! The shoppers themselves revealed another reality; the surfeit of joy, the bedlam of the season, was all too apparent in the faces of drudgery, the quick slaps practised on young children who did not cease whining for presents beyond their parents' means. Their faces seemed to cry out, *We're not deceived! We know there's no structure to this, no beginning, middle, and end, but an endless, implacable, piteous year!*

I looked into the eyes of some of the persecuted mothers sick of substantiating the Santa Claus myth. *Her* words had a sudden piquancy: 'Life is pain; menses, child birth, you're growing up.' Had it been a portent? Was there no way back? Were there no choices at all in this? *Was there not a page I might turn to find out my fate before actually entering into it?*

I was standing by Mum in the lingerie department. She was muttering about elastic quality and durability, announcing, for the amusement of the sales assistants and the women around us, 'You know all this lace is just an accessory. What you need is just a bra, plain and simple, none of this contour accentuation rubbish, Lycra, or the like. Just a plain and simple brassiere . . .'

Her voice trailed and I found myself gravitating toward the toy section. I walked past a girl of my age accompanied by her mother.

I overheard the girl say, 'Mum, I'm telling you I don't need it. I've got enough underwear to last me each day for a year.'

I examined the article in question: a peach-coloured satin bra with false pearls grouped in a flower in the centre.

'I know you do, but I want to get you a present, don't you understand? I'm your mother, after all. If your father buys you whatever he fancies, I don't know why I can't either.'

I thought from her countenance that the mother might burst into tears, but the daughter yielded smoothly and hugged her with not a remonstrative word more.

I remembered *her* words to me: 'I want you know that whatever happens I'm your mother.'

I thought again of the vaginal cross-section she had brought to my attention, but the words of the anatomy I beheld at that moment were written in an even more inscrutable script, an indecipherable cuneiform: *divorce, lives with father, mother is very sad.*

('Dolores! She said your name, Mama, didn't she?' Shanti had screamed.)

I suddenly saw the bold, definitive lettering of my destiny at the bottom of the page; this was no palimpsest: THE END, it read with crude finality. I was lost and alone, like Ariadne, ready to meet my Minotaur in the labyrinthine sections of Target. It was too late now to choose another fate, make my way back, endure and savour the innocence of my dear youth with all its minuscule trials and tribulations. Instead, the monsters of adulthood seemed to lurk in each new aisle; I got lost amongst the maternity wear: oversized padded bras and dresses as wide as bed linen. When finally I recovered my bearings, I wandered off, bored and terrified, to see if I could steal Strawberry Creams from the confectionery section, leaving Mum twittering to herself and testing cotton fibre between her fingers.

A child, balancing an icy cola in one hand, was struggling with a dispenser of Milk Bottles. I helped him. He smiled gratefully and skipped off toward his parents. I then shovelled as many Strawberry Creams as I could into my hands without anyone's noticing and stuffed them into my mouth. I was thirsty and thought that I might like an icy also. After all, it wasn't so far from Target to the milk bar that sold those drinks; she would barely notice my disappearance.

I escaped from Target, relieved of the bright lights, and skipped happily toward the icy shop. I chose a raspberry one and watched as the soft ice swirled into the elongated cup. I considered buying one for Quentin as a kind of peace offering, but it would have melted by the time we got back, and besides, I thought, I would probably spill it in the car, thereby destroying Mum's deep belief in my newfound maturity. I paid the woman – a blond woman with extremely large breasts whose smile haunted me – and walked back slowly, relishing the fizzy snow gradually rising through the straw and arriving on my tongue.

When I got back to Target I waited outside. There was a cool evening breeze.

'Mummy, I'm hungry.' 'Mummy, I'm tired.' I heard the soft symphony of infant grievances, so visceral and primitive. It was music to my ears.

I began counting the stars. The moon was a half-crescent; the whole sky a brilliant anthology.

I was peacefully identifying the Southern Cross, when Mum – Janus, not Minotaur – emerged.

'What, you just decided to leave, or what?'

'I was thirsty.'

'I have been hunting all of Target trying to find you!'

She grabbed me by the hand and dragged me inside, mumbling, 'Always a performance, always a great drama.'

A voice-over was calling: '*Mina Pereira, Mina Pereira, could you please come to Information where your mother is waiting for you!*'

Mum proceeded to the information desk, towing me behind.

'I'm sorry, I've found her,' she told the sales representative. 'Wait here,' she ordered me. 'Always a performance, always a great drama,' she kept on articulating.

She soon returned with the same bra she had been inspecting upon our arrival: a bone-coloured nylon affair, unadorned.

In silence, we proceeded to the checkout.

'Will that be cash or credit?'

'Cash,' my mother said, the last word she spoke that evening.

The bra remained abandoned in its bag on the dining table the whole next week. Dad finally told me to take it to my room one evening after dinner while he was disconnecting the lights on the Christmas tree.

I was eating a mango, had finished with the cheeks, but the bata kept slipping like soap from my small hands.

'I don't want it!' I suddenly said, a golden sap running down my wrists, pulp covering my mouth.

Mum was ignoring me; she was sitting peevishly enthroned in the armchair by the fake arbour, pecking at the synthetic holly berries which adorned the branches.

At that moment we heard a small explosion.

'Ouch!' she shrieked and jumped away.

I looked over and Deepa looked up from the Aragon book she was reading.

'Mummy took all the trouble to go and get that for you,' Dad said sheepishly, rushing about and trying, with his bare hands, to put out the ignited ends of the synthetic branches where the fuse of a few lights had just blown.

'I don't want it, I never wanted it!' I shouted. 'If you want it, you keep it, otherwise take it back!' I told him.

I hadn't noticed, but tears were also running down my face. I was taking in large gulps of air and almost gallons of snot began to pour forth with my sobs.

Dad began to ask Mum whether Target had a policy of returns on lingerie. Mum didn't answer. I could see the gratuitous glee had dissipated from her aspect, that disturbingly false mirth; and in my heart I was glad, mildly triumphant, that she had returned to her schizoid old self.

I got up from the table to blow my nose.

'Oh, don't worry about her,' I heard Deepa express as I exited. 'She's in denial. It's quite common.'

As I blew my nose in the bathroom that evening, a strange thing happened. Whole streams, estuaries, oceans of snot seemed to flow through my nose, and then – to my great astonishment – two small brown balls, the peas, preserved in the state they were upon entry, dislodged themselves and promptly fell out. *Denial*; I mulled over the charge while washing my face, staring at the top half of my visage, the only half I could see in the mirror that was still too high for me. *Denial?* What was Deepa talking about?

I mean, certain things had changed, that was for sure. Small, soft fields of black hair had sprouted in that cavity beneath my arm, a place I had held sacred all the days of my girlhood, happy with its bald shallow. When I was cold, I knew I could place my hands there in the middle of the night and loosen my stiff fingers with the warmth that emanated from its secret hollow. This was a comfort on which I could no longer depend. Now I felt my arms being ambushed by something, and I know it wasn't the hair itself but the sense that there was no discrete beginning, middle, and end to these developments. And this small change had given way, it's true, to certain other trauma-tising manifestations. My chest had taken on the shape of a wide cleft and was, I noted with some alarm, deepening. As had once happened only with my feelers, the landscape of my entire body now threatened to erupt with these subtle mutations, and I vowed then and there – a New Year's resolution – to never affirm them in the mirror.

Even a mother has her revenge. When you are twelve years old, you are not, whatever they might tell you, an auton-omous human subject. Plans are invariably provisional, resolves easily broken. The summer diminished, the days became shorter, the evenings darker sooner. For my own personal reasons I advised Quentin that I would be seeing less of him.

The river was still replete with abandoned balls. Once

or twice I made my own way there on my bicycle but did not feel like entering the dirty water and so just stood lonesomely contemplating the minnows and the tadpoles making their aimless way among the water lilies. The notion that those small creatures could be the antecedents of real frogs seemed an accomplishment, a feat almost as great as that of the engorged penis.

'We don't have to go,' I had said, handing her the letter one evening as she was making salmon cutlets, hoping she would dismiss its contents as quickly as she signed my absentee notes and excursions slips, permissive only by neglect.

The Christmas break was over. I was now in senior-primary, but in fact I felt as tiny and disoriented as those little tadpoles. My new uniform hung long on me like a shroud. The boys had left us; there was suddenly no place for them. They now made their way to a school at the end of a steep hill more than ten minutes away; the 'brother school' they called it, as if they intended us to remain part of the same species, much less united in fraternity.

'We're going!' she had said as she'd snatched up the epistolary encumbrance with one hand and with the other rapidly driven a knife through a clump of coriander.

I was a senior but I was still blighted by the same problems multiplying and dividing decimals, came up against the same barriers equalising fractions, finding the hypotenuse of triangles. I was a senior but I felt burdened, weakened, by the knowledge of my ascendancy and began to walk around the school, my face scrunched, my eyelids firmly shut, as if waiting for a great blow. Here, too, we were inundated with appellations that baffled me, some of us endowed with the harrowing honour of Prefects and Captains.

The only encouraging development, so far as I could see, was that the curriculum had been expanded and we were now offered ancient history.

In the first week of class we were taught about a queen who usurped the young Tutankhamen's regency, Hatshepsut. Queen Hatshepsut, we were told, felt aggrieved by the patriarchy of the time, which had robbed her of her right to the throne. The process of her demagoguery was arduous; Middle Kingdom Egypt was a paragon of custom. In order to legitimise her right to rule, she claimed divine parentage, enthroned herself over the child Tutankhamen and spent her reign in drag. On all the public works she commissioned she depicted herself in male garb; on statuary as on sphinxes, obelisks, and the paintings of even her mortuary temples, she represented herself as a man. I was awestruck, admired her tenacity; she became, in these precious moments of my senior year, a model to me in my own efforts at androgyny. I replaced my collection of *The Thousand Story Book* with a mammoth text I'd discovered in the school library: *Ancient Egyptian Civilisation*.

But then that missive had come, a clear omen, and thwarted my plans.

We had been advised to read the letters ourselves and then pass them on to our parents. We were big girls now, seniors; they trusted us. *Why would we want to keep secrets from our beloved parents?*

I had read mine walking back from school, my feelers frantically spinning. I had thought it was all over, thought I'd already endured my denouement, but I had been wrong; again, I would have to offer myself and again be obliterated.

Dear Parent,

This time in your daughter's personal development is tender. The school, in this complex age, must be an instrument in the service of a holistic life wisdom. We must strive to offer the most satisfying life paths to your child's future, whatever her particular talents and capacities. The task, you will agree, is a daunting one.

In previous years we have been fortunate to have access to the services of the Life Knowledge program. You may already be aware of this program. Briefly, the Life Knowledge fund was established twelve years ago under the auspices of the child psychologist Dr. Freida Roman and her gynaecologist-writer husband, Dr. Charles Roman, to deepen the general awareness of school students in their personal development, issues of sexual and psychological health most importantly. Since its inception, the fund has grown and expanded to other states and most recently received a $1.5 million grant from the federal government to continue its noble work.

It is our pleasure to have Drs. Charles and Freida Roman once again host a special symposium we have arranged for the girls of seventh form on Thursday, March 19, at 6.30 P.M. Other schools from the Rain Hill vicinity have been invited, among them the boys of seventh form at St Mark's. Parents are welcome and, indeed, encouraged to come. There is no cost for attending. However, as seating may be limited, we would appreciate if you could RSVP to the school

secretary, Mrs. George, by February 27. Light re-
freshments will be served.

We look forward to your company at this highly
engaging event.

Yours faithfully,
Sister Anne Kelly, RSM, Principal

There should have been nothing surprising about my fate:
I had had it confirmed in *Ancient Egyptian Civilisation*.
The history teacher, Mr. Hughes, had conveniently failed
to mention the end of the Queen Hatshepsut saga: the
savage demolition of her temples; the desecration of all
artworks; the thorough effacement of her name from
every pillar, annal, and document of the dynasty. Even
the peasants turned against her, partook of the sacrilege, I
had learnt in those pages. In short, Hatshepsut's annihila-
tion. If the Egyptians had exacted the revenge they'd
wanted, the book had said, we would not even know
of Hatshepsut's existence.

I was remembering the way my mother had demolished
the coriander with the knife; I was remembering the way
her hands rotated expertly, almost in a dance, around the
small, soft balls of salmon; the way she had crushed green
chili, onions, and paprika into the pink flesh; and finally, I
was remembering the way she'd sadistically stood, sighing, oblivious to her carnage, flattening those fishy spheres
into disks with her fist.

She had reminded me of Salome as she had carried the
platter to the oven and, I guess I had been waiting, when
she had said, 'We're going!' for her to have set down a
blood libation.

I was remembering all this several weeks later when we were in silence driving to the school.

I don't know how it had happened, but Quentin was sitting in the backseat next to me. I imagined her having furtively approached Mrs. Soyer one weekend, going next door – 'just to say hello' – and mentioning that this would be a wonderful opportunity for Quentin.

I could imagine poor Mrs. Soyer, dishevelled and lonely since her husband had left, complying with Mum; I could imagine her placing her confidence in Mum's Spockian conjecture that the symposium was sure to be useful, that these Drs. Roman seemed a most enlightened and progressive pair. I could imagine Mrs. Soyer looking very distant, thinking of Quentin, her only son, the grand pressure she felt, alone, in raising him. She was nursing that night: *Would Mum mind very much taking Quentin?* And I could imagine Mum's greedy exhilaration in then saying, yes, that, of course, it would be no trouble.

Whichever way it may have gone, there was an obtuse fact: the boy to whom I had not spoken at great length or played with in a while; the boy whom I had, in twelve-year-old style, subtly excommunicated from my life, was staring blankly out the back of the car window, staring through the vast, suburban trees; jacaranda, casuarina, eucalyptus.

'Did you have some dinner?' Mum asked him as she parked the car.

'Oh, yes,' Quentin said, unbuckling his belt, hopping out.

'Mama, why didn't you park the car in the school car park? This is so far away.'

There was a legitimate reason for my complaint: I knew I might want to make a quick exit.

She was ignoring me; I had exacerbated her displeasure by delaying, taking a lengthy shower, wanting to crimp my hair.

'Always a performance, always a great drama!' she had burbled as I had run into the car.

She was wearing a blue blouse on whose fabric a series of enormous foul daisies were flowering and, as we now walked toward the school hall, me straggling behind her and Quentin, I began to understand the logic of her own manoeuvre: the parking lot was chock-a-block; even the street we had parked on was crowded with vehicles.

Inside the hall there were what seemed at least a thousand faces, some familiar, some strangers, and all of them terrifying. I thought again of the blond woman with very large breasts, her mouth a slit, her head aslant, and her face a rictus of pain. All these faces seemed to turn to me now with the same expression.

We were late. The speaker, I guessed it was Dr. Charles Roman, was gesticulating and smiling as he lectured; people laughed now and again and agreeably shifted their knees to let us pass as we found three vacant seats.

I did not look sideways at Quentin beside me or search for the familiar faces of my peers. There was laughter, yes, but as I settled in my chair, it slowly registered with me that not one child was humoured. Boys beside me, some of them my former classmates, their legs barely reaching the ground, were anxiously kicking the toes of their shoes across the parquet.

I was touching my hair, crimped only on one side, when

at a distance I now suddenly made out the figure of Amen Anthony on the other side of the hall. *Yes!* I thought, *It was Amen Anthony*, restored to privilege, flanked by the pillars of his parents – his mother whose hair was set in a tight perm, a contented Jezebel in a red pant suit, and, his stoical proud father. It was a site of private dignity. ('You're *very* sexy. You're *very* sexy,' I had murmured to myself).

And I now recalled the packet of condoms – its use-by date expired – that I had discovered in Mum's dresser drawer while she had been at the 'beautiful house' in the 'bush'. *Had she also put those away for later?* I now silently speculated.

An intermission finally came and I was glad for it, because not only had I not been entertained, but I was heavily perspiring.

'Want to get a cordial?' Quentin asked me.

'Oh, no, you go. I've got to go to the bathroom.'

Mum was talking to Deepa's form mistress, accepting a showering of congratulations, I presumed.

I dashed toward the bathroom before having to endure that humiliation, smiling pathetically at some of the girls in my year who were milling around their parents and lifting their hands into small salutes as they saw me go past.

I locked the door of the cubicle, pulled the toilet seat down, sat, and tried to catch my breath. *She's mad*, I suddenly thought. *She's mad*. And as I wondered how long I could plausibly stay in the cubicle until the symposium resumed, my eye caught something on the back of the door. Scrawled in blue, red, and black ink – in places scratched into the timber of the door itself – were conversations, whole discourses. I began reading them and stopped when I came to one in particular:

Helen Newman sucks Alan Turnball's cock and loves to swallow the cum.

I turned and flushed the toilet, opened the door, and fled toward the taps, where I drenched my face with cold water. I left the bathroom and turned into the hall. People were settling into their seats again. I saw my mother and Quentin and squeezed toward them. Quentin handed me a tumbler of green cordial.

'Thanks,' I said.

Still my mother did not utter a word to me.

Soon Drs. Roman had returned together to their places at the lectern.

'And now we would like to answer commonly asked questions from the children themselves,' Dr. Freida suddenly said.

I looked again from the corner of my eye and caught sight of Amen Anthony, his head now solemnly bowed.

Drs. Roman asked and answered in partnership. First there was a question about wet dreams:

Q.: At what age might I start to expect a wet dream?
A.: Well, it varies, depending on the person. Some boys have their wet dreams very early, about eleven years old, others don't have them at all.

Q.: Should I be embarrassed about my wet dream?
A.: Oh, no, the wet dream is a perfectly normal and healthy response of the body to a boy's development.

It means that the hormones are functioning properly, producing sperm for later adult life when it will be possible to impregnate a woman.

Q.: Is there something wrong with me if I don't get my periods with all my friends?
A.: Girls have their own menstrual cycles and there is no 'good' or 'bad' time as such to start bleeding. You will bleed when your own body is ready. In fact, you should not feel left out if your friends start before you, because they have to put up with this monthly for the rest of their lives. There's a reason why the period was once called 'the curse.' Of course it's not a curse; it's a miracle, for it means a woman can have a baby.

On and on in this fashion they went, answering their own contradictory and tautological questions like a couple of fools, the adults in the audience nodding their heads in quiet approbation.

At one point, Dr. Freida said, 'Now I'm going to ask whether someone might be brave enough to answer this question.'

Q.: Can a girl get pregnant when she is having her period?

Silence swelled around us. The heat of the hall was enough to make me asphyxiate. I felt like slipping the straps of my sandals off my ankles, undressing, and sitting naked save my singlet and panties, as I would in the summer when Dad would carry the huge blue Panasonic fan to the dining table for us to cool off.

No child made a sound; there was only the wooden echo of the boys' feet as they swung their legs and lightly tapped the parquet with the soles of their shoes.

Q.: Is no one brave enough to answer?

Parents, teachers and even Dr. Charles chuckled to themselves. Slowly a hand rose, the large, doughty arm of Anita Cooper, a prefect, and a voice that seemed to ring across the hall.

A.: No.
Q.: And what's your name, darling?
A.: Anita.
Q.: Well, Anita, can you tell us why you think that?

Pause.

A.: Is it, cause there's no egg?
Q.: Does anyone else want to have a go? Mums and Dads, want to help Anita out?

Laughter.
Mrs. Hammond, the form mistress, boldly raised her arm.

A.: I would say it's true that the egg does fall away, but that it's impossible to tell whether or not a woman can get pregnant.
Q.: Well, yes, Mrs. Hammond has the right answer. Women have been known to fall pregnant even whilst menstruating. That is a very important piece of in-

formation. Next question. Who's brave enough to tell
me what I mean when I say the word *masturbation*?

Silence swelled and this time threatened to engulf us all.
People were more undaunted now, at least the parents; my
mother, among them, had her hand raised.

Quentin nudged me and I nudged him back.

Q.: Yes, the lady in the blue floral shirt, please?

Oh, mother! Oh, mother! I wanted to cry out.

A.:Oh, my daughter can tell you that.

I opened my eyes; this time my cheek was burning and I
felt the sting of the slap throb over my face. The boys and
girls beside me were now looking at me wide-eyed, ex-
pectant, some of them on the verge of smiles.

My feelers grew wild.

Q.: And what's your name, sweetheart?

I closed my eyes; again I felt another huge blow throw life
out of me, my body being pummelled.

A.:Mina.
Q.: And, Mina, sweetheart, can you tell me what I
mean when I say the word *masturbation*.

I then remembered the minnows and tadpoles running in
the river with no apparent purpose; the aluminium cans,
plastic wrappers, drenched cigarette butts, all irrelevant to

those creatures. Their pleasure was autonomous and distinctive.

A.: Oh, it's touching yourself, I think.

Peels of laughter now burst forth from my previously repressed colleagues. I smiled shyly and then slowly lowered my head. Quentin nudged my ribs again, all thirteen of them, and I nudged his twelve back, harder, punitively.

Q.: Yes, that's correct. For a boy this sometimes produces a nice sensation and for a girl also, something like a sneeze. Although, a white fluid – semen – might come out of the boy's penis. The nice sensation is called an orgasm. Now you must understand that masturbation is also a natural and healthy activity, you should not be ashamed for it . . .

I don't know how I made it out of that crumbling school hall alive.

Again Quentin nudged me, I nudged him back, harder this time. I sat in the backseat next to him and, now and again, caught Mum's pert eagle like reflection in the rearview mirror. The air was cool, colder; I could see the first golden leaves of April scattered about the trees under the huge street lamps. I think I knew she was mad, then. Not just thought it, but really – *as only a twelve-year-old girl can about her mother* – knew that she was truly mad.

I rolled my window down and drank in the fresh air. I would have liked to open my door, to have stumbled out onto the rough bitumen. Instead, I masterminded another plan. I would assess my sneezes over the next few months, record them, investigate this stupid sensation – which I personally had only known to be annoyance – and then maybe if that brought me to ruin, I, too, would seek retribution.

'Want to play bulrush?' Quentin said as I moved toward the house now, stoical as Mr. Anthony.

'Let's get one thing straight,' I said, not knowing where my sudden verve had its origins.

I was savvy then, savage. Play was over. I had to make arrangements for my forthcoming reality. I was not a child anymore; I could not stand aimlessly between trees, running indiscriminately from a fabricated enemy. I had to be firm; it was not my prerogative but someone else's.

Deepa's example was appealing; I reached for it.

'Bye, Quentin!' I called indifferently, walking slowly into the house.

'*Bye, Mina*!' he sang after me, sad and elegiac.

WD40

A nd then it all flared up and fell away. I should have
known it was to end that way; I should have known
the beginning of the end was nigh when Dad, coated in
sawdust and grease, suddenly surfaced from beneath the
house one evening bearing a can of WD40 in his hand.

'Whenever things get a bit sluggish,' he had energeti-
cally announced, 'just apply some of this and you'll be
amazed how much life it supplies!'

The way he spoke of this lubricant I imagined him doing
television commercials for it. It unnerved me; he was an
optimist, yes, but his was a happiness indexed to what
seemed aeons of defeat; he was an enthusiast who held his
head in his hands a great deal. Not just downcast; Dad
could be found, literally, *down*.

Yet WD40 seemed to have given him a new lease on life.
As if the waters of a baptismal font flowed from the nozzle
of that can, he hereafter spent whole days roaming above
ground like a missionary, ardently preying on all manner
of household appliances with WD40.

'Whenever things get a bit sluggish,' he could soon be
heard uttering any time of the day, as if it were a song

stuck in his head, 'just apply some of this and you'll be amazed how much life it supplies.'

I didn't buy it. It sounded to me like the other essentially hopeless tune of his repertoire:

Smile, though your heart is breaking
Smile . . .

I knew he was no holy man, that he was just a sad, deranged repairs man, rescuing hinges in the most obscure places; lost laundry screws, bolts, and nuts (one morning about this time he even recommended that I rejuvenate my performance by trying WD40 instead of resin on the bow of my violin). Washers that we didn't know even existed became so viscose in his hand we could hear them clinking to the floor in the middle of our dreams. I pitied him because I knew that he was applying himself to the more feasible of tasks, taking control of the accessories, maintaining the insubstantial gadgets of the world, the few circuits that remained within his dwindling power.

I didn't buy it; I was beyond believing in a revolution, I was past praying for a renaissance of any kind. What's more, I'd *seen* his sunken face earlier in the day of the great WD40 discovery, earlier, as she'd escaped through the door again, red ripped raincoat gripped in her hand, her exit was so swift.

She was frying vegetable pakoras, and then, her descent as fast as her departure, had dropped everything and headed for the door.

'Maybe,' she screeched, her voice reverberating through the derelict house for hours after the door had slammed, 'you should have just gone and hired a womb!'

At that moment I was crouched in the bathtub, writing up my physics report on motion, felling figures, annihilating the method as I went, hoping to have time to slaughter the few problems we'd been set for tomorrow's class. The conclusion was the same each time and brought me a certain satisfaction:

Object accelerated when velocity was increased.

As she left, I climbed out and followed her to the door, a position that I'd come to occupy like a sentry. The evening hung in twilight shadow. She was fast, seamless as a swallow. As she swooped passed the porch and crossed the front garden, I saw agile Shanti flipping her supple body over and back in midair somersaults on the lawn. As if all those years of passive televisual spectatorship had, without our even knowing it, trained her for the feats of flexibility that one would ordinarily impute to characters from Looney Tunes cartoons, it didn't disturb me to look out from the bay window and frequently find Shanti these days doing callisthenics on the lawn, lithe and fluid in her breakfast-smeared pyjamas.

Truth be told, the transformation had been induced because the television, her longtime soporific, was not working; the birds, we suspected, had in their belligerence damaged the aerial antennae so that the picture on the screen, a series of crooked lines, bespoke cardiovascular chaos. The scarecrow was now a doubled-over centrepiece in the yard; a fallen, emaciated soldier stranded in enemy territory. Not only had Dad's former contra-avian plan failed, it had backfired, for discovering in the scarecrow's billowing nightdress a familiar and affectionate remembrance of the woman who would each morning scatter fresh seed on the lawn for them, the birds had gathered with even greater glee, nestling in the crippled figure's facial features; its armpit; around its single crutch like foot.

They were not only a menace but had in time become a serious health hazard, pecking at Shanti's limbs and descending on my antennae as we ran with our bags over our heads for the school bus.

On heeding her squeals one morning this autumn, I had run into our bedroom and found Shanti sitting on her bed weeping and vigorously scratching her scalp. She had silently lifted her T-shirt to reveal enormous inflammations and welts that had spread across, totally ravaging, her skin. Upon inspection, I also found lice to have thoroughly buried themselves in her scalp.

I tried to immediately communicate this news by Morse to Dad, but he had not responded; when finally I had knocked on the door of the manhole, he had, blind and sleepy as a bear in hibernation, told me to pour – of all things – turpentine on Shanti's head.

The lines of communication thus down, it was extremely difficult to make any kind of plan. Such simple needs took days to be adequately satisfied; applications had to be made months before the most basic desideratum would now be provided for. When you are knee-deep in degeneracy, your appeals must be lodged way ahead of time.

In the kitchen roaches scurried from unwashed dish pans and maggots crawled out of griddles encrusted with rancid ghee. Mould bloomed across the walls and cobwebs cascaded from the ceilings. We all suffered various acute forms of sinusitis. These conditions, given that

Florence Nightingale was otherwise engaged, were not only left untreated but steadily worsened.

In fact, the rot had accumulated to such a degree that simple tasks were perils. We could barely move in the rooms of the house without tripping over, falling onto, or bashing into things. Leverage was offered by, for example, the two cubic meters of the bathtub, where Deepa and I – when she was not frisking around with male miscreants from school and the neighbourhood – would vie for space to do our homework. The dining table was overflowing with unpaid bills, unanswered letters, and a mammoth pile of Mum's unopened journals. Secondhand garments – from where they arrived we did not know – burst from various wardrobes.

When one day I rode my bicycle past the curious spectacle of a desperate destitute diving into the nearby Anglican Charity bin, my heart had skipped a beat as I'd discerned that the pair of shoes on this stranger's airborne feet bore a striking affinity to Mum's own tattered bed slippers.

Shanti was now blithely oblivious to Mum's passage across the grass and, watching her, I wondered whether she had been preparing herself for psychological suppleness all those years ago when she'd swing herself round the Clearwater Park monkey bars as smoothly as she'd turned somersaults in Mum's womb. All this while I had trouble letting my feet off the ground on the swing sets.

Ulti Bacha: this was the Hindi conjunction for 'Vomit Child', which Deepa had picked up one year in India and from time to time injuriously inflicted upon me. Ulti

Bacha: this because the journey from Sydney to Canberra in the car had an emetic effect on me, which, en route to India, was magnified ten-fold. They'd tried everything: antinausea pills, 'sea bands'; Dr. Levy had at the time said it might have something to do with the feelers retaining a large amount of fluid from the aural passage. It never had occurred to them to treat my motion sickness as a kind of emotional cathexis.

Indeed, since those days of our youth, the farthest I'd seemed to come manoeuvring myself around despair had been with that fluorescent hula hoop and, even then, all I'd really been doing was, quite literally, going round in circles. That circumference of my childhood sadness hung abandoned on a nail in the garage, no longer luminescent. Even its wide diameter could not embody the immense mounds of joylessness that had amassed themselves at my thirteen-year-old feet.

I neither yielded nor could yield to any law other than that of my own body. I was rigorous in a way they had thought me previously inept. I'd become so punctilious I even *aspired* to rigidity. I took pride in, enjoyed, for instance, the stiff feel of my boardlike back against the high wooden laboratory chairs as Mrs. Riley, the physics teacher, stood talking to us of the principles of velocity and acceleration.

'Distance over time equals velocity,' she wrote on the blackboard both in principle and algebraic notation.

For me, though, who still laboured over the most rudimentary mathematical paradigms, no time seemed to separate the trauma of my contemporary situation, make the tragedy of it any more remote, though I dearly longed for vast space, epochs and eras of time. These days in class I would sit inert, taking copious notes on Motion, hoping with all my heart that the formidable formulae might carry me away or at least strengthen me, hold me together, in the event of sudden turbulence. I'd come to feel I was leading my life on a long, long aeroplane journey; but I was strapped to my seat, and there was neither take-off nor landing, no final destination to speak of.

As she fell through the air, I noticed Shanti's hair was still oil-slick with turps and her body glistening with the ointment I'd found in the first-aid cabinet, beside the old tube of mercurochrome, to soothe her itchy wounds. *Pliable as pastry, based in grease*, Deepa and I had once teased her as she'd been oiled to filo-perfection by Mum. And, yet, it wasn't so hard, seeing them now, child and estranged mother (*though the one body had been borne of the other; though the one had leaked from the other's very loins*) to imagine that floating, leased womb Mum had mentioned. Maybe, I thought, this was the way it was: the placenta a sweet, nutritious weed that the child fed from; the uterus a lagoon she never thought she'd lose. You cannot mortgage life, though: It evicts you. No wonder a child cries upon entering the world.

It was her comment about the womb that had done it.

Soon after, I had seen Dad creeping out of the hovel towards the garage.

'Are you all right, Daddy?' I had said, lifting the roller door to find him, his body buried inside the veneer cupboard in which he kept his most useful tools, a rough coffin into which, I thought, seeing him smothering his brave, tear-stricken face with his hanky, he might have comfortably settled, closed the door (only the key of that door never *did* fit the latch).

'Fine, sweetheart.'

'Sure?'

'I'm fine. If only I could just find it . . .'

'Find what?'

'Find the . . .'

'What?' I said, 'What, Daddy?'

Triumphant, he now retrieved the can of WD40. 'Found it!'

Did I have the gumption to tell him then that velocity equalled distance over time, that you would need the object to succumb if you wanted to make motion, that dementia is one step beyond languor, that with a pathology like hers he ought to be maintaining not the washers, screws, and bolts of the house but the mechanics of his own heart?

No, I stared instead at that dulled yellow loop of my youth on the wall behind his workbench.

'You better do something about dinner, Mina,' he told me. I returned to the house, went to the freezer, and took out a pack of frozen pies.

Deepa and her current interest, a boy called Walter Lockwood who lived two streets away, had come home and were lying, enveloping each other, on the brown cord sofa in the sunroom. Walter reminded me of Shaggy from Scooby-Doo with his long red bangs falling over his dopey eyes, his complete impotence in the face of – indeed, blind surrender to – Deepa's domineering tactics. As I stood in the kitchen, I couldn't see them, but I could *hear* their frolicking and cavorting. I attempted to ignore it, but of course, knowing I was there they wanted to give a great concupiscent performance. At one moment I looked over and had a hard time admitting the fact to myself: They were kissing. *Kissing!* My feelers rose anxiously.

'Oh, Walter!' Deepa squealed salaciously now and again.

Oh, and I remembered now how I, too, had almost been kissed! I had wanted to take my bicycle into the hills in Goa and Dad had insisted that either Shanti or Deepa accompany me. I had been quarrelling with Deepa, and Shanti had said she had no desire to go anywhere. I had moped about all morning until the servant boy, Tomas, fiddling with the figurines in the crib, had turned to me and asked why I had such a long face. I had put it to him plainly – nobody loved me – and I must have done a good job persuading him because he had simply left unfinished the carving of Balthazars and led me by the hand towards the hills. Buffaloes, we saw, farm children, women working in the valley rice fields, but not once did I see the movement of a serpent. My head bowed, searching for something sleek between the leaves and rocks, I almost screamed when Tomas brushed my hair back and drew his cheek close to mine.

'What are you afraid of?' he'd said, smiling cheerfully as my little heart fluttered.

Now, though, thinking of Walter's dim-wittedness, I could only hope that Deepa had not made any elaborate mental plans for marrying the boy. I would not put it past her. Her mind, as I have elsewhere noted, was capable of *anything*. I pottered about the kitchen, preheating the oven, making noise enough that they might divine I was not impressed. From the corner of my eye I could see Deepa's hand delicately extended from the sofa. In it she held open a copy of Bataille's *Story of the Eye* and, running her hands through Walter's straggly hair during intervals of passion, she turned her head and read aloud to him

> '*To others, the universe seems decent because decent people have gelded eyes. That is why they fear lewdness.*'

'Oh, Deepa,' I heard him drone, when once she got quite absorbed in the passage about eggs and urine. 'Why've you always got to have a book between us! Can't you just relax for a second.'

At this I coughed, a loud disrupting whopper of a cough.

'Come on!' Deepa said, grabbing Walter's hand, running upstairs to her bedroom with him.

I thought, *This was the level of depravity to which we'd sunk!* My bookish genius of a sister bedding the boy next door. Well, not next door exactly. God forbid, the boy next door!

I emptied the pies out of their foil trays and put them in the oven to bake. The rusty old hinge on the oven door creaked as I let it down and I wondered whether I should inform Dad of it now that he had the WD40 near at hand. No, it could wait.

I returned instead to the bathtub and the problems Mrs. Riley had set for homework. I'd become a master of the laws of motion, was able to cruise through each question using the same old principles with ease. *Distance over time taken equals velocity. Distance over time equals velocity. Velocity divided by time equals acceleration.* The laws of motion brought me comfort. It was the same solipsistic succour I'd derived swinging that circlet round my waist when I was nine years old and found myself all alone in a fast depleting universe. An onanic kind of eroticism, I was now relieved by the fore-drawn dimensions of the scenarios, the simple, hermetically sealed psychology of the various narrative conceits:

A boomerang is thrown vertically and takes 3.6s to return.
a) What was its initial velocity?
b) What was the maximum height reached?
c) How long did it take to reach its maximum height?

But then, just as I'd settled into them and the pace had picked up, I realised I was contending not with the laws of aerodynamism. The turbulence came and I found, as on those long sixteen-hour Air Indian Boeing 747 flights to Bombay via Singapore, the air-sickness bags tucked like a bib into my tracksuit top, that there was no foreseeable end to my agony. The text book dropped a bombshell:

Provide an original example of something moving with a constant velocity.

I panicked at this entreaty. *Something? Original?* Was I to randomly select from the multiple objects in my life that continuously moved, ran out on, abandoned me? Oh, no, I didn't want to dwell on those! I needed concrete, localised, placed objects; even a tree sloth riding up a tree would do, a girl running to a bus stop, a yo-yo on its return. But *something?* At a loss for ideas, annoyed that physics was demanding more than it had advertised, I left that particular question blank. *Mother*, it occurred to me to write in the void beside the question, but Mrs. Riley had even less imagination than I and would no doubt have been nonplussed by such an answer.

At this moment, Dad entered, changed out of his grubby overalls. He was garbed in a pair of khaki pants and a freshly starched Indian khadi pyjama shirt, groping for outmoded icons while the infrastructure of the modern nation threatened to collapse.

'Dinner ready yet?' he said with curious alacrity, spraying the tracks of the sliding door he'd just come through with WD40.

I got out of the tub, went into the kitchen, opened the oven door, and stabbed with a fork the centre of one of those vile Anglo-American culinary travesties.

Before I knew it, Dad, having heard it, was standing behind me, inspecting the rasping hinge. Like a zealot, he coated it thoroughly with WD40.

'Mina,' he proselytised, indicating the can, 'whenever things get a bit sluggish, just apply some of this and you'll be surprised just how much life it supplies.'

'*Dad*,' I wanted to say to him, '*when velocity and acceleration are in opposite directions, speed decreases.*' '*Dad*,' *I wanted to say to him, reminded of the words of my omniscient physics author,*

'Case studies of motion, in which it is definitely not ethical to ask for volunteers, can yield important insights.'

I shovelled the rubbish onto the floor and arranged five plates on the table, as Walter would no doubt be joining us. I then went to the door to call Shanti.

I was breathtaken more by the stamina of that child than by the contortions of which she was actually capable. She was still hurling herself through the air and, with the streetlights now on and the stars blinking above us, she reminded me of a genuine open-air circus acrobat.

'Dinner's ready, Nadia!' I called out. She had requested that I relinquish *Samosa*. Now it was Nadia Comaneci, first Olympic gymnast to have scored a perfect ten.

'I still haven't got it,' she rebuked herself, unsatisfied with her landings.

At least, I thought, *you, dear sister, have access to the ground.*

'I think I need more of a run-off.'

'*Yes*,' I wanted to tell her too, '*Velocity equals acceleration by time.*'

'Your pie'll get cold.'

'Oh, pies!' she groaned.

Again I had the impulse to say to my sister,

'*Case studies of motion, in which it is definitely not ethical to ask for volunteers, can yield important insights.*'

I then made my listless way up the stairs to Deepa's bedroom. I was about to knock when I was struck by what I thought were wrestling noises coming from the other side. One person breaking another and screams of pain? Or were they gasps of delight? Was it war or love being waged beyond that door? *Coupling or killing?* How strange to think that it was from friction that gratification might be derived, that a scream of agony might be indistinguishable from that of glory. Was coitus the only domestic pursuit in which the attempt to sublimate, make another person shout – draw blood even – did not result in casualties?

I now had a sudden vision of Walter's freckled, pimply face; his restless, nervous hands; the fire-coloured strings of his hair sloping down his long, dull face. His yearning nauseated me. I knocked hard and abusively on the door, smashed my fist against it.

'Dinner's ready!'

And Deepa: 'All right, all right, we're coming!'

I turned and, as I reached the landing, braced myself because I now believed I heard Deepa say to Walter *(though the lining of that room, the walls of the house, were supposed to protect me from all umbrage)*, 'Don't worry, she's just jealous!'

'Where's your Mum?' a stunned Walter asked at the dining table. With all the solemnity and habit of a tribal rite, we'd collectively raised the flaps of our pie pastry with forks and were waiting respective turns to flood the insides with chilli and Tabasco sauce.

Walter had liberally applied tomato to the surface of his own pie.

'She's gone out,' I answered sternly, carelessly smashing the bottle of chili sauce on the table and wiping the dribble at the rim with my fingers.

We ate in silence, hardly relishing the meal.

'What are all those suitcases for?' Walter said pointing to the luggage that could still be seen jutting out of the hallway.

Deepa, Shanti, and I looked up at once and in unison said, 'Business trip'.

'Oh,' Walter said, disconcerted.

I'd impaled my pie but could not take a single bite to my mouth.

'I was hoping you guys would be having curry or somethin',' Walter now said.

That was it, I thought, *I've had more than enough of this idiot!*

I got up from the table and carried my plate to the garbage bin and did away with the pie.

'Where are you going?' Dad asked.

'I just remembered I've got some physics problems to complete by tomorrow.'

'Gosh,' I heard Walter say on my exit, 'everyone's so serious in this house, so – '

' "Studious" ?' Deepa, aiding him, pragmatically offered.

'Yeah,' said Walter, scratching his head, baffled by such a big word, but sensing that if it had come from Deepa's mouth it surely had to be accurate.

And, as I rose up the stairs, steadying myself against the banister, he had the audacity to further comment, 'Mina's awfully skinny, isn't she.'

My nodes grew taut and the ground seemed to fall away from under me.

'Oh, no,' Deepa said, 'she's just small-boned. And, besides, she's been sickly since childhood.'

' "Sickly"?' (He suffered a major vocabulary deficiency.)

'Motion sickness,' Deepa, lover *and* thesaurus, qualified. 'Cars, planes, even bicycles, would you believe!' She giggled.

Motion sickness. 'Don't worry, Baba,' Dad would say, gripping me by the forehead as the plane shuddered into Changi or Sahar airport, 'You'll feel better once we've landed.' They'd take turns nursing me. 'If you don't think about it, it won't happen. It's just that simple,' *she'd* tell me. All the while the dark, sympathetic faces of fellow passengers, registering the tremendous diasporic burden I, regurgitating, carried on my young shoulder.

Motion sickness. Little did they know that I had out-grown that infantile propensity. I was no longer that feeble-bodied child whose form convulsed at the slightest bit of turbulence, whose nausea had once formed the centrepiece of Deepa's dinner-table jokes. No indeed. I'd readied myself for a rocky ride.

In my bedroom I quickly completed the remaining pro-blems, closed my physics exercise book, and lay down on my bed to meditate. I'd since moved on from survivor narratives to embrace Gandhian models of self-sacrifice. I considered my own famine to be a fast in the larger, loftier interests of peace and nonviolence. *The Story of my Experiments with Truth*, a text that my grandfather, hoping to help me overcome my grotesqueness, had once given me as a gift, now lay beside my bed. To my delight these were experiments whose hypotheses consistently and accurately matched their conclusions.

I fell in love with my own relinquishment. At school, for example, I felt a certainty, a certain self-governmentality, my twiglike legs aching as I stood in those science classes with Mrs. Riley, designing experiments to demonstrate the speed of a Matchbox car as it ran down a timber incline.

Having acquainted myself with satyagraha and ahimsa,

I made suffering an aesthetic of the highest order. *Renunciation without aversion is not lasting*, I'd remind myself, living on the tart acid of a Granny Smith apple for a whole school day. Dreaming of the Mahatma's strength of will, adamant, bound to the struggle for self-determination, I made my own salt marches downstairs to the kitchen, where, each night before going to sleep, I had taken to drinking a litre of brine so as to retain my precious fluids for an endless ramadanic vigil.

Renunciation without aversion is not lasting, I now repeated to myself and, lying alone in my bed, I placed my hand down my pants and sated myself the same way I'd once sated myself inside a hula hoop, hating her, loving myself with my own hand. I would abnegate everything but my own body; I would not be subject to any alien force, I thought, while that thin onanic sensation of pain or pleasure – or what I was not sure – shuddered and brought me to land, and now cascaded like disembarking passengers down my inner thigh. *Renunciation without aversion is not lasting: renunciation without aversion is not lasting*. I made a masturbatory mantra of this maxim.

Renunciation without aversion is not lasting, I was repeating, when I suddenly heard the keys of Heaven jangling in her hand as the front door – another sluggish hinge – ground open.

I heard a stranger's voice boom, 'Just as long as you know next time that you can be fined for this!'

I got up from the bed, drew the curtains apart and rattled open the stiff window.

A Rain Hill council truck was parked, the engine still running, out the front of the house and Ranger Samuels, the local parks overseer, was standing on the porch.

He now removed his felt hat, solemnly pressed it to his chest, before presenting the circumstantial evidence before Dad.

Squinting, I made out that, indeed, she had made quite a killing. From a distance, in Ranger Samuels's open hand, it seemed a whole stack – maybe seven or eight – nests collected during her short time away. I also saw that she was dishevelled, that her knees were wrecked, and that she was guiltily concealing something – *More eyries?* – beneath the opening of her raincoat.

Ranger Samuels shook his head.

'You can't just go stealing little birdies' nests like that. There are laws against such things,' he admonished her as if she might in her red raincoat have really been the distracted, insolent infant she so much seemed – except that instead of fidgeting obnoxiously Mum was staring into the inky sky, starting up her familiar swan song.

Dad was pledging that it would never again happen; he could not imagine what had come over her; things were not going too well for his wife these days, he told Ranger Samuels.

'Antifaunal obsessions. Ornithic fantasies. We have names for these illnesses now,' I heard Ranger Samuels say as Mum fluttered past them into the house.

'Ranger,' Dad said mechanically, demonstrating the WD40 on the hinge of the front door, but this time with much less ebullience, 'whenever things get a bit sluggish, just apply some of this and you'll be surprised how much life it supplies.'

'Yes, I'm sure, sir,' the ranger said before replacing and tipping his hat and starting quickly toward his truck.

I closed the window and returned to my bed. Again and

again I touched myself. *Oh, and it was nothing like sneezing!* Suspended in climax, my feelers throbbing, it was now that I envisioned the tragic vanity of my sacrifice; that the house had been, was going to be, partitioned regardless of the extent of my suffrage; that a nation had to be born even if that meant it was swaddled in blood, if the fruit of the mother had to be ripped right apart. Passivity is an effective tool for a public kind of protest. For those that are seeded and nestled in the womb, only for these whom we intimately loved, are we quite willing to have ourselves a massacre. Atrophication; self-mutilation. The self fells itself. We kill our own kind: What more could be concluded of the personage of the Great Soul's assassin? Millions lay torn across the battlefields.

It was not long after Ranger Samuels had made his house call, then, that I arrived home from school to find Dad reincarnated back in his overalls.

He was leaving by the back door – still sluggishly grinding in its tracks – when I caught him, sad and vanquished, clutching the WD40 to his chest like an urn that contained the ashen remains of his beloved.

He did not stop to remark on his defeat but simply headed for the garage, passing the lopsided scarecrow in the yard, the mop head frayed, the nightie tattered and weather-beaten with holes.

Mum was nearby, chirring affections and endearments to her alliary allies.

'Too bad Inspector Gadget!' She cawed after him as he lifted the garage door.

Mournfully, he replaced the WD40 on its shelf.

His head was cowered and when he glanced up, only

once on his way back toward the house, his face was a sacred river, a silent stream of tears.

'Just going to double-check I insulated those new fuse connections properly. You know, Mina, a live wire is a hazard whose potential people grossly underestimate,' he finally said, bereft as he saw me, gesturing toward the door of the manhole.

And down he slowly went.

I now moved melancholically into the living room.

Shanti was pacifically poised in a headstand. The television was on, still a medium of fuzz.

'What's wrong with them?' she now asked me, inverted, making me queasy just watching her.

'Wrong with what?'

'Your tentacles. They're drooping.'

I had thought only I had felt my feelers hanging passionless on my head while the world had these last weeks been breaking down around me.

I had noticed them before school while encountering my reflection in the bathroom mirror; they were sagging, not in sadness, but like a thirsty plant. When I'd drawn closer I had discovered that, in fact, the base where they rose was unusually dry, peeling in part like a mending scab. At first I'd suspected bird lice, but the irritation I was experiencing was sensory not epidermic. I had abstained even from my recently discovered ritual of self-gratification, thinking it the cause. I had tried to conceal the discovery by vigorously teasing my hair, but attuned to my unease, Deepa had more than once broken into the chorus of 'An Octopus's Garden'.

'I don't know,' I now confessed to Shanti.

Indeed, as though my own signal programming system

were malfunctioning, the nodes were failing to perform in concord with either sentiment or stimuli, and I had paranoiacally wondered when the sensation might dim and diminish entirely.

Before I could convey any of these fears to Shanti, though, a deafening drilling started up, rumbling the ground beneath us.

Shanti, like a true bodhisattva, remained unmoved by the turbulence while I myself gripped the nearby table leg.

Mum suddenly swept into the house now, flailing her arms and wauling about Dad's incipient excavations.

Then without even a cursory recognition of us, she fell mysteriously silent. Her eyes grew wild, as if with distant hypnotic recognition. Before we knew it, she was slipping on her raincoat and fleeing out the front door again.

'Give it up, Inspector Gadget!' I heard her cackle a final farewell from the driveway as the fulcrum of the door creaked dolorously behind her.

My stomach cried out ravenously after her, but this time I refused the inner impulse to trail her to the door. Instead, I made my way over to the refrigerator. I put my hand to the cool interior where liquids had spilt, fermented, and hardened like agar jelly. I wondered what critters might be slyly incubating there. *If you don't think about it, it won't happen. It's just that simple.* I longed to be obstinate; I yearned to not succumb, but could not help myself.

I knelt before the soft light and began gorging on whatever I could grope and grasp with my famished hands. *Renunciation without aversion is not lasting*, I whispered to myself, imagining I was eating from the vegetation of her womb, swallowing nectar, grubs, and seeds already masticated by my mother's tongue. I knelt there for what seemed hours, sucking my fingers and licking my hands.

Then, swallowing the last mouthfuls of food, I silently proceeded to the bathroom, where the same way I'd learnt to put my finger to a different orifice, deriving pleasure and pain in equal quantities, I this time put it to my mouth.

Slinking towards my own room, I now saw that Deepa's bedroom door was ajar. The evening light fell, illumining two pair of writhing legs. I heard the muffled movements of two bodies colliding, the muted harmony of two mouths moving one against the other, producing no movement but procuring pleasure all the same. I tilted my head slightly, wishing to confirm the perverse inverted physics principle, and suddenly saw in Deepa's arms not the straggly droopy face of Walter Lockwood, but a boy who'd once loved me in a totally innocent way, told me his sorrows and given me his eye to play with: *It was Quentin!*

Now I began to run. I ran down the stairs past Shanti still standing on her head and, as I fled through the front door, I swung it so hard that I imagined it unhinging and flying blindly through the wind behind me. I dashed down the long driveway, onto the bitumen, leaping and charging, the sound of my sobs ringing out disconsolately throughout that silent, fading street.

I knew neither where I was nor where I was going but only that I had to run. And I felt myself running from incidents faraway. I felt I was running from my grandfather trailing me down Clare Road in Bombay, a magnifying glass glinting in his frail, jaundiced hand. I was running from the house in Goa where my grandmother was snoring and sleep-talking in a small damp room whose whitewashed walls swam with the shadows of a million luminous moths.

As I ran I found myself being chased by my own shadow, warped on the moonlit tar. I ran and had a sudden vision of the room into which I had long ago been led by Quentin, the lugubrious upstairs room of the Soyers' house, wallpapered with maps. I was eloping with the evening as I now recalled those myriad rivers and lakes, the tributaries and estuaries, the promiscuous liaisons where the land met the sea so frequently. I had once longed to lie down on those cartographies, but now, wide awake, I believed I was tearing through them, running, ripping, tripping, and falling over the accident of my being in the world, the daughter of my mother the child of my parents.

As I bounded forward I heard the ducks of Clearwater Park in quiet conversation; I heard a train, far off, leaving a station, emptily, like all those things that do not wait for a response from other beings to make their exits, close their doors, and depart. I made my reckless way through the park and, running between the dark mass of trees, I, too, now momentarily wanted to sink into the soil and be absorbed by the sweet earth beneath my feet.

I was running in Rain Hill, but in the passport of my soul I was encircling the city of Sydney, crossing whole continents and vast tracts of land. I had spoken all the idioms and minor vernaculars that are lost in the blood that is shed when you lay yourself down at the borders of the world. I felt I had loved and lost and mourned too long! And where, I now wondered, was a lap on which to lay my woeful head, where the arms of familial love to pull me back each time I came to that precipice and looked down, as I called my mother's name and it echoed back from the deep valley of lonesomeness, echoed back and enveloped me?

I ran over and over echoing the well-like vowels from which all aloneness in my life had issued: ovaries and operations. 'Oh!' I cried through the barren branches, 'Oh, oh, oh!' I ran, wondering where in his native Ireland Mr. Heaney may have gone, whether he had reached his ailing mother before the poor woman had perished. I ran dreaming of do-si-doing with Daniel Hoolahan and of chocolate eclairs stuck to my milk teeth. I ran imagining firecrackers exploding and the night shuddering into blissful climax and Shanti's eye bleeding and Dad cursing the name of Queen Elizabeth II. I ran with a passion borne not of joy but of a deep ineluctable sadness, seeing the Tower of Babel teetering above me and hearing the deep reverberations of the well at the back of the house in Goa, beneath whose water Karena would keep the coals smoking for my bath and into whose depths, I would, on occasion, have very much liked to drop. I ran remembering Dad tucking me in at night and talking to me about the world. Oh, how I enjoyed our little discourses, me a child and he an adult, but he never condescending me! I ran contemplating Mum's kisses weighted with a mercy so sweet, the kind only a mother may discharge. And as I ran I suddenly saw looming above me the gigantic hallucinatory figures of Drs. Freida and Charles Roman, their mouths moving in hysterical circumlocution. I thought of Mum demonstrating the vaginal cross-section and, laughing rapturously as I ran, I saw Mrs. Soyer staring blankly back at me with water banking in her own plentiful sockets. 'You laugh like that,' she warned me, 'and you'll end up crying.' I ran remembering Jacinta Tyler squealing as she released the springs in the multiple mattresses she'd mutilated in the house. And I ran thinking of what we had recently heard; that Jacinta's eldest brother, Stephen, had had to drive Mr. Tyler in the ambulance to the very same hospital to which he had, like a man destined to die, made his perfunctory passage for the last forty years and whereupon it was confirmed that he had suffered a burst brain aneurism. 'Stephen,' I now imagined Mr. Tyler gasping between consciousness and everlasting life, 'please, son, turn the siren off.' And I now ran into the fast-receding evening envisioning Mr. Malone, poor Mr. Malone, crushed in the wreckage of the Malone family automobile, wondering at the provincial fate of Lucy Malone. I ran remembering murmuring to rheumy-eyed Father Murphy that I'd stolen sunshine from a dying man's daughter, and as I kept on running I now imagined I was flinging myself into the open arms of the man who had saved my life when I was once about to plummet from the guttering of the Opera House in the first grade. I ran seeing myself fleeing, my bow in hand, from the monolithic spectre of the Sydney Conservatorium of Music and now longed to run into my bedroom again and caress again my violin, that sad surrendered child of strings, let the tuning fork resonate over and over the note of my youth: a perfect B-flat. I ran feeling all the world sliding like loose kaleidoscopic shapes inside my heart and suddenly glanced up, imagining her, alar, lost to those trees, screeching words that were supposed to cocoon me, turn into a creature of belated volant beauty, though with a pair of wings forever punctured. Closing my eyes as I crashed headlong with the night, I now wondered whether I'd not felt this same exhilaration years before, while writing my mortal name on the frosty glass, while flying against the jambs, of the doors of our home, that lost carapace, me its disfigured daughter, its mutant crustacean who'd grown too large.

I felt as though I had been running through a burning summer and a freezing winter. I ran as a somnambulist. I ran as an interlocutor in the dark. I ran as if gazing out the window of that remote math classroom and, witness to the fading and dissolution of my phantasmagoric universe, I now screamed:

> *The eyes are not here*
> *There are no eyes here*
> *In this valley of dying stars*

Weeping and flailing my arms, I ran now yanking from my head, the tendrillar, wasted remains of my feelers; I ran crying and tearing those rotted knobs from my scalp. Gone for good my umbilical cord to the world! *Gone my chrysalis!* My antennae ripped forever from my skull, I finally knew while I ran what it was to feel the blood that might previously have surged to those organs flowing in predictable patterns only through my veins.

And, as if in a last rite, as though they were two blood-saturated plaits with which I was to make an offering to the gods, I now clutched the dead, severed ends of the antennae in my vermilion hands and slowly turned homeward.

As life retreats, so too does it return and choose us. We do not beg to be born but frequently find ourselves aging at the most inopportune moments. I had believed that, should I have willed it that way, I might have remained forever young. I had believed that love could neither break nor burst, that a heart could not be overloaded. I kept believing this even as I returned home this evening to find my mother finally transported, my father finally at peace; she aloft and he entombed in the sacred grave into which he had so long been inhuming himself.

As I approached from the corner of the street, I could hear a great intercontinental flock of birds crying, rising and thrashing about; the egrets, after a long sojourn, turning like resigned exiles towards the park, the cockatoos screeching maniacally; even a lone kookaburra from a nearby telephone wire, not laughing its signature laugh, but weeping, really weeping as even kookaburras sometimes must. Currawongs, galahs; I could even make out a rainbow shower of rosellas, desperate in flight, tasting smoke with their small, taut tongues.

I neared with trepidation and now also saw the rest, witnessed the utter devastation; the flames and sparks rising from the debris as if in a display of pyrotechnic wizardry. I edged slowly forward and as it all now dawned on me, as it registered in my wide eyes, weepy with smoke, that this was my house afire – *my own house ablaze* – I did not drink fear but was lost to glorious exhalation. It was as though I were now, now in this dark, final, smog-saturated moment, truly gulping life, breathing for the very first and falling to the earth from a great height.

Several fire-rescue trucks and ambulances, their sirens blaring, waking up the languid neighbourhood, had surrounded the glowing house.

The entire Rain Hill Fire Department appeared to be on call.

Hoses were strapped to various taps, from pumps in vehicles, extending like obese slugs across the garden and yet seemed to do very little in reducing the extent of the conflagration.

I stared on, dumb with joy, for as one section of the house was doused another roared in a sudden burst of flame from below the ground.

'I can't believe this, it all seems to be simmering from underground!' I suddenly heard one official in bafflement bellow from a loudspeaker.

The house and the front garden had been cordoned off up to the driveway and letterbox.

Neighbours stood ogling behind yellow tape. Quentin, Mrs. Soyer, old Mrs. Rabe, even the Russian with his ferocious Alsatian were now looking on, aghast, at the flaring calamity wrought by our father's failed underground operations.

Feverishly, I sought Deepa and Shanti in the crowd and in silence clung as never before to them.

Amid the incendiary catastrophe, thunderous subterranean explosions were incessantly erupting, spouting, and spitting, among other things, charred wire, seared gaffa tape, pliers heads, mangled drill pins, the scorched remains of a camping tent, the blackened dented pieces of what could distinctly made out to be a portable aluminium cooking stove.

The pungent perfume that hung in a thick vapour above us was that of a vast spice warehouse burning to the ground. I could smell vast vats of mango and lime pickle; the bittersweet of cardamom spores that, with the intensity of the heat, must have prematurely burst from their pods; peppercorns and paprika; turmeric, tamarind, and bay leaf; all these now lingered and mingled in a masala of mixed messages with the certain scents of dried cloves and the singular aroma of coriander.

One firefighter, sweat trickling down his ruddied cheeks, suddenly emerged from the back and shouted on a loudspeaker. 'We can't get him out. He's literally buried beneath the structure, and I'm afraid, even if we were to try, it would be too late anyhow!'

'He's dead, isn't he? He's dead,' Shanti murmured, over and over.

'All those wirings and connections, all that mysterious recircuiting and mining, it was a tragedy waiting to happen. Truth is, he didn't know the difference between an AC or DC power socket,' Deepa lamented.

Two more men now attempted to enter the burning manhole but escaped quickly, coughing and spluttering and shaking their heads, confirming what had already been suspected. Timber was crashing and I heard the last birds cry and flee overhead; the sky, too, as though scorched and torn apart, was turning violet and mauve and ultramarine all at once, such was the carrion. I waited for the earth to crumble in on itself, literally fall beneath my feet.

'There's no way we're going to be able to reach him,' one of them relayed. 'So much has caved in, it's like a whole separate strata down there now!' Then, wiping either a bead of perspiration or a tear from below his eye, he heaved again, 'There's absolutely no way!'

I looked up into the clotted sky, to the liberated dust of decades, to the ash rising and sinking like burnt snowflakes or charcoal petals, to the sun on its urgent journey below the horizon. I had believed that paradise was only a figment of my fecund imagination; I had waited at the edge of that precipice for her, but now, as she departed my heart, my mother swept and rose and it was I who retired, I who fell as the shudder of her wings carried me down, drowned and emptied me into the vast unsteady air.

Soaring through the slaughtered sky above our ruined home, she was now crying with all the contentment of the newly free, the wild joy of the recently emancipated. No force could reach her, no creature ever before her flew with such sublimity and there was no name for the glorious phoenixlike form she had now assumed.

Watching her fly, I felt it all compress as if I were gawking at the long wide, vision of my girlhood. I saw her slip and drop between the evening clouds and felt the same twilight now leap and lead and enclose me like an eyelid into darkness, darkness and dilapidation. I am suddenly blind in the rooms and moving shyly in the ill-lit passages. I retrieve marvellous things, deep, arresting flashes of insight; at other times, I lose myself, want to lie down to die in the wreckage.

And with the last beat of her wing, the final clear sight of her encircling in the dim haze above his fire, I know that it all comes to this: I spent a great time of my life, the most tender part, wishing I had not been born. I was so long on the verge of losing everything and then, when I closed my eyes because I could not bear to be this way anymore, the one whom I loved most in the world vanished; that gentle face so much my own, those eyes that doted, the tender but somewhat clumsy hands that had bathed my infant form and that had held my face away from the gaping canyon of my mother's elusive misery.

I will not say that I did not love my mother; I loved her – dangerously so. But a time came when I could not keep waiting at the edges of my dreams for her. It was now that I looked at her with new eyes and saw a great shadow sloughed off from my own reflection. It came to me that all this lost time I had been wandering the earth, staring down steep ravines, gulfs of pitch darkness, hoping that if I called her beautiful name long enough she might return to me, beguiling myself that if I began where she ended, then surely my mother would be interminably connected to me.

But it was a vigil maintained in vain, for we begin at a time beyond the womb, a disjunct moment; and we love after having survived the unnameable and unmasterable miseries of the past. And on and on each one of us arrives and advances, flying with her face forever gazing at the nebulous sometimes hideous and occasionally divine shapes of the history from whose thigh she sadly slides.

ACKNOWLEDGMENTS

I would like to express my gratitude to Tifanny
Richards, my agent at Janklow & Nesbit
Associates in New York, for her insight, guidance
and unfailing commitment to seeing this novel
enter the world; to my editor, Karen Rinaldi,
at Bloomsbury USA, for her critical acuity,
original eye and belief in the book. Finally,
I wish to acknowledge the generous support
of Peter Bishop, Executive Director of the
Varuna Writers' Centre, Katoomba, Australia,
who nurtured this project from its inception,
provided me with hours of his time and,
under the auspices of the Eleanor Dark
Foundation Ltd, a safe haven in which
to work.

A NOTE ON THE AUTHOR

Suneeta Peres da Costa was born in 1976 in Sydney,
Australia, where she has been an award-winning
dramatist and short story writer. She is currently
a Fulbright Scholar, living in New York City,
and studying for a Master in Fine Arts degree
at Sarah Lawrence College. *Homework* is
her first novel.

A NOTE ON THE TYPE

The text of this book is set in Linotype Sabon,
named after the type founder, Jacques Sabon. It
was designed by Jan Tschichold and jointly
developed by Linotype, Monotype and Stempel,
in response to a need for a typeface to be
available in identical form for mechanical hot
metal composition and hand composition using
foundry type.

Tschichold based his design for Sabon roman on
a fount engraved by Garamond, and Sabon italic
on a fount by Granjon. It was first used in 1966
and has proved an enduring modern classic.